The Glory Boys

GLORY: 1 exaltation, praise or
honour.   2 Something that brings
or is worthy of praise.   3 to triumph or exalt.

The New Collins Concise Dictionary
Of The English Language

The Glory Boys

The True-Life Adventures of Scotland Yard's SWAT, the Last Line of Defence in the War Against International Crime

by

Steve Collins

Century · London

First published by Century in 1998

Copyright © Steve Collins 1998

Steve Collins has asserted his right under the Copyright, Designs and
Patents Act, 1988, to be identified as the author of this work

First published in the United Kingdom in 1998 by
Century, 20 Vauxhall Bridge Road, London SW1V 2SA

Random House Australia (Pty) Limited
20 Alfred Street, Milsons Point, Sydney,
New South Wales 2061, Australia

Random House New Zealand Limited
18 Poland Road, Glenfield
Auckland 10, New Zealand

Random House South Africa (Pty) Limited
Endulini, 5a Jubilee Road
Parktown 2193, South Africa

Random House UK Limited Reg. No. 954009

A CIP catalogue record for this book is available from the British Library

Papers used by Random House UK Limited are natural, recyclable
products made from wood grown in sustainable forests.
The manufacturing processes conform to the environmental
regulations of the country of origin.

ISBN 0 7126 7733 X

Printed by Mackays of Chatham, plc, Chatham, Kent

FOR MY BROTHER

THE GLORY BOYS

From the realms of imagination
Through the darkness of the night
From the heart of a Nation
Through the glare of an Armalite
Come the Glory Boys

From the eye of a villain
Through the barrel of a gun
From the haze of a barrage
When there's no place to run
Come the Glory Boys

These men of granite, these nerves of steel
These men who serve, these men who feel
These men who live to tell the tale
These men of men dare not fail
Hail the Glory Boys

Vivemus Morimur Nunquam Deficemus
We live, we die, we never fail

Laurence Michael Hayes, 1998

Contents

Acknowledgements

A lot has happened for me since the publication of my first book, *The Good Guys Wear Black*, and as a result I am deeply indebted to a number of people, many of whom I now count as personal friends rather than merely associates. I am of course talking about my publishing team at Random House. Those singled out for particular thanks must be: my editor, Mark Booth, undeniably one of the best around, and an excellent lunch partner; his right hand, Liz Rowlinson, who I know Mark wouldn't be without, and who has helped me tremendously; Katie White from Publicity, who worked so hard to bring it all together; Bob Hollingsworth and photographer Andy Kingsbury, for their excellent jacket designs; and of course the entire sales team, too numerous to mention, but whose drive is second to none.

On a personal note, I'd like as always to thank my wife Jill for being by my side and believing in me; Mum and Dad, my greatest advocates; brother Dave and good pals Clive and Dave for making the jacket photograph a success; my hard-working agent Barbara Levy for her guidance and support, and without whom none of this would have been possible; and finally reporter Lee Brown of the *South London Press*, for all his research on my behalf, often at the drop of a hat.

Last but by no means least, I must thank my friends and former colleagues at SO19, who ask no reward, yet lay their lives on the line daily to protect the public. To you, we all owe a great debt of gratitude.

Author's Note

Due to the type of work undertaken by SO19 specialist teams, a large number of operations can be termed 'covert', with their operators often working in plain clothes, out of the public eye and under a blanket of secrecy. No role, however, can be more dangerous than that of an undercover officer. Perhaps supported by SO19, but more often alone, these operatives work unarmed to infiltrate major organised crime groups. It is they, and the painstaking intelligence they gather, that makes it all worthwhile. For the most obvious of reasons they cannot be named here, and to this end (at their request and in the interests of their own personal security) the names and identifying features of those people and some other individuals in this book have been changed.

Preface

Scotland Yard: worldwide, the very name is synonymous with policing excellence. And these days it is its Special Operations wing that people talk about, its experience and expertise that is in constant demand around the globe.

It is a commonly held fallacy that, since the service was first set up, the traditional British Bobby has patrolled his beat unarmed. In fact, up until 1936 officers patrolling on night duty were entitled, at their own request, to draw a firearm for personal protection.

Today, though, a more systematic approach is called for – the stakes are far higher. With the collapse of the former Soviet Union, the demolition of the Berlin Wall and the construction of the Channel Tunnel, Europe's borders are shrinking at an alarming rate. Many Governments are almost powerless to hold back the flood of rising crime, and a new breed of criminal. In Britain's capital city the culture of the gun has regrettably become a way of life. This is a city ravaged by violence, where international crime syndicates and the law of the gun have seized a vicious stranglehold on the once 'honourable' manors of the London 'firms'. The East End, where once the Krays' sinister influence prevailed, has now fast become a melting pot of hate, where Asian street gangs and Turkish extremists rule with an iron fist. Similarly, in the south of the city, Jamaican Yardies have introduced a violent and bizarre culture where drugs are the currency, respect the question, and death the answer.

In early 1996 there were five fatal shootings in Brixton alone, two incidents within the space of three hours, placing Brixton – with the Watts District of Los Angeles and South Africa's Soweto – as one of the world's most notorious trouble-spots.

At the forefront of the battle, taking the fight to the very heart of organized crime, are SO19, the Metropolitan Police Tactical Firearms Unit. The men in black. The Glory Boys.

Prologue

Crack! Crack! The Glock bucked in his tightly gripped hands, but not so tightly that it made him tremble. He applied just about the same amount of pressure as a good, firm handshake, just as he'd been taught all of those years ago, just as he in turn had taught others.

The first Winchester nine-millimetre jacketed soft-point round left the muzzle of the weapon at a speed far in excess of thirteen hundred feet per second, the recoil forcing the slide rearwards, with the extractor and ejector discharging the spent case from the ejection port in a spiralling upwards motion. As the slide snapped back forward, driven by the powerful recoil spring, it stripped a second bullet from the top of the seventeen-round magazine, seating it firmly in the breech. Then, with a further press of the trigger, the second round joined the first.

The whole sequence of firing a pair of shots had taken no more than a second, both rounds finding their mark, tearing through flesh and tissue. The small, round entry holes hardly bore testimony to the damage inside the body, as gas, dirt and minute particles of damaged clothing were sucked into the void of the gunshot wounds.

Hit twice, David Ewin – a violent criminal fuelled by a cocktail of heroin, cocaine and strong lager, who had survived two murder trials and had a string of more than forty previous convictions – stared in amazement at the wounds before slumping forward, his head coming to rest on the steering wheel of his stolen Toyota MR2. Only moments before, with a total disregard for public safety, he had attempted to use this vehicle as a weapon, to ram his way to freedom.

Not twenty miles away across London, I sat in a small room. By my side my unit waited – Black Team, SO19. The door opened, and all eyes swung round to take in the duty officer.

'It's Pat Hodgson,' he said quietly. 'He's just shot somebody in Barnes.'

1

The Great Black Team Skip Caper

'On Yer Knees!' proclaimed a jubilant headline in the *Sun*. 'Crawl!' echoed a triumphant lead in another tabloid, while the more sedate *Daily Mail* merely announced, 'Bomber at a Bus Stop!'

As we had swooped on Robert 'Rab' Fryers, top IRA enforcer in north London, a photographer had captured the entire incident on film from an eyrie high above and with incredible timing, clicking away as the drama unfolded below. The result? An exclusive set of photographs that were made immediately available to every newspaper in the country.

It did our little known department a power of good, of that there is no doubt, and as a result morale was at an all-time high. But what the papers didn't reveal was the fact that the unspeakable had almost happened.

We'd tailed the suspect for some weeks, and as with most SO19 covert operations we'd crewed up in the rear of Anti-Terrorist Squad vehicles, or gunships as they are commonly known. The surveillance team had eventually located Fryers at a bus stop in Crest Road near Oxgate Lane in Cricklewood, north London. In his hands was a bomb consisting of two and a half kilos of Semtex attached to a further two litres of petrol. His intention had been to strike a blow for terrorism in the heart of London.

The radio had crackled, 'I have control, I have control.

3

Over to you, Steve.' And it was at this point that things had started to go dramatically wrong. Checking my Heckler & Koch MP5 in the rear of the lead vehicle – a black cab, or flounder – the convoy of gunships had started to snake their way cautiously along Oxgate Road. But for some reason known only to himself our squad driver had totally cocked up the geography of the plot, and as a result the team had sailed past Fryers' location. Had it not been for the quick thinking of two of my lads – Sinex and Ninja – the day would have been lost. Bailing out and challenging Fryers, they'd forced him to his hands and knees, relieving him of his lethal cargo which was later defused.

The rest is history.

I'd arrived wearily the following morning at our base in Old Street, a dowdy old Victorian-style police station on the outskirts of the East End, still on a high from the previous day. But life had to go on – and with the six teams carrying out hundreds of armed operations a year we were obliged to remind ourselves of the well-worn saying within the department; 'You're only as good as your last job.' Pushing open the heavy doors I was immediately hit by the oppressive heat in the basement, and as the smell of toast and freshly brewed coffee reached me, tiredness left me and I looked for the rest of the team.

Sipping a hot, sweet coffee I laughed at the newspaper accounts of the ambush in Cricklewood. Once again many of them quite wrongly stated that the SAS were believed to be involved, which really gripped my shit. Any spectacular operation on the mainland, particularly involving terrorism, is invariably accredited in the tabloids to special forces. The reality is that they are nearly all down to SO19. Once again we would not even get a pat on the back, and unlike the SAS and their Royal Marine counterparts the SBS, who both get special forces pay, officers in SO19 receive no more salary than their colleagues in the office or on the beat!

Throwing the *Sun* on to the stack of newspapers I picked

up the *Mail*. 'Bastards!' I spat.

'What's the matter?' asked Ninja.

'They've cut me out.'

'What?' he gawped.

'They've cut me out. The bastards have cut me out!' I held up both newspapers. 'I'm in the *Sun* and the *Mirror*, but not in the *Mail*. They've cut the bottom off. The best-looking face on the team and they've cut me out!'

'It was only a shot of your arse sticking out from behind a wall anyway,' quipped Neil, an ex-shield training instructor, munching on a piece of toast.

'That's what I mean! The best-looking face on the team and it's been cut out!'

As the remainder of the team arrived that morning I could tell they were on a high; one good job always seemed to shake out the cobwebs and set you up on a lucky roll. Hopefully today's operation would prove me right.

Finally Andy appeared. Andy was a tall, fit, dark-haired inspector, who possessed an uncanny knowledge of the law and a remarkably quick wit. Not only was he a friend, he was also Black Team's duty officer. He was accompanied by Bob, an old pal from his Special Patrol Group days. Bob was a sergeant on division who had managed to obtain permission to shadow a team for a few days with a view to joining the department. As a result he had sat with Andy the previous day in the control vehicle.

Now an almost open-faced innocence clouded his tanned features as he beamed with uncontrollable excitement. 'I still can't believe what happened yesterday,' he said victoriously. 'That was just fantastic.'

'Yeah,' I replied somewhat sarcastically. 'Seen the papers? They're talking about nothing else.'

Bob stooped and picked one from the pile. 'Brilliant photos.'

'Yeah,' I snorted. 'Little *too* brilliant, don't you think?'

Bob's forehead creased into a frown. 'What do you mean?'

I smiled, looking around the now quiet room. 'Well, call me Mister Cynical, but this job has done MI5 a power of good. With public confidence at an all-time low and pressure on to get results, they pull off their greatest coup.' I jabbed a finger at the photograph Bob held. 'And the grand finale just happened to be captured on film by some good samaritan who wishes to remain anonymous.'

Bob thought quietly for a moment. 'What? You're not saying . . .'

Holding up my hand I cut him short. 'Bob, if you ever do get on this department, you'll learn that there are many things left unsaid.'

'Fucking right,' said Chris, my tall, stocky number two, who stood silhouetted in the doorway.

I looked up. 'All right, mate?'

But he just grunted, pushing his way towards the locker room.

'What's with him?' Bob asked.

'Fuck knows. Probably got the hump because he wasn't in the paper.'

When the job went down a number of pedestrians and shopkeepers had come out on to the pavement. Realising we had Fryers well under control, Chris had ushered them to safety. He'd returned to the corner shop when everything had blown over and picked up a can of drink. Taking it to the counter he'd ferreted in his trouser pocket for change.

'Forty-five pence, please,' the shopkeeper had said.

Chris held out his palm and counted the coins. 'I've only got forty-four pence left.' Then he'd winked. 'Still . . .' He nodded out of the window, where the SOCO was still working. 'I guess we've just saved you all from being blown up.'

The shopkeeper had looked him up and down – body armour undone and hanging loosely from his square shoulders, holstered Glock self-loading pistol and high visibility baseball cap – and returned the wink. 'Only forty-four pence, eh?'

Chris had nodded.

'Well, you'd better put it back, then!'

After our light breakfast we dragged our bergens from the shelf and pulled on the heavy coveralls and boots before checking the rest of the kit we'd need for the job later that day: ballistic helmets, heavyweight body armour, belt rigs and gloves. Linking up with some members of Blue Team, who'd be working with us in plain clothes, we booked out our weapons from the small armoury before trudging silently into the yard. The morning was already hot, and I cursed our luck, knowing full well that we'd be cooped up in the back of the Trojan horse for a couple of hours. With the excess kit weighing in at around four and a half stone it was sure to be hot and uncomfortable; looking up at the watery sun I knew that by the time we were ground assigned it would be almost unbearable.

When we arrived at the anonymous-looking flying squad office, deep in the heart of London's East End, I pressed the buzzer and announced our arrival as the drivers parked the vehicles. Repeating our details, the owner of the faint voice at the other end pushed a button which disengaged the electronic lock with a loud *thunk*. Pushing open the doors we entered, climbed the stairs and headed towards the faint aroma of coffee.

Leaving Chris slouched in a chair, Andy, Bob and I made our way towards the hustle and bustle of the busy squad room.

Pushing open the door, we were met by the fug of a roomful of heavy smokers, which coupled with the din of conversation, gave the general impression of an illegal gambling den rather than an orderly office.

I searched the sea of familiar faces, veterans of many a street ambush, until finally my eyes fell on Mick, the officer in the case. Short and stocky, with a ruddy complexion and bushy moustache, he had the type of face that could make you laugh without his even trying.

Making our way towards his desk we were intercepted by

a familiar voice. 'Boys! How you doing?'

I turned, a broad grin on my face as my ear tuned in to the heavy Glaswegian accent. 'Gordon, how's it going?' I said, pumping his outstretched hand. Gordon was a DS on the squad, who in the past had fed us some good quality blags, the last of which ended up with one of our team, Nigel, shooting a robbery suspect as he took a post office guard prisoner in Crouch Hill, north London. As a result – and in strict accordance with departmental policy – Nigel had been taken off ops during the Police Complaints Authority investigation. He had only recently returned to the fold.

'How's Nigel?' Gordon asked.

'Great,' I beamed. 'Back on ops. He's in the other room.'

'That's brilliant fucking news!' Gordon said genuinely. 'I'll go see him in a minute.' Then he lowered his voice to a whisper. 'You boys on that job yesterday?'

I smiled. 'Yep. Black Team strikes again. You seen the papers?'

He nodded. 'Fucking great job! I guessed you'd get in on it somewhere down the line.'

'Yeah,' I grinned. 'Well, we're on a roll. You think this will go today?'

He turned up his nose. 'Who knows, Stevie? The whole job would be a damn sight easier if the blaggers came to the briefing – at least that way they'd fucking know what they were supposed to be doing!'

I laughed out loud. 'We'd better go and see Mick. Catch you later, Gordon.'

Huddled in the briefing room, the tall, almost larger-than-life DI – who, with his craggy, weatherbeaten face and long, unkempt hair was a ringer for Mick Jagger – set to work.

First he outlined the background. Marsh Lane, Leyton, London E10: a quiet, non-residential side-street. Hackney Marshes lay off to the south-west, and the only other feature worthy of note was a clothing recycling factory opposite St Joseph's Roman Catholic Infant School. The geography – and the fact that a lone Securicor vehicle delivered wages to

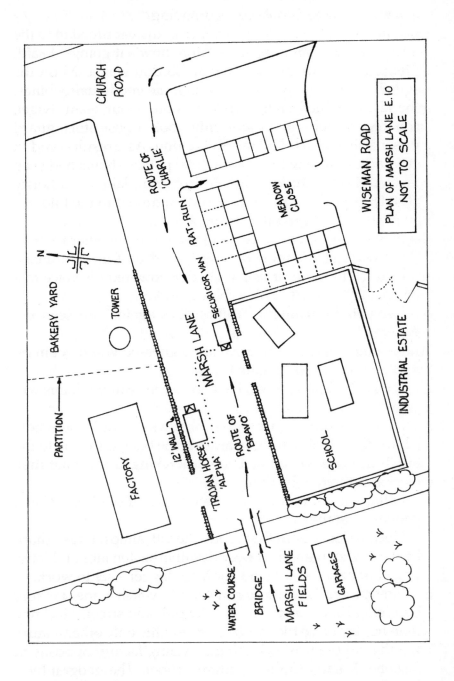

the school – made it the ideal setting for enterprising young robbers.

Over the past month or so the squad had lain patiently in wait as two known criminals, Nicholas Drakou and Edward Levy, had plotted the vehicle's movements, watched the guards, and bided their time. I too had spent my time surveying the ground, studying the photographs and getting a feel for the plot, until eventually, together with other officers from the squad, I'd hatched a plan I considered my most innovative yet.

The DI concluded his part of the briefing. 'Now I'll hand you over to Mick and Steve from SO19; they'll fill you in on the plan.'

Mick nodded, dragging himself to his feet. 'Steve's drawn up a sketch of the plot and will later go over the attack in some detail,' he started in his heavy cockney accent. 'We've got two OPs covering the ground. OP One will contain the boss here,' he nodded toward the DI, 'the SO19 guvnor, Andy, and the spare skipper, Bob. They will be responsible for calling on the attack and any tactical decisions that have to be made in the event of a cock-up. Further down the road will be OP Two. That will contain a camera – for evidential purposes,' he digressed, breaking into a grin. 'I've got to tell you, those trees down there are a bit urgent at this time of year. Twice this week I've been down there with a hedge-trimmer cutting them back. Should get some good photos now, though.'

I laughed at the thought of him cutting back the trees, but made a mental note of the camera and the need to reiterate its presence to the lads later. Although our practices were strictly above board, relying on SOPs honed by years of trial and error, it was always nice to know you'd be captured on film, just in case.

Having designated squad drivers and call-signs, Mick handed over to me for the tactical brief.

'Cheers, Mick,' I said, standing and moving to the head of the room. 'For those of you who don't know me, I'm

Sergeant Steve Collins, SO19. Most of us have worked together in the past so you'll know how we like to operate. When the attack is given, we will have in effect been granted control, and it will only be SO19 going across the pavement. Today will be a little different, but the rules remain unchanged: nobody gets between the suspects and the guns.'

This was the first law of every briefing that I liked to hammer home, having been on plots before when, at the moment the attack was given, certain squad men with tunnel vision and the bit between their teeth would rush towards the suspects armed with nothing but a truncheon, oblivious to the fact they were between us and the gunmen.

Speech over, I distributed a hand-drawn plan of the plot. 'OK. We've been told that there will probably be two suspects, and for our purposes the ground is ideal for an ambush.' I held up my copy of the plan. 'Marsh Lane runs approximately west to east.' I traced the road's line with a pen. 'Church Road is the main route in from the eastern end, and it is from here that the blue box will enter, drive down and park outside the school on the south side. As you can see from the plan and photographs on the board, the street is abutted on both sides here by a twelve-foot brick wall topped with razor wire.' I paused, clearing my throat. 'To the far west of the plot is a small water course, and the bridge across this leads to Marsh Lane playing fields. To the north of the plot, over the wall, is Percy Ingle's bakery, and next door to this is a textile warehouse which recycles old clothes.' I looked up, glancing around the quiet room. 'At first it looked nigh on impossible to lay down a jump-off wagon – any of our Trojan horses would look well sussy. But with the aid of Special Events we think we've cracked it. The horse has been converted to accommodate a team . . . I won't keep you in suspense any longer. It's a skip lorry.'

'Fucking hell!' came a moan from the back. 'You mean we'll be in the back of a skip?'

I nodded. 'Yeah, but no ordinary skip. This is a container

on the back of a lorry, hired from the guvnor's mate. Special Events have decontaminated the inside with disinfectant so it's clean, although it still smells a bit.' A laugh trickled through the room. 'At the back is a large opening covered with a tarpaulin. We've had a false wall made, to which they've nailed old clothes; it actually looks quite good and should pass anything but a very thorough inspection. If anybody does look inside they'll think it's just an old wagon waiting to be off-loaded in the factory.'

I sipped a cup of coffee to let this sink in for a moment, then continued. 'Fellas, it's important we box this one up tight. As I said, it's the ideal place for an ambush – with a good backdrop if the shit does hit the fan, but there's still that potential.'

I pointed to the plan again. 'East of the school, by these houses, is a small rat-run leading to Meadow Close. If they get through there we're fucked; likewise if they manage to get to Marsh Lane Fields. The only thing that really bothers me is the possibility they get inside the school playground. Now that just can't be allowed to happen. Apart from the unthinkable – a hostage taken or a gunfight – there's a high wall at the far end which leads into the Orion Industrial Estate, and once again, if they make that we're lost.'

I pulled out a separate sheet of paper. 'Postings: Black Team – consisting of Sinex, Ninja, Chris, Nigel, Neil and myself – will be in full kit and coveralls. We'll be in the back of the horse and will constitute the main attack. Call sign "Alpha".'

Due to the fact that robbers could go mobile, plots were usually covered by teams in plain clothes who, at the point of attack, would don high-visibility baseball caps as a means of identification. On this occasion, however, I knew the plot was static: we weren't going anyplace else; this was where the action would happen. It was also smelly and dirty, so in order to protect our civilian clothes I made the decision that the team would kit up in coveralls. The other advantage of this was the psychological effect the black kit had on criminals, almost as if you were some comic-book superhero. This effect often left them disorientated and overwhelmed before a shot was fired, and it was on this premise that I liked to work: fear, aggression and overwhelming odds.

I nodded to Sinex, 'We'll practise the jump-off order in the compound before we leave. The lorry will be parked facing east with the arse-end away from the plot; that should cover us when we debus. On the "Go" you open the false door and Spyderco the tarp.' Spydercos were the bane of the department: a small, scalpel-sharp folding knife that could be opened with one hand. Originally issued for cutting your abseil line in an emergency, they were now carried everywhere by the teams. But along the line they had claimed many fingers; immediately after issue one guy had even inadvertently stabbed himself in the stomach.

I continued. 'The team will drop down into the road, which will be our FAP.'

Glancing around, I found the familiar face of the Blue Team skipper. 'Gary, you'll be "Bravo". You'll come in from the west in a Range Rover. Apart from a driver you'll have an SO19 dog and handler and will be supported by a flying squad gunship containing two more of your team. I'll leave you to work out the postings and give the boss the list later.' Gary nodded as I pointed to the plan. 'You can self plot around the Marsh Lane Fields area – there's some open garages down there you might want to look at – but obviously you'll need to be out of view of any third eye sweeping the plot. Your job will be to act as cut-offs to the west.'

I cleared my throat. 'The same scenario from the east. Gary will nominate the Rangey and gunship crews to come in from Church Road. Again you'll have a support dog and handler; call-sign "Charlie". OK, fellas, we've got a lot to cover and a few surprises in store,' I added.

'Actions on . . .' Now I would cover the essential contingency plans to cover any foreseen (and sometimes unforeseen) scenarios, and the remedies taken to correct them. 'Firstly, the attack goes in and we have runners from the plot. If this happens, everybody stand still and let the dogs deal. Each handler has a nominated cover man for his own protection. Secondly, the Securicor guard or a schoolchild is taken hostage. In this event, Alpha will secure and contain the scene ready to negotiate. However . . .' Once more I indicated the map. 'Let me now bring your attention to this large tower in the baker's yard. Once again Special Events have come up trumps and have erected a screen around the top. The tower has a commanding view of the plot and will be manned by a flying squad observer along with Rick, the Black Team sniper. He'll be armed with a ninety-three. It will be Rick's responsibility alone to deal with as he sees fit; we must have the discipline to stand off and not get in his way.' I pointed Rick out. He was a relatively new member of the team who, with his short-cropped hair and bushy moustache, looked every inch the ex-21 SAS trooper. He nodded in acknowledgement. 'If by chance,' I continued, 'they make it to the playground, Keith and one other from the spare team will jump this wall into the playground and cut them off.' I indicated the wall and the adjoining industrial estate. 'To conceal them until the attack, the job has even gone to the expense of erecting a new shed in the garden of one of these houses. As you've heard, Andy, Bob and the DI will control things from this OP.' (I have deliberately left the location of the OP out of the plan as it would be wrong of me to include it. Police officers all across the country rely on the good will of local residents and traders who ask nothing in return when allowing their premises to be used in such circumstances.)

I concluded my briefing: 'Lastly, guys, Casevac. In the event of a shooting incident, SO19 will secure the scene. The squad drivers all know the local hospitals. If one of our guys is hit, he and another member of the team will be placed in a gunship and taken directly to hospital. If a bad guy is hit, our medics will stabilise him as best as possible and await the arrival of an ambulance.' This may sound callous, but the conveyance of anybody to hospital in a police vehicle is against regulations, and the commissioner could later be sued for lack of proper medical attention. In the squad's case, however, we were willing to waive this and get anyone hurt to hospital quickly. 'Police and civilian casualties will not go to the same hospital,' I concluded. This had happened in the past; police and villains had actually ended up in the same casualty ward. Apart from bad practice, the suspects' irate families have been known to turn up later looking for vengeance, resulting in a full-scale clash.

'Finally, guys: coms. We'll use Cougars until the hit. Then we'll go open on seventy-five, the Police National Firearms Frequency.'

I sipped cold coffee and regarded the attentive faces before me. 'Any questions?'

Somebody at the back laughed, slapping his forehead. 'Are there any fucking questions?'

I looked at my watch. 'OK, then. Black Team downstairs – we'll practise debussing from the horse. Everybody else, find your respective drivers and motors. It's seven forty-five. Ground assigned, eight thirty.'

Bob patted me lightly on the back. 'Good briefing, mate. I think I'm going to like it on this department.'

I smiled wearily. 'That was only the briefing, Bob. As Gordon said earlier, if the villains come they know what they've got to do. You think you've planned for everything; trouble is it invariably goes to ratshit.'

The team had made their way swiftly to the yard where, sitting in the centre in all its glory, was the horse.

'Fucking Hell' Chris said, tapping its side and causing a resonant metallic clang. 'We'll need to be dead quiet in this. One false move and the noise'll wake the dead.'

I smiled at the ingenuity of it all. 'Yeah, but if this comes off it'll be the dogs bollocks of all Trojan Horse jobs, don't you think?'

'Let's try it out then.' Sinex pulled his lanky frame into the back of the skip. 'I reckon it's about a four foot drop,' he said. 'With all the kit on we'll have to be careful we don't fall when we hit the ground.'

I laughed nervously as I visualised the whole team spilling out on to the pavement. 'You're right. Let's stack up and give it a go.'

Four attempts later and we had it off to a tee; now I could only hope we'd be as professional on the plot.

At eight fifteen our driver arrived. 'Looks like rain,' he said to nobody in particular.

Great, I thought. That's all we fucking need – first the heat and now the rain. I knew it was going to be hotter than hell in the back of that skip with no ventilation; having to bail out in the rain was the final insult. I looked at my watch and checked my kit before tapping the double magazine on my MP5 to make sure the magazine was properly seated. I'd heard of jobs before, where magazines had dropped out and left the operator with only one round in the chamber. That I needed like a second arsehole.

'OK,' I announced, 'let's mount up. But be careful; there's nothing to hold on to in the back, so it's best to sit down and try and get comfortable.'

One by one we climbed into the vehicle in reverse order – Sinex, the first man out, pulling himself on last. I looked around the team and smiled as the last of the light was blotted out totally as the driver positioned the false wall. This is a good bunch, I thought. Extremely professional and proud of their own unique style, even if the powers that be considered us somewhat maverick. I also knew that I could trust all of them with the one thing that meant the most to me: my life.

The lorry shuddered violently as the large diesel engine coughed into action. 'Fucking hell,' grunted a voice in the darkness as it lurched forward, throwing us across the floor. Finding my radio, I punched the press-to-talk button.

'A bit of passenger consideration please, driver,' I called.

'Sorry,' came the muffled apology. 'I've never driven one of these before; it's got more gears than a tank.'

'Now he fucking tells us,' I moaned.

The driver slowly got the hang of the cumbersome vehicle as he cautiously weaved through the early-morning traffic. Sitting in the back, each of us was deep in his own thoughts, mentally running through the actions-on situation and each individual's responsibility. With well over a thousand operations between us, another robbery plot was nothing new. We all had experience of staring at a suspect through the sights of a gun. We also knew that we could well be cooped up in the back of this stinking motor for hours on end – but that was one hardship we were used to.

Disorientated as we were, ten minutes later I was aware of the lorry manoeuvring back and forth, and could only assume it was being parked. This was confirmed seconds later as the engine spluttered and died.

In the inky blackness, Chris held the cougar tightly to his ear. 'Yes . . . yes," he whispered, then addressed the team. 'OK guys, he's laid it down outside the factory, arse-end away from the plot. It's pissing with rain, and the distance from the horse to the school is about twenty yards. There are no other motors about, and no update on the blaggers.'

'Well there's fuck-all we can do about it,' I hissed, 'so we just sit tight and hope it comes off.' Somewhere outside, the cut-off vehicles and gunships, under Gary's command, were already roaming the streets looking for a spot near enough to the plot to hide up and wait. Everything was in place; we'd done our part. Now it was up to them.

Oblivious to the police activity, Drakou and Levy had decided to go ahead with their plan. Not a stone's throw away in the back-streets of Leyton, Levy had donned the guise of a road sweeper, the finishing touch being a hand-held council cart stolen for the job. In his pocket was a small self-loading pistol. Drakou on the other hand was not so covert: in dark clothes, and with a baseball cap pulled tightly down over his head, he fingered the trigger of a

Brazilian-made Taurus .38 Revolver, loaded and ready to go.

As the optimum time for the delivery drew slowly nearer, nobody dared move. For the last hour I'd been trying to avoid fidgeting, as every move was accentuated with the ominous *clang* of metal. The heat was stifling and the smell of rotten vegetables nauseating, and even after all this time our eyes had not become accustomed to the dark. 'God, it's like a fucking morgue in here,' Chris whispered. 'A metal fucking coffin.'

I chuckled softly. 'Talking of morgues, you heard the story about that bloke in the county force?'

'No,' came Nigel's hushed voice, surprisingly close to my ear.

I lowered my tone. 'I don't know if it's true or not, but this is the way I heard it . . .'

Upon joining the police service, every recruit is obliged to undergo a two-year probationary period during which time, if he fails to come up to scratch, his services may be dispensed with. Police officers are by nature practical jokers, and in common with employees in many other walks of life like to play jokes on the new boy.

As part of his day-to-day business, a police officer is more than likely to encounter the odd dead body, be it from a road accident, a suicide or just a plain old sudden death. Whatever the cause, he must overcome his initial revulsion and get used to it. So part of a probationer's training includes a trip to the local mortuary where, if you're extremely unlucky, you may even get to see a post-mortem.

It was one such training trip that sparked off the following chain of events: one of the older members of the shift was approached and asked if he would like to take part in 'setting up' the new probationer, who was due to see his first dead body at the mortuary later that day. He volunteered immediately, and was told that he would play the part of the corpse. Covered only by a thin white sheet, he would lie in the drawer of the cold storage unit. When the probationer arrived and the drawer was opened, he was to jump up, wailing and scare the living daylights out of the new boy – great joke! Arriving with his crewmate shortly before the new guy, our volunteer went straight into role-playing, covering himself with a sheet and climbing on to the slab. With the drawer shut, all he had to do was wait – and wait.

Lying inside the freezer he suddenly became quite chilly, and after five minutes decided that perhaps this wasn't such a wheeze after all, in fact it was getting beyond a joke. After ten minutes his mind began playing tricks on him and, glancing around the interior at his fellow corpses, he decided that when he got out he'd give his mates a bollocking. After fifteen minutes he gave an involuntary shudder.

That's when the stiff beside him complained, 'Fucking cold in here, innit?'

Our man screamed in terror, sat bolt upright, and knocked himself out!

The first I knew about it all coming on top was when Chris urgently whispered, 'The blue box has just pitched up.' With only one encrypted radio set between us, Chris had been tasked with monitoring the traffic; the rest of us were getting it second-hand.

I looked at the faint glow of my watch: 10.16a.m. 'Stand to,' I called into the gloom, rising silently and letting the blood flow back into my legs. 'Number off.'

'One,' came Sinex's faint reply from the far end of the horse.

'Two,' came another, and so on, until finally we were stacked up and ready to go.

What exactly was happening outside I've yet to fathom; suffice to say that fate and circumstance had come together to create the world's largest clusterfuck. 'India One on the plot,' Chris relayed, his normally monotone voice rising with excitement. 'We're fucking game on, boys.' At the far end of the street Levy had started his approach, pushing the cart towards the Securicor van which by now had come to a stop outside the school. But unbeknown to the team Drakou, the front marker, had walked on ahead. Whether he had sensed a trap, or it was part of the plan or he'd simply lost his bottle I'll never know, but with collar turned up and baseball cap pulled tightly over his head, he strolled straight past the van, hands in pockets.

If it was ever put up by the OP, this information was not received in the horse.

Levy, on the other hand, seemed to have tunnel vision, and his eyes locked on to the guard as he climbed from the cab. At the same time a local council surveyor walked out of the school entrance into the middle of the plot.

'Stevie,' Chris whispered, 'they want us to move to the FAP.'

Up ahead, Sinex was already moving the makeshift wall, and with his Spyderco glinting ominously in the dark he set about slicing through the thin tarpaulin. One by one we dropped silently into the bright light of the day, blinking rapidly in an attempt to accustom our eyes to the change.

Chris peered round the corner of the van. 'Fuck! Back up! Back up!' he called, having seen Drakou but not realising he was a suspect; even if he were an innocent bystander we stood out like a bulldog's bollocks, and as a result could well blow the job.

With the tarpaulin now hanging in shreds, the skip offered no cover, and the only apparent place to go was the narrow gap between the lorry and the wall. I squeezed in tightly, joined by Sinex. 'Push up, push up,' he hissed as the rest of the team shuffled up behind.

'I can't,' I said, hugging my MP5 to my chest. 'It's parked at an angle and gets narrower.'

'Well try.'

Gritting my teeth, I sucked in a breath and squeezed in as far as I dared. 'Fuck it!' I muttered, now well pissed off.

'What?'

'I've just trod in dog shit. Smell that!'

When an attack is given, different people react in different ways; one may lock directly on to the gunman, while another will just see the guard. It may all be over so quickly that some may see nothing at all – it all depends on what position you are in at the time. It's not engineered that way. It just happens.

My seventy-five set burst into life: 'Alpha. Stand by, stand by. Attack, Attack, Attack!'

Having seen the guard, Levy had abandoned the cart and drawn his weapon. Taking the terrified man with one hand, he callously pressed the pistol to his head in an effort to persuade the driver to open the door.

I moved fast, legs pumping, adrenalin coursing through my veins, weapon raised.

A number of things were now happening at once. Amid shouts from all sides of 'Armed Police! Armed Police! Drop the gun! Drop the gun,' Levy's gun flew from his fingers and dropped to the floor at the feet of the panic stricken guard as he thrust his hands high in the air.

With a desperation borne of fear, the unwitting surveyor darted swiftly into what he believed was the safety of the school playground. Believing him to be the second suspect, I gave chase as the squeal of tyres and cries of the cut-off teams swept hurriedly through the plot.

'Attack! Attack! Attack!' This was the moment Keith – in the garden shed – had been waiting for.

'Suspect into the playground,' I called into the radio. 'Support.'

Throwing open the door to the shed, Keith covered the distance to the wall in three strides, MP5 at the ready. As Sod's law would have it, he cleared the obstacle with ease and landed heavily in the strategically placed wheelie bin on the other side.

Drakou pushed on, sensing something had gone drastically wrong, and as Gary and Bravo team came sweeping on to the plot, debussing with dogs barking excitedly, he suddenly realised he had nowhere to go. Diving into the doorway of the factory, he quickly went to ground.

'Armed Police! Armed Police!' I screamed, safety off and finger on trigger, as I levelled the five at the head of the hapless surveyor. 'On The Floor, hands behind your back!' Grabbing him roughly with my left hand I pulled him to the ground, and shaking like a leaf he complied without protest.

Suddenly I heard running footsteps from behind as I was joined by Keith. Covering him, I called, 'Got any cuffs?'

Keith produced a set of plasticuffs and immediately went to work securing the prisoner. Taking in Keith's dishevelled appearance, I asked, 'What happened to you?'

'Had a fight with a fucking wheelie bin,' he replied matter-of-factly.

'He's one of us! He's one of us!' came a panic-stricken female voice off to my left. Looking round, I saw a middle-aged woman standing with both hands held tightly to her face. 'He's a surveyor! He just left here – he's innocent!' she called, calming slightly.

'You're sure?' I asked, pulling him up so she could see his face.

'Yes. Yes, that's him. I can vouch for him.'

'Bollocks!' I cursed, letting him drop. 'We're one adrift.'

Handing the questionable suspect over to the squad, Keith and I sprinted out of the gates and into the chaos of the street. Outside, Bravo and Charlie teams scoured the road while I silently fumed. If we lost the suspect now we'd look a right bunch of tossers. Something had very obviously gone wrong the other end, but now was not the time to dwell on it. 'Somebody went into the factory as the hit went in,' Rick called from his perch high above. 'Couldn't have gone anywhere else, it was bottled up tight.'

Charging across the road, weapons ready, we hit the factory door, crashing it inward against the wall. The hum of machinery was deafening. Met with a large, open expanse of factory floor, I quickly made the decision to fan out and conduct a slow, methodical search.

Minutes later I heard a shout off to my right: 'Over here, guys. Have a look at this.'

Poking my head through the door, I grinned as I was met by the sight of Drakou sitting naked on the toilet of the small cubicle, clothes and gun wrapped in a bundle and stuffed behind the door.

Protesting his innocence, he was cuffed and lead away.

As the adrenalin rush subsided I suddenly felt quite tired. It had been a good job, but also a bit of an anti-climax. Like the day before, something had gone terribly wrong, something that potentially could have blown the job or got somebody killed, had it not been for the professionalism of the team – and that left a bad taste in my mouth. I thought back to my days of selection and the words of a wise old sergeant we'd affectionately nicknamed Mr Pastry: 'Remember, no matter how well you plan and brief a job, things can still go to ratshit. It's at that point you must pick up the pieces and, even if colleagues are injured, be professional enough to carry on. After all, who else is there?'

Accusing fingers were later pointed in all directions. As far as we were concerned, the squad had fucked it up; to them it was our responsibility. Whatever the case, both Drakou and Levy were later convicted at the Old Bailey.

Downing a well-deserved pint, I put the empty glass on the bar and nodded for another. I'm getting too old for this crap, I thought. The pressure had been on for a while for me to take an instructors' course and have a little rest from ops – something I'd fought against for ages. Now, however, the concept was beginning to look slightly more attractive: monday to friday, eight to four, and no pager. When I was in moods like this it almost seemed quite appealing. After all, at thirty-nine years of age, did I really want to get up at 12.30 for a 2a.m. start every day? Did I really need to be called out at three and four in the morning? As it was, the job had already taken a toll on my health, and my body's clock was totally fucked. I was shitting when I was supposed to be sleeping, sleeping when I was supposed to be eating, and drinking far too much. My body just didn't seem to have the resilience anymore, that resolve that it had once had. Perhaps the pressure was getting to me. But I was too stubborn and pig-headed to accept it. After all, even with the unswerving loyalty and commitment the teams gave to the job, we were still only treading water, making no headway. It was almost as if we'd sighted our objective in the distance but couldn't reach out and grasp it, sucked down as we were by the mire of rising crime. I shrugged off the thought.

'Oh well,' Chris smiled, raising his glass. 'Who dares wins . . .'

I nodded, sipping my beer. 'Who cares who fucking wins?'

2

UK SWAT

Beep Beep Beep . . .

I groaned and rolled over in bed, fumbling for the annoying object that had practically ruled my life for the past three and a half years. Picking up the pager, I shut off the noise. On the other side of the bed Jill was already sliding into her slippers, pulling on her dressing-gown and knotting the belt. She ran her fingers through her tousled blonde hair. It was one thirty in the morning and I was on call. Like every other team member's wife, Jill was as much a slave to the job as me. Flicking on the light, she crept silently down the stairs to the kitchen.

I reached for the phone.

'SO19,' snapped the baseman.

'Yeah,' I replied, phone gripped between my shoulder and ear as I danced around the bedroom pulling on my jeans, 'I've just had a U101. What you got that's so important the ARVs can't handle it?'

'Job down in Stoke Newington. The guvnor's down there at the moment, wants a team. Something to do with a Yardie gunman. You want a fast run in?'

I looked at the clock. 'No point. The roads are clear – forty-five minutes tops. Tell whoever gets in first to load up two Rangies, full kit. And in the meantime dig us out a safe route to the RVP. I'll see you shortly.'

Taking the stairs two at a time I grabbed the cup of coffee

from Jill's outstretched hand and drank it on the hoof as I headed for the door. Again, like all wives, Jill never pried, knowing I'd bring her up to speed when time permitted. Kissing her briefly on the cheek I waved and climbed into the car. Shivering involuntarily in the early-morning chill, I gunned the engine and headed off into the night.

I was once asked by a neighbour who knew a little about my occupation, 'You deal with the dregs of humanity every day – notorious hard men and killers, but if you could put your finger on any one particular group, who are the worst?'

Somewhat taken aback I said, 'I'm scared of no man,' but, working it out later, my thoughts were that, though categorising any group is dangerous, if I were to do it loosely I'd have to say that druggies are commonly cowards. Sure, they frequently carry guns for their own protection (and occasionally to rip each other off), but SO19 are way out of their league so by and large they don't bother us. The second category would be the so-called Bermondsey school of armed robbers, good old South London gangsters, again quite predictable. If they see a way out then they'll take it, and if that means using firearms, so be it. Next come the terrorists. With those there's always a hidden agenda. Even if they appear unarmed there's always the strong possibility of a remote device ready to trigger an explosion. And lastly you have the Yardies, the black mafia posses. To me this group ranks as one of the highest threats: unorganised, totally unpredictable, and extremely dangerous. Posse – the name conjures up the image of a wild, untamed rabble riding in and shooting up the town. And that's exactly why they chose it. They have this image of themselves as badmen, who'd shoot you as soon as look at you, and for no other reason than to add to their street cred. No, these men are nasty bastards with a life expectancy of around thirty. And when they shoot at you, they empty the clip.

Yardie – at one time the given name to anybody from

Jamaica, much like a cockney comes from east London. Over the past few years, however, the name has become synonymous with a band of black desperados whose stock in trade is murder, extortion, drug dealing and guns, and whose evil influence has spread like a cancer throughout every major black populated area in the Western world. By the end of the 1980s the Americans, through agencies such as the DEA and the ATF, attempted to warn the United Kingdom of an epidemic heading their way. Sadly the advice fell on deaf ears, and by the time the bureaucrats had got their arses into gear it was too late – a foothold had already been established. The dealing had begun. And the war was to follow.

In the early 1990s, a report by the National Drugs Intelligence Unit warned of an influx of Yardie-type gangs heavily involved in the drug scene. They would stop at nothing, including the use of firearms, to achieve their ultimate aim: domination of their turf. Later, the National Criminal Intelligence Service would take up the reins. They also drew comparisons with the Yardie scene in the United States, and concluded that, although not yet commensurate with that of America, the threat of Yardie crime was on the increase.

The motto 'Who Dares Wins' and the winged Excalibur, badge of the world-renowned Special Air Service, is guaranteed to strike terror into the heart of any armed adversary. But it is lesser known as the unofficial emblem adopted by a US SWAT team operating on the dangerous and violent streets of California's capital, Sacramento. In the previous year Jill and I had taken our holiday in the States, and it was while on vacation that I arranged to meet my American counterpart in the Sacramento Police Department. Call me a sad bastard, but it was something I really wanted to do . . .

'Steve.' The short but powerfully built man had held out his hand, and shaking it vigorously I'd taken in his tanned good looks, shock of sun-bleached blond hair, and piercing cobalt-blue eyes. He looked every inch the all-American good guy I'd come to expect.

'You must be Pat.'

'Good to meet you.' He nodded. 'I've taken the liberty of arranging your day. I hope you don't mind.'

I shook my head. 'No, not at all,' I replied, somewhat nervously. Like Pat I was a veteran of many hundreds of firearms operations, but somehow the thought of riding out with a SWAT team, unarmed and in one of America's major cities, made me feel more than a little excited, even though I knew full well the likelihood of getting involved in anything was as rare as rocking-horse shit. But that was always the way.

Pat smiled and looked at Jill. 'My girlfriend is a patrol officer working the late shift. Would you like to take part in our ride-along program?'

Jill's face broke into a huge grin. To ride out on patrol in a black and white was something you didn't see in every holiday brochure! 'Thanks Pat,' I said. 'What's in store for me?'

He beckoned me to his waiting vehicle, calling to Jill over his shoulder: 'She'll pick you up at twelve.'

I climbed into the spacious interior. Through the thin cotton of my T-shirt my back burned against the sun-soaked leather seats.

'Well,' Pat started, turning on the ignition, 'I've arranged for you to go out with a couple of the guys. To justify a full-time SWAT team in such a small department the men carry out plain-clothes patrols between jobs. Unfortunately we don't have any live operations today, but after work we'll go back to my place, cook some steaks, drink some beer and tell a few lies.'

I laughed. Cops around the world are notorious for embellishing stories of derring-do. 'I heard about your hostage rescue in the civic building last year. Sounded serious.'

He nodded slowly, as if turning back the clock. 'Yeah, I'll tell you about it later,' he replied.

After signing the disclaimer indemnifying the Sacramento Police Department against any harm that might befall me while in their care, I was introduced to Mike and Steve, two of the team and my guardians for the day. Like Pat, both looked tanned and fit. Steve was tall and stocky with a friendly, smiling face and a mop of sandy coloured hair; Mike was darker, smaller, with a droopy, Mexican-style moustache. Both had an air about them and that made me feel safe.

After booking out the unmarked patrol vehicle I huddled down in the back seat, adjusting my Ray-Bans and feeling a bit of an imposter. We drove out of the compound and into the mid-morning California sunshine to cruise the maze of residential streets.

'What's your biggest problem in London?' Steve called from behind the wheel.

I studied his eyes, framed by the rear-view mirror. 'Much the same as yours, I guess,' I replied. 'The same old round of blaggers and druggies.'

'Blaggers?' Mike asked, glancing over his shoulder.

'Armed robbers,' I replied. 'I suppose the only thing we get to deal with more than you is terrorists.' I shrugged, knowing that many Catholic American police officers held a certain affinity with the Irish population. What really gripped my shit was the fact that New York officers would actively take part in the St Patrick's day celebrations with drums and pipers.

Steve nodded. 'Yeah. The IRA. I've seen that on TV. Terrible . . .'

I sighed and looked out of the open window. Gone were the plush houses with their neatly trimmed lawns; gone were the white picket fences and covered pools. Wooden homes now stood in close proximity, paint peeling from their neglected walls; tarmac drives held clapped-out vehicles, and the faces that now stared our way were predominantly black. The air here was one of distinct hostility.

'This is one of our downtown areas,' Steve explained pleasantly. 'We'll have a drive around and see what we can pick up.' He turned the wheel and we slid into a side-street. 'Do you have many drive-bys?' he asked with interest.

'Occasionally,' I replied. 'But I wouldn't say it was a great problem.'

'How about Yardies?'

'Yeah – some,' I answered. 'We get quite a lot of shootings in Brixton. How about you?'

He slowed the car to walking pace and pointed across the street. 'See that house over there?'

I nodded. 'Well, there was a drive-by here last week. The parents were standing in front of the garage with their seventeen-year-old son. He was hit.' He looked in the mirror, catching my eye. 'Third time this month – same house. You notice anything different?'

I studied the building. 'No,' I replied.

'It happens so often that they just can't afford to get it fixed. Even if they did, same thing would happen. I guess they gotta cover the holes with something.'

Swinging the wheel, he pulled over to the kerb. I removed my glasses and squinted, then burst out laughing – for, like some large, wounded animal, the entire house was covered in sticking plasters.

'SWAT teams here in the States,' Pat explained later, 'often devise their own tactics. About five years ago we started doing some work with simunition.' This is a coloured, waxy soap-based round used in exercises, when participants are wearing specially devised safety gear and goggles. Ideal for man-on-man scenarios, it is an invaluable training aid and something we in SO19 had just started experimenting with. Pat continued. 'In a hostage rescue situation it soon became apparent that, in more than sixty per cent of cases, the first man through the door was dead.'

I nodded. 'Yeah, that's something I'm deeply aware of, but it's an unfortunate fact of life. We've tried everything from stun-grenades to dogs, but if you've a dedicated professional in the room waiting for you, then he'll get off a shot or two before you can even react.'

I was in luck. As we spoke a call came in that there was a SWAT job scheduled for three that afternoon: a Yardie crack joint in a bad area of town. Out on patrol, Mike and Steve had stopped a scruffy-looking individual for a moving traffic violation and had quickly found drugs, discovered that the guy was on parole and in breach of his probation, and found a loaded rifle in the trunk of his car. Dumping their captive off at the local sheriff's central booking hall, they'd quickly made their way back to base, adrenalin pumping at the thought of a live op.

It was there that I now spoke to Pat.

'Looks like you're gonna get a chance to see some of the tactics we devised later this afternoon,' he said. 'I realised from our work with simunition that it was the silhouette of a man that the suspect was shooting at. It's what he expects. I reckoned, break up that silhouette and he becomes disorientated. First we added a ballistic helmet with a heavy visor. Then I started to experiment with cut-out wooden shields of different designs. Eventually, when I was happy with the shape, I had a company make one up: a round, twenty-two-inch shield. At first they were sceptical, but now they carry it in their brochure under the brand name the California Shield.'

'Good idea,' I said. 'How did the team take to the new tactics?'

Pat flashed me a toothy grin. 'At first I had a few moans,' he said. 'The guys seemed to think that it somehow detracted from the macho image a bit – you know, rushing into a room with a shield and helmet somehow took away the sporting chance aspect.'

I laughed as Pat continued. 'Unfortunately I'm not into giving people a sporting chance. I'm only here to save my guys' lives. I think I can safely say that I completely turned around the odds. Now, in sixty per cent of cases we are engaging the suspect first; and in those where we aren't the bunker man is taking a hit in the helmet or shield. The other plus I've noticed is that we can use the shield itself as a weapon, knocking any unarmed troublemakers clean into the cheap seats. I can safely say I've never lost a man yet using this technique. We were on the job a few months back. Mike was the point man, and because of the shield he could only use a handgun. We had an armed and barricaded suspect. Mike hit the door hard,' Pat smiled, 'and as he went through this guy pointed a rifle at him. Mike got off the first shot with his Sig, but he hit the back of the shield he was carrying. Even at point-blank range the bullet just lodged in the Kevlar without over-penetrating, which shows you the shield's ballistic properties. Anyway, the force of that first round knocked the shield to one side, helping Mike to get off a second round which hit the suspect square in the torso.'

'What happened?' I asked.

'He died,' Pat said matter-of-factly.

The team had begun filing into the room. The briefing (by SO19's standards) was short, sharp and to the point – but precisely the way I like it. To me it exemplified a team used to working together as one, and those words left unsaid spoke volumes. As the operation was somewhat impromptu, Pat had only managed to scrape together an eight-man team, or I should say seven men and one woman – Denise. Denise was somewhat an anomaly by SWAT team standards. Far from being the butch East-German-shotputting type you'd expect, she was small, almost petite. With a little make-up and shoulder-length streaked hair, she somehow had managed to maintain her femininity in this male-dominated environment. Apparently she was a crack shot, who had more than satisfied the exacting standards required to become a SWAT team member.

Looking around the small, cramped room, I was

immediately struck by the colossal size of some of the players. It was evident from their bulging biceps that upper body strength played a major part in their training.

Throwing me a set of heavyweight body-armour, Pat quickly explained that we would be driven to the venue in the back of the team's covert white van. The target address was a single-storey brown and white bungalow which had been recced earlier in the day. Special agents from the Bureau of Narcotic Enforcement – along with some local narcs would surround and contain the perimeter, co-ordinating with the arrival of the team van, which would stop directly outside the premises. The team would deploy, hit the address by forcible entry and secure the suspects inside. I smiled at the similarities in tactics and equipment, even down to the MP5s. It was a classic Trojan horse job.

I swayed with the rhythm of the engine as the horse took off from the compound and made its way slowly to the RVP, a small side-street on an industrial estate some distance from the plot. During the journey I joined in with the banter and pre-operational small talk of a team staring death in the face, though I still felt like an outsider. After ten minutes the van slowed, then juddered firmly to a halt as the engine died.

'OK, guys,' Pat announced happily, 'now we wait.'

Emerging from the back of the van I squinted against the harsh sunlight before jumping the short distance to the ground. In small groups stood a number of plain-clothes officers sporting blue baseball caps emblazoned with the word POLICE in yellow lettering – or in the case of the BNE officers an impressive badge with the words SPECIAL AGENT. Over the top of their body armour, all wore thin blue nylon raid jackets, again with POLICE stencilled across the back in large letters. It was imperative that nobody would be in any doubt as to who the good guys were, particularly the perps, Pat explained.

'Hi, I'm John,' came a pleasant voice from over my shoulder. I turned to see an officer dressed similarly to the rest of the narcs in tatty jeans and trainers, but with a tactical vest that was littered with a vast array of stick-pins and badges, all of which glittered in the sun. 'Steve's from the London SWAT team,' Pat told him. 'He'll be on the raid with us today.'

'Nice to have you aboard,' John said, patting me on the shoulder.

After five minutes or so I was aware of a change in mood. The radio had begun to crackle continuously and I instinctively knew we were about to get the go. Almost immediately Pat confirmed my instincts. 'Haul out, guys. They're home.'

While we had waited patiently at the RV, an OP consisting of undercover narcotic detectives had been watching the address waiting for a delivery of some gear, and the drop had apparently just taken place. Now the danger level was escalated, and it was down to SWAT.

With minor adjustments to helmet straps and belt-rigs, the team mounted up. Mike and Steve posed for a photograph for me as the van rolled along. Having clicked off a frame it suddenly dawned on me that the only thing I'd be armed with was a camera!

All of a sudden I was jerked to my senses. It was happening. The van shuddered to a bone-jarring halt, the back doors, already ajar, were flung open with a resounding crash, and sunlight flooded the gloomy interior.

'Go, Go, Go!'

The team disappeared into the streets, accompanied by the squeal of tyres as the back-up units arrived. *Crash!* Pat hit the flimsy door with the hand-held ram, imploding it inwards in a display of splintered wood and glass. Screams emanated from inside as the team filtered in. 'Swat! Swat! Down, Down!'

It was all over before I'd reached the door. A strange, uneasy silence hung in the air, then Pat emerged smiling, his heavy ballistic helmet swinging limply in his hand. 'Come and take some more photos, Steve,' he called.

Inside, the stench of stale sweat and human excreta permeated the fabric of the building. The suspects, all black, lay face down on the filthy, threadbare carpet, their dishevelled appearance and stained T-shirts testament to their devotion to crack cocaine. In the small, sparsely furnished kitchen, the thick layers of grease and fat were more than enough to sustain the appetites of the constant stream of cockroaches.

'Steve.'

I looked around to where John was silhouetted in the doorway. 'There's something I'd like you to see,' he said, beckoning me with his finger.

The soles of my trainers stuck to the grime as I made my way across the kitchen floor and into the hall. There I was greeted by a sight I'll never forget.

I looked down into the pathetic, dark, drug-saturated eyes of what at first I thought was a dwarf, standing some four and a half feet tall. Only as I let my eyes wander further downwards to the large pair of fibreglass ski-boots, did I realise that what I was actually looking at was a full-grown man, but a man so wasted by drugs that the bottom half of both his legs were twisted and deformed. Because his veins had all but collapsed through years of constant drug abuse, his legs were forced into ski-boots for support. The rancid, sickly sweet smell from his ulcerated, putrescent limbs bore witness to his addiction. Barely able to stand and oblivious to his surroundings, he merely stared into space, the only thing on his mind being the next fix.

'That's what we're up against in this wonderful, golden state of California,' John explained outside, pushing a souvenir BNE raid jacket and a special agent's baseball cap into my hands. 'For God's sake, don't let it happen in England too.'

It was still dark when I pulled into the yard at Old Street. Smoke plumes billowed gently into the cold night sky from the exhausts of the two black Range Rovers parked there.

Passing by on my way inside, I ran my hand over the sleek, dark lines of the three-and-a-half-ton armoured vehicles.

The locker room was a hive of activity. Jigging about on one leg, Chris was pulling on his dark blue coveralls as the rest of the team checked their personal gear and radios. He looked up and nodded. 'All right, Stevie? Motors are loaded up and ready to go. Don't know the full SP on the job, but the guvnor said we wouldn't need a van.'

I scanned the interior of the small room, making a mental head-count. 'I'll go and see what the baseman's got. How many more to come?'

'This was all they could get,' said Chris, pulling on the other leg. 'You, and five – minimum strength.'

I sighed, walking back to the door. 'Well let's hope we can get it done and dusted quick, so we can fuck off home.'

'I'll second that,' Chris called at my back.

Sitting behind his computer console, the ever-busy baseman looked up from his screen as I entered the control room. The desk was staffed twenty-four hours a day by a member of the ARVs, and it was certainly a job I didn't envy. Working alone, the operator manned three telephones, the Met Police radio, computer-aided despatch, and the teleprinter, all of which comprised the nucleus of SO19 operations.

'All right, Sarge?' the baseman asked, munching on a sandwich.

'Yeah, what you got?'

He swallowed hard. 'Like I said on the phone, job at Stokey. Some Yardie type has done a robbery. Handgun was seen and he's gone to ground in a spieler.'

I nodded. Often operating out of the fortified basements of run-down buildings, these illegal drinking and gambling dens attracted the more unsavoury elements of the local community. They stayed open long into the morning, so I knew it was likely to be still busy when we hit it. 'What's the SP so far?' I asked.

Taking another bite, he chewed slowly before answering.

'Locals have kept a watch on the place since he went in. The guvnor and a couple of cars are round the corner in case he comes out.'

I frowned. 'Why not simply take him when he leaves? A high-profile street ambush with a couple of ARVs would be safer all round.'

He nodded. 'Preservation of evidence, Sarge. He might not have the gear or the shooter when he leaves.'

'Fair comment,' I said, tearing a rough map of the route in from the teleprinter. 'But I'm well thin on the ground. See if you can get me some SO19 dogs.' In my mind there is no greater way of sorting out an unruly rabble than a good old snapping dog!

Joining the rest of the team in the armoury, I pulled my MP5 from the rack and instinctively checked the action, which slid back with a well-oiled click. Taking out a thirty-round magazine, I was about to load when a long, dark object on the rack caught my eye. 'Anybody taking the eight-seventy?' I asked, replacing the magazine and carbine.

'No,' they all shook their heads in unison.

'You're not taking that, are you?' Chris asked as he loaded and holstered his Glock.

'Fucking right,' I said, hoisting the Remington from the rack. With its folding stock forward, its entire length was only thirty inches – eleven inches longer than the MP5, but its overall appearance was something quite different. It had a pistol-type grip, and could chamber seven small-game rounds, and with each cartridge holding nine balls, each the size of a nine-millimetre MP5 round, the firepower was devastating. I estimated the spread of shot at seven yards (beyond the width of the average room) to be no more than about six inches, which also made it extremely accurate. Racking back the slide with one movement, I turned the weapon upside-down and rested the stock on one knee; then with my thumb I began to insert the rounds into the magazine. 'Nice one,' I said as the last round slid home. 'You know, there's nothing as reassuring as the sound of a pump-action being racked.' I snapped the foregrip forward and engaged a round in the chamber. 'It really is a great leveller.'

Climbing into the Rangey next to Chris, who was my driver, I turned on the blue lights and nodded. As the six-man team swept out of the yard and into the unknown, I grinned. 'Another day, another dollar.'

The Rangies pulled silently up to the kerb under the bright, artificial glare of the sodium street lamps in the dingy north London side-street. Shaking off the early-morning chill, Chris and I strode purposefully towards the vehicles and the small huddle of men standing nearby.

Andy, the guvnor, nodded in acknowledgement. 'All right, Stevie?' There was, he explained, no update since the initial call-out. The locals were still convinced the gunman was inside, and Andy was faced with a dilemma. With few misgivings he weighed up the odds – after all he was the boss, and it was his call. Did the importance of the evidence that may be disposed of due to a delay in entering outweigh the risk a rapid entry posed to a team? He decided that it did: to recover the firearm we had to move fast.

We were going in. And I for one wasn't about to argue. Still, I found the whining of the support dogs raring to go almost encouraging.

'Any of the locals been inside this place before?' I asked. We had just debussed at the FUP. 'If I could get some sort of interior plan, however rough, then it could be to our advantage.

'I have,' came a voice from the rear of the group. The speaker looked me up and down. 'I was the one who saw him go in. We've done this place before. Piece of piss.'

I eyed up the short, skinny frame of the plain-clothes crime squad officer. 'Oh yeah?' I raised one eyebrow. 'Then why the fuck do you need us, Rambo?' It was always a pain in the arse, especially after being dragged out of bed in the early hours of the morning, to meet gung-ho arseholes who thought they could get the job done without the proper support. Even in America, where every police officer is armed, they still await the arrival of a SWAT team for the risky assignments. But, with that stiff upper lip and Dixon of Dock Green resolve, the good old British Bobby still considered himself invincible.

'Chris,' I hissed. 'Go with him, have a look at the entry points.'

He nodded and moved off at a trot. Five minutes later he returned. 'Fucking place is a nightmare,' he said. 'Bars on the fucking windows, fortified doors, everything.'

I looked him in the eye. 'Well?'

He grinned. 'Door should go if it's not barricaded, but it may take some time.'

I smiled. 'That's exactly what I wanted to hear.'

Chris held out a rough sketch on his notepad. 'Guy reckons it's something like this, but I'd take that with a pinch of salt.'

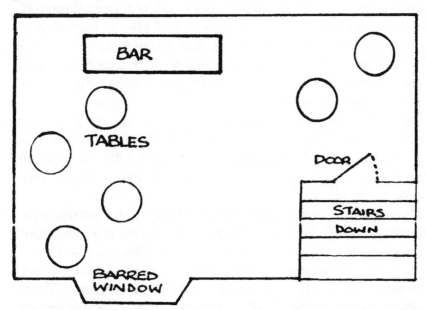

I looked up from the sketch at the somewhat arrogant face

of the artist. 'Yeah,' I said. 'Get kitted, get the guns, quick heads down then we'll do it.'

I looked around the half-dozen hooded faces, distinguishable only by their team numbers, emblazoned in silver on a black background and worn on the sleeves of their coveralls. I held up and pointed to Chris's small notepad. 'This is apparently a sketch of the interior, but don't take it as read. You all know what we're up against, and the latest intelligence – for want of a better word – is that there are only six people inside, our man being one of them. Chris will hit the door. I want a rapid entry, no time for those inside to react. Hit them and hit them hard.'

Their heads nodded in unison.

'Everybody will be placed face-down in situ. Group Two, in support of us, will be the dogs and ARV personnel. We'll cover, they'll cuff. Once, and *only* once we're secure, will the local arrest-and-search teams be called in.' I looked to Andy. 'If it's OK with you, guv, the team will pull out, leaving the ARVs as armed support while the locals search. No point in sparking a riot if they see the black kit.' Andy nodded. 'I'll stay anyway. You ready to go?'

'Ready as I'll ever be,' I replied, hoisting the menacing eight-seventy into the high-port carrying position. 'You sure there's only six?'

Chris gave the thumbs up, then with the small red enforcer slung across his broad shoulders he set off towards our objective.

Stacking silently in the litter-strewn back alley outside the basement flat, we adopted our final assault positions. No time now for chatter – radio silence had been adopted, leaving everything down to hand signals. Dressed from head to foot in the dark assault gear, the remnants of night in the sky made us almost invisible. Through the inky blackness I watched as Chris and his support man darted noiselessly towards the steel door before disappearing from sight down the small flight of stairs. Barely audible behind me was the strangely reassuring raspy breathing of the dogs, hand-picked for their stealth while moving and their courage once deployed.

I peered down the stairs as Chris looked up in my direction, his white eyes clearly visible through the round eyeholes of his hood.

'Stand by,' I whispered urgently into the radio. 'Go! Go! Go!'

Crasshh! The ram connected with the fortified door, a kinetic energy of four and a half tons slamming into the lock, which yielded slightly.

Crasshh! Chris hit it again. On the third attempt the lock gave up the fight, sending the door smashing inwards.

Suddenly I was up, sprinting full-pelt and taking the small flight of stairs two at a time towards the opening, where the gentle swirl of sickly sweet drug-laced smoke now hung in the chill night air.

MP5 now drawn, Chris blanked out the dim light from within as he and his cover-man silhouetted the door, then I was in, adrenalin racing as I scanned the small, cramped interior.

Something on the intelligence side was very obviously wrong. If there were six people inside it was more like twenty-fucking-six. At one table alone sat a posse, while at the bar, at the back and off to the left, people were milling around in their droves, talking, drinking and smoking ganja. We were in the shit!

Fuck, Fuck, Fuck, my brain cried out as I took in the sea of black faces staring at me! There seemed to be hundreds. It was Rourkes fucking Drift.

Coming to my senses, I levelled the eight-seventy, looking for any sign of the suspect, noise all around me as the full impact of the assault came to a head. 'Armed police!' I screamed. 'Down, down, down!' Still on the move, maintaining the momentum and aggression, I made for the round table directly ahead. Coins, notes, half-empty glasses of drink and playing cards lay haphazardly on its shiny surface. Around it, at least ten sets of eyes locked in my direction. It was impossible to see their hands, which in my mind constituted a threat so had to be treated as such.

Everybody has at one time or another watched a third-rate spaghetti Western with two gunfighters squaring up to each other on the main street, the camera flicking dramatically from one set of eyes to the other. What the fuck for?

Eyes don't kill you, hands do! And not at the unrealistic length of a main street, but at the width of a room – a room much like this!

Making the table within a split second of coming through the door, and with the eight-seventy held high, I lifted my boot and kicked it on the run, spilling its contents on to the sticky, wet, foul-smelling floor.

Movement, way off to my left. Chris screaming, 'Armed police! On the floor! On the floor!' accompanied by unintelligible Jamaican gibberish and the baying of the dogs, eager for action. Now I was fucked. I'd gone as far as I dare, and with ten suspects to cover I had to hold my ground, unable to move on into the unruly mob to back up the team – for in doing so I would leave their backs exposed, and if our man was at the table he would pull the trigger in an instant. No, all I could do now was cover the table and pray that the rest of the guys could cope.

Somebody had fucked up large. We were well outnumbered, and that in itself was dangerous.

Through the slits in my hood I stared at the large frame of the rasta opposite. Sitting in a chair, he had his hands clasped firmly on his head, fingers interlaced, his long hair hanging in true Rastafarian style in thick, matted dreadlocks. An ugly six-inch scar ran through his left eye and cut a deep furrow through his cheek before coming to rest at the corner of his mouth. Obviously no stranger to violence, he smiled defiantly, but I could see he was eyeing the eight-seventy with 'respec'.

Then, sucking on his teeth, he mumbled, 'UK SWAT,' in a quick-fire Jamaican accent. 'UK SWAT,' he repeated, louder this time.

'UK SWAT . . .' the contemptuous chant grew louder as it reverberated around the small room.

I grinned, and my earpiece burst into life. It was Chris: 'Room secure, Stevie, you can call in the arrest team when you want.'

Taking the big man by the wrist, an ARV crewman slipped on the thin, white nylon plasticuff, pulling it until it was tight; then pulling the rasta's arm behind his back, he secured the other wrist and placed him face-down on the floor. All around the room similar events were taking place under the ever-watchful and intense eyes of the dogs, who would occasionally bark at the odd stroppy prisoner as the chanting all but died.

Working their way slowly around the circle the ARV crew finally came to the last man who, in stark contrast to Scarface, was paralysed with fear. Sitting bolt upright in his chair, eyes wide and staring, he still had his hand of cards clasped tightly to his chest. Leaning over him I said, 'You bullshitting bastard! You should have chucked those ages ago!'

Before leaving the locals to clear up the mess, I made a quick head count. 'Twenty-four,' I mumbled. 'Twenty-four fucking suspects! Four times the amount we were told.' But it was pointless to complain.

As one job rolled on to another, I never did find out if a gun had been found – or for that matter even the suspect – and to be honest I didn't really care. All I knew was that we'd been called in to do yet another dirty job that nobody else would touch, and now, as always, we would ride off into the sunset.

3

The Russians Are Coming

In the months that followed I quickly came to realise that, for all their reports and no matter how well intentioned, the warnings from the Americans had come too late. And what I'd previously witnessed in that filthy house half-way around the globe was now fast becoming a reality.

The number of SO19 operations against the so-called crime gangs was rapidly on the increase, albeit at different levels. While the Yardies plodded along in their own disorganised yet indomitable style, dealing crack and killing anybody who stood in their way, other, more organised groups were also making headway, and the term 'Mafia', a word seldom before used in British law-enforcement parlance, was fast becoming commonplace.

To my mind, it was the Colombians who lay at the root of the problem. Their organised crime groups, the so-called cartels, were to prove ultimately responsible . . .

Thousands of miles away on a remote Caribbean island, a DEA informant was at work. An informant so highly placed, and with information so damaging, that he would eventually pay with his life. In the war that was to follow, SO19 would be at the forefront of the fight – a fight that would result in an enormous blow to the infamous Medellin cartel and the capture of a notorious drugs overlord.

'What the fuck is that?'

I gagged involuntarily, spitting a half-chewed mouthful of toast on to the stained brown top of the canteen table. Chris followed my gaze out of the window to the car park beyond the nissan hut.

We were at the Metropolitan Police's firearms training establishment at Lippitts Hill, situated in the leafy heart of Epping Forest. The camp consists of nothing more than three twenty-five-metre and one fifty-metre semi-open-air ranges, low level accommodation and administration blocks, and a wooden canteen. Standing in approximately twenty acres of ground and surrounded by high chain-link fencing, Lippitts Hill has remained practically unchanged since its days as a prisoner of war camp. It is flanked to the south and west by the West Essex Golf Course, while within the safety of the perimeter fence lies the helicopter fleet of the Metropolitan Police: the Air Support Unit. To the rear of the camp, next to an abseil tower and assault course, is a small grassy knoll with subterranean bunkers. This area is known as the Banjo.

'Looks like a Russian invasion,' scowled Joe, pushing back his chair and craning his neck for a better view – which could quite easily have been achieved if he'd bothered to get his arse out of the chair. Joe had recently rejoined the team after having fallen out with the guvnor, Andy, and having served his penance by driving a uniformed Armed Response Vehicle through the streets of London. Tough and outspoken, Joe was a likeable character – tall and strong, his hair cropped close to his head – and he had easily slipped back into his role as MOE man.

Outside, the three distinctly colourful uniforms had got out of the car and been greeted by the camp commandant. Now they strode purposefully our way.

'What you looking at, fellas?' Bill asked in his familiar Liverpudlian accent. Throwing his dark blue beret on to the table he slumped into the chair next to Chris. A stocky ex-Royal Marine who, after many winters spent in Norway, called himself the Arctic Fox, Bill was also a Black Team member, currently seconded to the Lippitts training staff. He sipped hot tea from a styrofoam cup and smiled. 'You know, we have a set of rules around here . . .'

'Oh yeah?' Chris said, taking his eyes off the visitors and eyeing Bill cautiously. 'What are they then?'

Bill put the cup quietly on the table. 'Well, the golden one is never look out of the canteen window in the morning.'

'Why?' asked Joe.

'Because,' Bill replied, 'you'll have fuck all to do in the afternoon.'

I bit off another piece of toast and swallowed it with a mouthful of coffee. 'That bad is it?'

'Bad? It's fucking dead! You have to make your own entertainment around here.'

I looked around the canteen and picked out the familiar faces of some of the older instructors – or 'staff' as they preferred to be called: immaculate in their training blues, berets on their heads (worn at jaunty angles of course) and trousers tucked into their boots (presumably to protect against snake bites). I'm afraid I just didn't get on too well with most of them – as the team well knew! They didn't like my methods, and I in turn hated theirs. Some of them had been instructing for donkey's years, yet still talked of the 'good old Streatham siege of ten years ago' as if it were yesterday – the 'good old bad old days', when the department was D11, the Blue Berets . . . the days when men were men, and boys were glad of it! To them, I was a maverick; to me, they were dinosaurs.

'The other day,' Bill said, 'I had some Royal Protection Officers and DPG guys up on a refresher. I told them we'd do some realistic training pertinent to their own roles. In the morning it was the royalties' turn – I had everybody jumping about and engaging targets all over the place, and when we went in for lunch they were really looking forward to the afternoon. After lunch I took them all into a room and closed the door. "Now we'll do some DPG stuff," I whispered, and asked for a volunteer. One bloke jumped up straight away. "Right, stand on that door," I told him, and called for another volunteer. Again one stepped up straight away.' Bill paused.

'What happened then?' I asked.

'Then I gave everybody else a magazine. "Right, sit down and read these," I said, and pointed to the second volunteer. "And in two hours I want you to relieve him on that door."'

We all laughed at that one: DPG work was as boring as the Queen's Christmas address to the nation.

'I was reading an article the other day,' Bill continued. 'Apparently they now reckon you can catch AIDS through your ears.'

'Fuck off,' said Joe. 'How?'

Bill jumped up and scooped his beret from the table. 'By listening to arseholes!' He walked towards the door.

I scoured the canteen, locking in on the old familiar faces. 'Yeah – and if arseholes could fly this place would be a fucking airport.'

'Fuck's sake,' Joe whispered as the three Russians strode purposefully into the canteen. I studied them curiously before deciding that the short guy in front must be the man in charge. Not only did he have a certain air of authority about him, but he had a hat you could land a fucking helicopter on. It was huge. And medals? He had more than the Imperial War Museum!

The little group was ushered out of the main canteen and into the small senior officers' dining room. We were quite used to seeing visiting dignitaries from all parts of the world; what they thought of Lippitts Hill, however, I'll never know.

Scotland Yard it seems is world renowned for its professionalism, and quite rightly that extends to firearms. Thus SO19 were seen by many as a flagship for the Met, the premier firearms training department for the United Kingdom, God help us. And therein lay the answer to the Russia contingent's visit: we were to learn later that, with the fall of the Soviet Union and the subsequent increase in criminal activity, the Russian police service were now desperately in need of a new training package – and like many before them they turned to the Yard for help.

The car screeched to an abrupt halt. With wide, panic-stricken eyes the screaming female was dragged from the passenger seat of the vehicle. The crazed gunman held the woman as a shield, and with his free hand brought up the pistol. *Bang!* A single shot rang out.

'OK. End-ex, end-ex,' called out the instructor. Flicking on the light he removed his ear-defenders and examined the screen of the gallery range: the neat, round hole beside the gunman allowed the glare of the backlight to flood through, indicating a miss.

The instructor looked up and smiled. 'Well, you didn't get him on this occasion, but don't worry – it's only an aid.' The Russian nodded as he continued. 'The film is controlled by a sensor; the noise of the weapon being fired is enough to freeze the image on the screen, enabling the back lighting to shine through the bullet-hole and indicate the fall of shot.' Having now grasped their full attention he added, 'This is an invaluable training aid which not only tests your accuracy of aim but also tactics and reaction time. It's often used as part of a comprehensive package to test an officer's mental attitude before he goes back on operations after being involved in a shooting incident.'

'I see,' said the Russian aide in his heavy accent. 'You can see if he is still mentally able to pull the trigger?'

'Not only that,' replied the instructor. 'More importantly, we can see if he is still able *not* to pull the trigger. You see, not all of these videos are shoot scenarios. It would be pointless for me now to play the conclusion of the incident you just dealt with; for all you know the suspect may have been about to drop his weapon and surrender. But that is academic. You chose to shoot him at that moment; you considered him a threat, so in real life the incident would have ended there.'

In fact, many of the videos used by SO19 for training purposes could be construed as being slightly ambiguous – incidents where different interpretations on what is actually happening could be applied. This of course is strictly intentional. By assessing the situation before him and applying what he'd been taught, a student must make a conscious decision to shoot or not shoot. Many would often react in different ways, simply because there was no right or wrong answer. All that is asked of the student is that, whatever his decision, he must later be able to lawfully justify his actions.

'You see,' the instructor continued, 'hindsight is an exact science.'

Again the Russian aide nodded. 'Yes. I like this, I can see it has great advantages.'

'Would you like to try, sir?' the instructor asked the man in charge.

The aide bent over and whispered an urgent translation into the short man's ear, and suddenly his face broke into a huge grin and he nodded enthusiastically. He rose from his chair and headed for the point.

'OK sir,' the instructor started, 'this weapon is loaded. For the purposes of this exercise, you are an armed police officer out on patrol, and you simply have to deal with what happens before you in any way you see fit.' He ran the video on to a new scenario. Bending to turn out the light, he looked up and froze in horror, for standing at an angle in front of the screen was the Russian officer, his left hand placed firmly on his hip with his arm crooked, the pistol in his right hand pointed skywards.

The instructor groaned. 'Sir, please, I've already explained range safety. The weapon must be pointed down range and towards the screen at all times. You must remember this one has a particularly light pull on the trig—'

Bang!

Fine white powder floated lazily down from the torn ceiling. 'Oh fuck,' the instructor muttered, looking up at the jagged hole and thinking of the mounds of paperwork. Taking the weapon gingerly from the officer's fingers he asked, 'This may sound odd, sir, but have you ever had any formal type of firearms training?'

The Russian smiled in response. 'Officer, in my country I have but one particular task: the *coup de grâce*.'

'OK, fellas, listen up.'

The hum of conversation died and I looked up to see a tall, thin, flame-haired figure dressed in dark coveralls. It was Tony, a legend within the department, and an SO19 veteran who, after singlehandedly gunning down three robbers on an ambush, had been given the nickname 'The Equaliser' by the national press.

Tony waited until he had the group's full attention before commencing his briefing. Following the collapse of the Soviet Union and the Eastern Bloc alliance, he explained, fierce gangs of Russian mafia cut-throats and racketeers were able suddenly to flaunt their trade in weapons, drugs and prostitution in the faces of the vastly inadequate local police forces. As Tony elaborated, the presence of the visitors began falling into place. The Russian senior officers were so desperately seeking new ideas from Scotland Yard, worried perhaps that these criminal gangs would find new frontiers open to them, free from the constraints of communist Russia, and gain a foothold in Western Europe and its major cities. London seemed the ideal spot.

Tony pointed to an immaculately drawn set of plans attached to the white board. 'The Hilton Hotel, Park Lane, W1.' For the next fifteen minutes he covered the plan, postings, actions on, contingencies, casevac, re-org, handover, withdrawal, and debrief. By the end of the lecture each man within the team was a hundred per cent certain of his task within the op.

Ten minutes later I was climbing into my coveralls and pulling on the heavyweight body armour, pausing only to drag the heavy ceramic ballistic plate from the bottom of my bergen. Ripping open the Velcro pocket on the front cover, I slid the plate in easily before sealing it shut.

'Fuck's sake,' said Chris from across the small briefing room. 'Do you know something we don't?'

I laughed and tapped the front of my armour reassuringly. 'Nah. Just got a feeling; you know what it's like sometimes.'

He nodded. It was strange – sometimes you'd have a little niggling doubt about a job. Invariably nothing happened, but upgrading the ballistic property of my body armour to stop a 7.62 round had a strangely calming effect. Since we'd been told that you stand a seventy per cent chance of surviving a head shot, yet a seventy per cent chance of dying from a groin wound, I'd noticed that a lot of the guys had taken to wearing the detachable groin protectors.

From our base at Old Street we mounted up into two covert vans and made our way slowly to Scotland Yard for the final leg of the briefing. That in itself was strange.

I checked my watch: 1.15 a.m.

Having finally managed to get past the miserable jobsworth on the gate of the Yard – they always had spaces for senior officers, and how the fuck could the compound be full at this time of the day? – we filed into the large, airy briefing room.

'Lovely view,' said Chris, pulling back the bomb-proof curtains.

'Gentlemen!'

I spun round at the sound of the authoritative voice. 'Fucking hell,' I whispered to Chris and Joe. 'I didn't know it was fancy dress. I'd have worn stockings and slingbacks.'

Chris laughed.

'Thank you so much for coming . . .'

I took in the large, almost portly figure before me, dressed immaculately in a dark three-piece suit, a blue and white polka dot tie secured firmly at his throat and a matching handkerchief cascading boldly from his top pocket helping to complete the flamboyant image. There were grins all round, but one thing was certain: he'd certainly captured the attention of the teams.

He continued: 'I have the privilege of being in charge of this operation, but I'll be running it from here.' He nodded to a smartly dressed woman seated to his right. 'The detective inspector over there will be on the ground with you; besides, I'd only be in the way!'

We laughed. The guy may have appeared eccentric, but he had the right attitude and I was actually beginning to like him.

'I don't know what you've been told to date, but let me bring you up to speed on the information.' He peered round the room to ensure he had captured everybody's attention. 'Now – what's the best way to put this? We have received information from the Russian authorities that three so-called chetnicks are staying in two rooms at London's Hilton Hotel, Park Lane.' He paused and nodded to Tony. 'I believe your colleague has the details.'

Tony nodded.

'These three men are believed to be planning the kidnapping and execution of a prominent American jewish businessman and his family.' He paused for effect. 'Gentlemen, the home secretary, the commissioner and Her Majesty's Government would like it made clear to these people that they are not welcome in this country. And that we do not wish them to return. Do I make myself clear?' he smiled.

'As fucking crystal,' I muttered.

'What the fuck does he want us to do?' Chris asked quietly.

I grinned. 'I think he's telling us to teach them a fucking good lesson, don't you?' The murmur that ran through the room suddenly died as the guvnor continued. 'Gentlemen,' he said quietly, 'before your colleague runs through the plan, there's a word of Russian you may like to use. You see, these guys are terrified of their own special forces. If they thought they were involved, it may have the desired effect. The word is simply *"militia"*.'

'Militia,' I said. 'Yeah, I like it.'

'Do we have any indication of weapons?' asked a member of Green team.

'Good point,' he replied. 'We have information that they stopped off in Germany en route, and the intelligence is that they picked up some weapons. The type and calibre is unknown, but I think we can assume that it's handguns.' Pointing to Tony he nodded, and for the second time that morning for the benefit of the arrest and search teams, Tony outlined the plan.

The twenty-eight storey, four-hundred-and-forty-six-room London Hilton Hotel stands grandly on the east side of Park Lane. To the west, it commands stunning views across the green expanse of Hyde Park and the Serpentine, while to the south-east lies Buckingham Palace, Constitution Hill and, ultimately, the Thames.

Pulling off Park Lane, the Range Rover, accompanied by two innocuous-looking white vans, glided silently to a halt in Hertford Street, stopping just short of a small flight of steps that announced the tradesmen's entrance of the hotel.

The plan in itself was relatively simple: the hotel security manager had provided each team with a masterkey – a small, white plastic card about the size of a credit card. The locks of the hotel, he explained, were constructed in such a fashion that, when the key was inserted into a slot in the door and quickly removed, the lock would disengage and a small light on the door would turn from red to green to indicate that the procedure was successful. The whole operation was virtually silent, which suited our purposes adequately.

Now that we knew we could gain entry we considered any possibilities that could baulk our progress, and came up with two. First, the door could be barricaded from inside but unless they were extremely paranoid this seemed unlikely; second, and more likely, the security chain would be fitted. Both eventualities had to be covered in the contingency plans, so the MOE men (in this case Joe and Chris) had equipped themselves with bolt-croppers and a small hand-held Enforcer battering ram for smashing down the door, should it be required.

Using hotel porters as guides, the teams were to be led up the tradesmen's stairs to their respective corridors (the Russians had split up prior to checking in, and were staying in two rooms on different floors). Green team, with Tony in charge, were to take out the head honcho, leaving myself and Black team to take out the two so-called 'soldiers' who were sharing a two-hundred-and-sixty-pound-a-night twin room overlooking the park. The hits would be co-ordinated by radio. Once entry had been gained and the suspects secured (providing there were no incidents, of course), the arrest and search teams would be called in to take over and our teams would withdraw. That was it, plain and simple. A bread-and-butter job. And if all went according to plan, the other guests wouldn't even know we'd been there!

With a final equipment check completed, the two teams climbed silently from the vans and stacked up in their respective positions, ready for the off. Having decided earlier that this should be a relatively low-risk operation, we'd opted to wear coveralls and full kit instead of plain clothes. We'd be working in the dark and in quite a small area – the width of a hotel bedroom - but as always the first man in was well on offer. With this in mind, the 'fear factor' was brought to bear: shit them up, cut down their reaction time with 'SAS' – surprise, aggression, speed – our tried-and-tested method.

It was because of the possibility of cramped conditions that I'd opted to discard my MP5 and work solely with a Glock and a three-cell Maglite. Made of aircraft aluminium, the torch was ideal for belting anybody who got in the way. And because of the fact that, as I had the masterkey I would be the first man in, I soon realised that I might well need the manoeuvrability a handgun provided.

As previously instructed, our hotel guide stopped just

below our target landing. Tony held up a gloved fist, barely visible in the dark gloom of the stairwell, and behind him we stopped. From here, we would leave the guide and make our way up the next flight to the landing, Black team's FUP. Green team's suspect was located on the floor above ours and at the far end of the corridor. Their plan was to go a floor higher, pass along the corridor and exit into the main stairwell, where they could come down a level and stack up on the target door.

After a momentary pause, Green team started to move and within seconds had disappeared from view into the darkness. It was three in the morning and, although at this hour we assumed the suspects to be home, and though checks with reception had confirmed this, we didn't know for sure that they hadn't slipped out. If that was the case, and if they decided to return, they'd have to approach their room from the main stairway – in which case they'd bump us. The corridor man was here for just that possibility.

Pulling open the stairwell door, we exited into a brightly lit antechamber which led through a door directly into the corridor. From the plans I knew that, once past the connecting door, our target was the first door on the left. Looking round, I nodded to the team.

On his head each man was wearing dark headgear pulled tightly to the scalp and at the moment much resembling a sailor's watch cap. Reaching up, we pulled down the flimsy material over our faces. With two circular eyeholes and a single round mouth-vent, the 'rapist' hoods completed the sinister image.

No sooner was this done when Tony's voice crackled quietly in the radio earshell concealed under my hood. 'Trojan two-seven.' My callsign. *Click, click, click.*

I responded by pushing the PTT switch on my set, being too near now even to whisper. Every communication from here on in would be in hand signals.

'Trojan two-seven, three clicks received.' Tony's voice again.

'Trojan two-seven,' he called again after a brief pause, 'Mike India FAP.'

This meant he wanted us to move in to final assault positions – the point of no return.

Click, click, click.

'Trojan two-seven, three clicks received.'

Drawing my Glock from its holster, I placed my hand flat across the top, then pointed out of the door and along the corridor, the signal requesting cover. Bringing his MP5 to bear, the corridor man nodded. With my free hand I quietly pushed open the connecting door. Silence. Nothing stirred in the dimly lit corridor as the cover man darted out of position, slipped silently past the target premises, and adopted a kneeling position covering the main stairwell.

We moved off, and in my mind's eye I could visualise Green team doing the same above. Reaching the door, I stepped to the right and slowly inserted the masterkey. Although the walls were flimsy I figured that, if somebody were waiting the other side, they'd decorate the door first, giving us time to react.

To the left of the door stood Chris, MP5 dangling loosely from his shoulder, in his hands a large set of bolt-croppers ready for the chain. Beside him stood Joe, the Enforcer raised and ready, and to his rear the two back-up guys waited, armed with fives.

'Trojan two-seven, Trojan two-seven . . .'

Click, click, click.

'Trojan two-seven . . . Attack! Attack! Attack!'

I eased the card to its limit to engage the mechanism, then pulled it out sharply. Red light on. Green light on . . . 'Go! Go! Go!' I shouted, lifting my left boot and kicking hard. The door swung rapidly into the room, striking the wall hard. No chain! Dull light from the corridor flooded into the interior of the darkened room. In one practised movement I pulled the torch from my assault vest and, continuing the momentum of my kick, charged headlong into the room. I made a conscious decision: fuck the bathroom on the right,

I was making directly for the bedroom, the stronghold. Reading my mind and knowing the cover men would back-fill the bathroom, Joe and Chris were hard on my heels.

In a fraction of a second I had covered the short distance to the bedroom and pointed the beam of my torch in, scanning from bed to bed. 'Militia! Militia!' I screamed in Russian like a crazy man.

In the bed to my right a figure cowered beneath the duvet; on the left a man merely stared at me, ashen faced in the yellow beam. 'Militia!' I called again, ditching the torch and pulling frantically at the bedclothes – although we had the upper hand it was the suspects' hands I was worried about, and I couldn't see any.

Pulling off the duvet, Joe grabbed the guy on the left and dragged him to the floor. The space was cramped, but with one easy swipe of his boot he kicked the bed aside. I tore back the covers from my man, who lay screwed up in a foetal position, hands between his legs. Grabbing him by the hair I pulled him sharply from the bed. The front of his underpants were stained dark with piss. Throwing him to the floor, I saw that his hands were empty.

It was then that an incredible wail started up from the back of his throat, gathering to a crescendo as it reached his lips, where it turned into a piercing scream.

Holstering up, I grabbed his arms and pulled them tightly behind his back as Chris covered. Joe was doing likewise to his man, who still appeared to be in shock. Pulling out a couple of sets of plasticuffs, I threw a set to Joe then went about securing my man's wrists.

The screaming got worse.

'For fuck's sake, Joe!' I called. 'Do something about this cunt! This was supposed to be a quick in and out – he'll wake the fucking dead!' Outside I could already hear the corridor man calling, 'Armed police! Get back in your room.' Curious guests were evidently craning their necks out of their rooms.

Joe plucked a pillow from the bed, and ducking down he

placed it over the back of the suspect's head, heaving down with both hands in an attempt to drown out the noise. But rather than muffle the screams (as Joe had obviously in mind) this had quite the reverse effect and the shrieks rose about a half-dozen octaves. On top of this, the guy's body began to twitch and convulse violently, legs kicking out in all directions as the screams got louder.

In the heat of the moment the cause hadn't dawned on me, but suddenly the penny dropped. 'For fuck's sake,' I called to a bewildered Joe. 'Take it off him. The silly bastard thinks we're going to slot him.' Sure enough, when Joe removed the pillow the Russian immediately sensed that danger had passed and broke down into quiet, animal-like sobs.

I shook my head. 'Let's hand over and get away from this fucking zoo.' Calling forward the arrest and search teams, our role was quickly over.

As the search teams applied regulation metal handcuffs, we snipped the plasticuffs and left them to it. As I walked from the room, the screamer regained some of his composure and, sitting on the end of the bed, tears streaming down his face, he cursed us in his own language. I stopped and walked back to face him. Staring at his stained briefs with disgust, I reckoned he got the message. He remained quiet until we'd left.

Linking up with Green team at the RVP, we exchanged our tales. Their job had been smooth, no problems – and even from the floor above they'd heard our circus. I explained what had happened to a chorus of laughter.

'Still,' I added, 'it's not every day you get to take out three commie bastards.'

'They might not have been commies, you know,' one of Green team pointed out, stowing his five in a slip.

'Well ours fucking were,' I replied seriously. 'They were wearing Red underpants.'

Arriving back at base I de-kitted and threw my coveralls into a stinking heap in the corner. 'Stevie,' Bob's familiar voice called across the room. Bob had finally made it into the department and was now in charge of the Orange team; although I liked to wind him up I actually liked him immensely and found him quite professional.

'All right, mate?' I answered. 'You're up early. Shit the bed?'

Bob laughed. 'No, I've been waiting for you. What you on tomorrow?'

I looked at my watch. 'I'm at fucking court in the morning. I'm just about to get my head down in a grot. Why?'

Bob lowered his voice. 'Got a two-team job on. Big crack place. Yardies. I need you and your boys for a rapid. You game?'

I sighed. It was standard practice for skippers to put jobs the way of their mates, so I couldn't really turn him down.

'OK. Leave me a note with the start time. I'll get the blokes to parade for the briefing and if I can't make it I'll catch you up later.'

Bob nodded. 'Cheers, mate. You'll like this one, it's a belter.'

4

The Glory Boys

'Team Bravo,' said Bob, 'will take the first floor. It will be a ladder entry on to the balcony, then in through the patio doors.' He flashed a casual glance around the thirty or so team members packed tightly into the small briefing room. 'From the recce, Clive, it's difficult to tell if the doors are single- or double-glazed, so you'll need facilities for both.'

Clive looked up and nodded curtly. 'We'll discuss our options later,' he said without moving his lips. Clive, the Orange team leader, was having a serious day, and was making copious amounts of notes throughout the hour-long briefing.

Bob continued. 'You'll be supported by a secondary team entering through the front door. Your objective will be to secure the living-room, which has been designated the main stronghold.'

It was three thirty in the afternoon, and I stared bleary-eyed at the meticulous plans attached to the board behind Bob. While I'd been at court my team had been called out for a robbery plot, where they were now, under the command of Stevie, a new team leader who was being groomed to replace me when eventually I went training. Stevie had been a PC on the department for years prior to being promoted, and was now hungry for his own team. Of course he was extremely capable and professional and a lovely guy, but it still left a bitter taste in my mouth.

With Black team now pulled off Bob was one team down. As a hasty replacement he had brought in Green team, but they were skipperless. That's where I came in. And I was already seven and a half hours into my day!

This particular operation, Bob was telling us, centred around a crack house in north London that had plagued the local division for some months. Previous operations had been mounted to take it out, but all had been blown out of the water at the last minute.

Call me Mr Cynical, but the one common denominator in all these operations seemed to be the local liaison committee, so-called 'community leaders' who were always informed and appraised of up-and-coming police operations within their area. The result was that many ops were aborted at the last minute, thanks to the committee's apparent paranoia that our actions would spark off some sort of civil unrest. The frustrating part about it all was that, in these predominantly black areas, the majority of decent people wanted the drug dealing stopped.

Apart from a full-blown hostage rescue, rapid entries are probably the most dangerous activities a firearms team can undertake. The reasons for this are twofold. First, you are moving at breakneck speed into relatively uncharted territory which probably contains an armed aggressor. Second, you may force a reaction from the suspect who, because of the speed of events unfolding before him, is unable to weigh up all of the options open to him. Rapid entries, therefore, are not undertaken lightly and have to meet certain strict criteria. This particular operation, Bob explained, was to be a three-pronged attack. The first phase was to insert an OP, something that had not been attempted before on this particular plot. Many of the teams had at least one trained rifleman who could quite easily adapt and double in this type of role. Malc was one such man. Beneath his quiet exterior beat the heart of a true professional – one who would take hours moving into a position where he could be of maximum benefit to the team. Once there he would if necessary construct a makeshift Hide – or, using personal camouflage, blend into the surroundings. Once ensconced he would be totally self-sufficient and able to remain in situ for hours if not days, relaying any movement from the suspect address. This was a particularly cold and lonely aspect of the job and not a task I would relish. It was, however, what Bob described as 'what Malc did best'.

'Your task, Steve,' said Bob now, 'Will be as OIC of the second floor. Your stick will hit the front door and take the stairs as Clive's accesses the balcony. It is imperative that we dominate the toilet area, as the information we have is that one of the dealers has been nominated to flush the gear in the event of a hit.'

As the main briefing came to an end all three teams broke off into their own little groups to discuss the tactics they would use within their own specific LOEs. With thirty men entering a building using every access point available, it was inevitable that guns would be in danger of pointing at each other. With this in mind, strict limits had been set up within the building, with a link man posted from each team to liaise in nominated areas such as the stairs or the living-room doors. Safety, as always, was paramount.

'Before we break, fellas,' I called to the assembled room. 'Jump off practice for the White teams will be in the yard at five thirty sharp. Full kit and weapons.' Taking a felt tip pen, I drew a rough box representing the jump-off wagon on the wipe board, then ran through the stacking order of the eighteen assaulters and ladders that would be housed in the rear. On this occasion the horse would be a large, unmarked van that would deliver us to the front of the building (or nominated 'White' aspect) and our FAP. From here there would be no going back.

The briefing room suddenly became a hive of activity, with individuals wading through Bergens of kit and teams discussing then rediscussing tactics until each man was sure of his role within that particular sphere of the operation. Runners returned with piles of fried chicken, kebabs and chips, but I chose not to eat, even though I knew full well that, once we reached the forward holding area, it could be a long night.

At five thirty we gathered around the board, each man fully kitted for the dress rehearsal. As stun grenades or gas were not going to be used, we'd opted to ditch the resis in favour of face veils and ski glasses, but still opted for the high-profile heavy assault kit with elbow pads and leg guards. Over his body armour each man wore a quick-release vest of black suede, consisting of a load-bearing waistcoat customised to carry equipment such as the Cougar radio, spare magazines for both the primary and secondary weapon, plus torch, field dressings in case of injury, carry sheets for casevac, and a large quantity of plasticuffs. On top of this, each man would carry a baton and personal breaking equipment (such as an axe), as well as the assault ladders and entry gear.

Having previously been involved in large drugs operations of this type I fully understood the logistics of planning, and had therefore decided that each man would number off in the order he would leave the vehicle. This would avoid confusion later when it became dark. I'd developed a system whereby each man would chalk his designated number on his helmet and on the back of his vest. The numbers would then stack up in the rear of the horse in reverse order, number one being the last man on and subsequently the first man off at the FAP. I was number eight, and would be situated in the back behind Pecky, designated seven. Like myself, Pecky was ex-level two, and a veteran of many hundreds of firearms operations. A small, affable Welshman, what he lacked in size he more than made up for in tenacity and guts.

I looked at the eighteen bulky figures, the MOE kit and the ladders, sure they'd never all fit. 'OK, guys,' I said enthusiastically. 'Number off.'

'Fifteen.'

'Fourteen . . .'

The van rocked slightly as we mounted up. Crammed inside finally, the doors were closed.

'OK. The first practice will be a DA. That's a covert approach – at this stage we have not been compromised. So let's go as quietly as we can while we have the advantage.'

A few minutes later the van came to a shuddering halt in the small back yard. 'Go, go, go,' I whispered, and the entry team quickly debussed, stacking up on the imaginary front door. Next, and right on our heels, came the climbing party who, placing the ladder against the wall to our left, began to ascend until the four main assaulters crouched side by side at the top of the Double German ladder.

'How was it?' I asked Bob, who had taken time out to watch.

'It was fast,' he said. 'I can't believe how fast . . . But it was noisy. The ladder hit something on the way out. This was a DA, remember? Let's slow it down a little and try not to compromise ourselves.'

I nodded, knowing that we were always over-critical of ourselves, and that inside a well-built house with music blaring we'd never be heard outside. But that wasn't the point; the point was that we were professional.

'I think we need a little extra padding on the ladder,' I said, detailing two men to go and find more hessian sacks to tape on to the ends.

'The other thing is you all look the same in the dark,' said Tony, the MOE man who was to breach the front door. 'You're nine, Steve, but in the heat of the moment I'll probably miss you.'

Tony's role was to hit the door, gaining access for the first- and second-floor entry teams. He was then to fall in behind me in the centre of the stick.

I thought for a moment, 'OK, Tone, I'll accept that. What I'll do is wear a Cyalume on the back of my helmet – that should help. When you see the light get right up my arse.' Cyalume lights are six-inch plastic tubes containing two different chemicals, one of which lies within the other encased inside a thin glass vial. When the plastic tube is bent the glass snaps and the two chemicals combine to emit a surprisingly intense light which much resembles a small fluorescent tube. They come in a variety of colours and have a number of practical uses.

After two further attempts at the DA, Bob was happy. 'Perfect,' he announced. 'Dead quiet – and I couldn't believe the speed! Now let's try an emergency reaction . . .'

By six forty-five we had practised and re-practised both options on our imaginary address until both were honed to perfection. There being no point in flogging a dead horse, it was time to move into phase two of the operation: the formal briefing at the FHA.

'Jesus! They've got more fucking guns than NATO!' exclaimed the young Territorial Support Group officer as he peered into our holding area.

'Yeah,' interrupted a surly-faced sergeant. 'Fucking glory boys!'

'What do you mean, Sarge?' asked the slightly bewildered first man.

'Like I said – glory boys. They fucking ride in on the back of everybody's hard work, shoot up the place and grab all the glory.'

'Not true,' I piped up from inside, unable to contain my temper at having recognised the sergeant's voice. 'And having just failed a firearms course, you should fucking know better.' I stepped into the doorway. 'Our job is hard enough without people like you stirring the shit.' I jabbed my finger in his direction, and was joined by Pecky.

Ashen-faced, the sergeant managed to mumble an obscene riposte.

'Bollocks . . .' I slammed the door in his face.

'What was all that about?' Pecky asked.

'Sour Grapes,' I replied. 'Wanker's just failed a firearms course and all of a sudden he's an instant expert. Should have been a fucking guvnor.'

Pecky grinned at my anger – and I smiled. 'Said we were just a bunch of glory boys.'

'Well we are, in a way.' Now Pecky was smiling too. 'No paperwork . . . do the hit, then ride off into the sunset.'

'I know that,' I said. 'But still . . . what a tosser. They ruined a fucking good arsehole when they put teeth in his mouth!'

Gathering our kit we moved out of the side room and into the rapidly filling auditorium. The TSG officers were there to provide the arrest. Specialist Pulsar search teams mingled happily with drugs dogs and handlers, who in turn were joined by local crime squad officers in their 'uniforms' of torn jeans and trainers. In the fourth row from the front sat SO19, joined only by our uniformed ARV crews, who would provide the inner armed cordon to give us the sterile working area we required to operate. Outside of these would be the unarmed support services, creating a further barrier between the public and the guns. It was a strange atmosphere, huddled in their own little groups, nobody seemed to approach the team. There were simply a few hesitant looks in our direction, almost as if we were taboo.

'Fuck's sake,' said Billy, the Green team medic, sitting up with a start. 'The job's got to be off!'

From beside him I looked up and followed his gaze to the door. The tall black man in his early forties wore a crumpled suit beneath an ill-fitting trenchcoat. Looking around the assembled room, he smiled before taking a seat in the front row.

'Yeah, looks like the job's been fucking blown all right,' said a voice from behind me, as we took in the dark features.

A hush filled the room as the uniformed chief inspector took centre stage. 'Thank you all for coming,' he started. 'I am Gold Control, and I'd like to welcome you all here tonight. Thank you SO19, TSG, crime squad, and our colleagues in the London Ambulance Service.' He nodded towards the front row. 'I'd particularly like to welcome Chief Inspector . . . from Kenya. He's here as an observer to see how the Met do things.'

Raising my hand to my mouth, I quickly stifled a laugh as the man in the front row stood, turned, and broke into a broad grin, arm raised in acknowledgement.

Bob launched himself into yet another complex and time-consuming briefing. But it was imperative that at its conclusion everybody in the room knew exactly what would happen when the job went down. A second OP had been set up somewhere near the front of the target address, a three-bedroom town house on a notorious estate. This OP could effectively monitor movement to and from the address and subsequently call on an attack at the optimum time, i.e. when the maximum amount of suspects were inside.

It was not a job for an amateur.

As the briefing came to an end the room began to thin out as people did a last-minute check of equipment and vehicles. It was nine o'clock when Bob suddenly shouted, 'Malc! Time to move out.' He had decided it was now dark enough to insert our eyes and ears on the wasteground at the back of the premises.

Grabbing his kit, Malc stood and made his way swiftly towards the door, equipped with the latest technology. He would be using a powerful night scope – an invaluable piece of equipment, which made his task that much easier. Drawing on all the available ambient light, the night scope enables the operator to focus on a particular object or location during the hours of darkness. Seen through the viewfinder, the object in question is shrouded in a low-intensity, almost eerie green glow.

With scanning prevalent on the estate (listening in on police radio frequencies with the aid of a special monitor), and in an effort to cut down on non-urgent radio transmissions, Malc also carried a GSM digital cellphone. That way, if all the radios went to ratshit we could still communicate.

With Malc gone, the waiting had started.

'You on this "remount" exercise next week?' Pecky asked with interest.

'Yeah.' I nodded. 'Can't say I'm too fucking happy about it, though.'

'Remount' was the name given to a joint anti-terrorist exercise conducted by the police and the SAS, which involved a great deal of planning and personnel. Needless to say, SO19 figured high on the list and always provided at least two teams. As the Regiment always ended up going in on the final assault, for us it was almost an exercise in logistics – which I, for one, hated.

Pecky smiled. We'd been through a lot together over the years, and he knew that my attitude had often got me into trouble with the hierarchy. 'Should suit the fucking yellow-arses, I suppose.'

Yellow arses was a term used in SO19 for guys on the unit who considered themselves pseudo SAS. They seemed to follow the doctrine of the boys from Hereford so closely, it was commonly considered that – if for some dubious tactical reason the Regiment decided to paint their arses yellow – they'd be round B & Q the very next day buying up their entire stocks of primrose gloss!

Bored, I stood up and shrugged off the day's fatigue. Wandering off in search of a Coke machine, it suddenly dawned on me that I'd been on duty for thirteen hours.

Bob interrupted the chatter soon after I'd got back. 'OK, fellas. Dealing has begun at the address. Alpha team, be ready to move in fifteen minutes. Thirty minutes from now, White team's Bravo and Charlie will mount up and move to the FUP.' I checked my watch and mentally made a note of the time.

In the earlier briefing it had been agreed that Alpha team, led by Bob, would be dropped off at a nearby building site. Once in position they could covertly make their way across a railway line and some thick undergrowth towards the rear of the target. Malc, monitoring their progress through the night scope, could also spot a potential compromise; in effect he was their rear guard. With each team member carrying his four and a half stone of kit it would be a difficult enough task to undertake the thirty-minute covert approach. On this occasion, however, they also had the thickets to contend with and were carrying assault ladders and breaking kit.

'OK. Number off,' I shouted for the hundredth time that day.

The van swayed slightly as the eighteen heavily laden men clambered into their allotted positions. It was eleven o'clock and Alpha had already started their approach.

Suddenly, out of the blue, my earpiece burst into life. 'Hold! Hold! Hold!' It was Don, the duty officer. 'Team leaders, we have shots fired. That's shots fired at the target address.'

Clive and I immediately debussed. 'What's going on?' I asked urgently. 'Has Bob's team been compromised?'

'Perhaps Malc's slotted someone,' came a voice from the darkness of the van.

Don cupped his hand to his earshell. 'We're just getting information that shots have been fired inside the address. Bob is in no way compromised, but armed-response vehicles have been allocated by the Yard.'

'Bollocks!' I protested. 'That'll fucking ruin everything. We may just as well turn it in.'

'Wait!' Don held up his hand before speaking into the big set. 'This is the SO19 duty officer,' he started. 'We have an operation running on this estate. Call off the ARVs before they compromise our position.' He turned back to me and Clive. 'The OP hasn't heard a thing. It could be a hoax . . . As shots have not been confirmed we're going in. Mount up.'

We were later to learn that the main dealer, remarkably enough a woman in her late fifties, had been involved in an argument with her son, a drug dealer in his own right. In a fit of rage he had left the house, and had placed the bogus firearms call in an effort to have his mother arrested; that way he would then be able to move in on her operation.

When it came to drugs, blood was by no means thicker than water! The offshoot of the call, however – and one that he could possibly have never known – was that it only served to heighten our awareness of the potentially lethal situation we were moving into.

Stacked up in the dark confines of the horse, each man slipped deeper into his own world in an effort to shrug off the discomfort.

Occasionally a crackling radio message would penetrate the blackness. 'Don, Don. Bob.'

'Go, Bob.'

'Don.' Now urgent. 'We are baulked, repeat baulked at the railway line. Half the team is across, but a punter from the address is parked up at the back in his motor. We'll hold momentarily. Stand by.'

I thought of the lads out there in the darkness, slightly surprised they'd made it at all. With the early-evening drizzle and the fact that electric railway lines are notorious for arcing on metallic objects, I knew some of the guys had expressed concern about the carriage of weapons and ladders. Apparently they were fears unfounded.

'Steve.' The radio.

'Go, Don.'

'Yeah, reference Bob's last. We'll hold off and see what develops.'

I acknowledged.

It was five agonising minutes later that Bob eventually came back. 'Don? Bob. Still baulked – will attempt a covert crossing in five minutes from now, but we may have to take him out. Oh fuck . . .' His voice rose an octave. 'There's a train coming . . .'

When Bob recounted the tale later, we learned how the team had thrown themselves flat on the embankment as the Intercity train had hurled past, picking out the prone black figures in its headlights. Later the driver would probably stop to report men with guns on the track – but at this stage of the game we knew it wouldn't jeopardise the operation.

Back in the van I stifled a laugh. 'That'll be Bob spread across three miles of track, then,' I whispered in the dark.

'Yeah, or forty feet in the air,' somebody giggled nervously.

I checked the luminous dial of my watch: 11.45 p.m. At the start of the evening it had been estimated that we'd be in the horse no more than fifteen minutes before moving off. Now, as the full weight of the kit bit into my shoulders and aching legs, I pushed the hardship to the back of my mind. 'Wouldn't happen on training department,' I muttered, shaking my head and realising how tired I'd become.

For ten minutes, nobody spoke. Then suddenly Pecky shattered the silence. 'Steve?'

'What?' I hissed, making out the whites of his eyes and mouth concealed beneath the ballistic helmet, large and unwieldy on his head.

'I love you,' he said flatly.

The horse shook as eighteen bulky figures suppressed their laughter.

'Don. In position,' Bob's voice suddenly crackled into life. And in an instant, gone was the fatigue as the adrenalin coursed through my veins, senses at an all-time high. 'Move up. Repeat, move up.'

Alpha was at the back door!

'All units, stand by, stand by,' Don ordered as the horse roared into life.

'Turning right . . .' Don kept up a running commentary from his perch. 'Target premises thirty yards – that's thirty yards. No compromise, no lookouts . . .'

I tightened my grip on the MP5.

'Ten yards, ten yards.'

The excitement mounted.

'Five yards. No compromise. Target address on the right.'

The horse shuddered to a standstill.

'Go! Go! Go!'

Clive, crouching behind me, cracked the Cyalume tube on my helmet, and immediately the darkness was punctuated by a bright green glow as the rear doors silently opened and the horse spilled its cargo into the road.

Only the distant rumble of traffic could be heard as a strange quiet hung over the plot. Following the stick out of the horse, I instinctively looked up for danger. There was none. Only the balcony door was visible, and – I couldn't believe our luck – it was open!

Stacking on the front door, I snapped open the retractable stock on the MP5, which I jabbed hard into my shoulder. With my left hand covering the torch mount should the need for additional light be required, my right index finger resting lightly beside the trigger, I was combat ready.

Tony held at the door. Still no compromises, as the other team moved swiftly into position. Beads of sweat soaked into my face veil and ran into my eyes. Come on, come on, my brain screamed as the ladder to my left was placed silently against the wall.

In seconds the first two assaulters reached the top and were over, quickly followed by Clive and his party. Refusing point blank to wear the number thirteen on his helmet, Clive had opted for 12A, which was now disappearing from view over the parapet.

In the split second that followed, two things happened: 'Go, go, go!' Don's detached voice blasted through my earshell, and in the same instant the night was shattered by a piercing scream from within the premises.

'Compromise, compromise! Go, go, go!' I heard myself shout.

Bang! Tony hit the door with the hand held enforcer. It imploded with a loud crash, followed immediately by the long stick of black figures piling headlong into the corridor.

More screams, louder now and accompanied by shouts of 'Armed police! Down, down, down!'

At the entrance, Tony tapped each man's shoulder as he filed past. My turn. 'On me, on me!' I shouted as he fell in step behind. As planned, I now had support.

The cloying, almost choking smell of crack cocaine

permeated the air, immediately bringing back memories of Sacramento. To my right I was aware of Alpha team as they smashed their way into the kitchen, entering through the shattered double glazing from the enveloping darkness of the garden, shards of glass bouncing from the threadbare lino, almost like raindrops, before coming to rest in a large, glistening puddle.

A black figure silhouetted the kitchen door, nodding as I passed. It was the Alpha link man at his LOE. Things were going to plan.

I hit the staircase to my left. A black male blocked my path. No weapon. *Crash!* I ran through him with a bone-jarring crunch, leaving him cowering and sobbing on the stairs. 'Suspect down,' I called, knowing full well he'd be scooped up by the team behind.

'Secure,' called Don almost before I'd reached the top of the stairs, my legs pumping harder as I caught up with the elusive and bobbing 7 on Pecky's helmet.

Another landing, still onward and up. Until finally . . .

Stevie, the tall south-Londoner, reached the objective first, veering left. Pecky went right. Instinctively I followed Steve, knowing full well that Tony would be at Pecky's shoulder. The sacred rule: never let a man go in a room alone.

Steve raised his large, booted foot, kicking the bedroom door hard and slamming it back against the interior wall lest a would-be aggressor be hiding there.

We were met with a wall of darkness. I tapped Stevie's shoulder and he immediately went right. Hard on his heels I went left. Flooding the four corners of the bare room with a greenish light, I sensed rather than saw movement beside the bed. Closing it down rapidly I screamed, 'Armed police!'

The large black man squinted in the glare of the torch, his craggy features ravaged by years of drug abuse. Again thoughts of that drug raid in Sacramento flooded back and in a fleeting, unguarded moment I almost felt sorry for him.

Grabbing him roughly by the collar I felt the brittle bones in his emaciated neck and flushed with anger. 'How could people do this to each other – peddling this fucking crap!' Pulling the plasticuffs tight around his thin wrists, I laid him face down on the filthy quilt.

'Clear,' I announced, leaving the room. 'Reorg on me.'

I passed back through the shattered building, ballistic helmet hanging limply at my side, sweat now running down my face and soaking into the already sodden coveralls. All around me, team members stood guard over plasticuffed victims. Glass and debris littered the hall, crunching loudly underfoot. The front door hung, battered, by one hinge.

Our part was over – and I smiled at the blank faces of the arrest-and-search teams assembled outside. They were in for a long night. I felt sorry for them; they now had the long and laborious task of taking the place apart in an effort to secure the evidence needed to support a conviction.

Climbing in the back of the horse, I sat on one of the hard bench seats and massaged my head where the helmet's lining had chafed my scalp, my shoulders aching from the weight of the equipment – things you never thought about in the adrenalin rush associated with a hit.

We drove silently back to the forward holding area, only the new guy gobbing off about what he had done. These fucking blokes have forgotten more jobs than you'll ever remember, I thought as I mentally marked his card. He wasn't on my team, and perhaps it was first-job nerves, but I'd be watching him in the future.

'Any comments?' Bob asked by way of a debrief.

'Yes,' I replied, taking a deep draw on the can of lager being passed around. 'Excellent briefing. Well planned, and thoroughly executed. Well done, mate.'

Bob eyed me warily. 'Thanks,' he stammered.

'No problem. In fact, so much better than the normal Orange team fuck-ups I've come to expect.'

'Bollocks,' he retorted.

Changing into civvies, I reflected on the week. It had been hard – harder than normal, and by the time I left the base I'd have been on duty twenty hours.

Aiming the crumpled tin at the bin, I nodded. 'See you Glory Boys in the morning.'

5

The Demise of Crazy Ken

The next few days passed slowly by, with the usual monotony of early-morning dig-outs and the boring prospect of the Remount exercise looming largely in my mind.

The Government had just managed to fix it so that every chief inspector and inspector in the country was to be salaried. This was implemented by taking away overtime payments and replacing them across the board with a fixed sum of £3,500 in lieu. What this meant in real terms was that, by taking away his overtime, the average Inspector on SO19 would be poorer by between ten and thirteen grand a year, whereas the non-overtime-earning court inspectors and desk jockeys would be richer by three and a half grand. Talk about robbing Peter to pay Paul! To make matters worse, rumours were rife that sergeants and PCs would be next. The result was that morale hit an all time low.

The Inspectors – quite rightly, in my humble opinion – refused to work their bollocks off for such a paltry sum. But shit has a habit of rolling downhill, and inspectors were now in a position where they saw sergeants and in some cases PCs earning more than they did. As a result, some refused to authorise overtime apart from in exceptional circumstances, the job in general suffered, and for a while a dark cloud hung over Old Street.

An offshoot of this new regime was that team leaders (who by virtue of their position were, like inspectors, Force Tactical Advisors) now found themselves being posted as duty officers whenever an inspector was either unable to or refused to cover a shift. Again, this presented problems. The ARV sergeants saw it as an affront to their ability to perform the role, and as a result I often sensed some underlying discontent. And the inspectors resented the sergeants called in on their rest days to cover their shifts earning still more overtime.

It was one such unsettled day that I was called in to work. I climbed the six steep flights of stairs and pushed open the heavy, brown paint-chipped door to the sergeants' locker room next to the canteen. Moving along the rows of dull grey metal lockers I found the one I'd been looking for. The inscription on the door in black felt tip simply read 'Dolph'. Nicknames within the department were commonplace, and I felt long ago that if I was going to be given a moniker then I may as well choose it myself. I felt that Dolph – the name of the tall, good-looking, muscular, blond film star Dolph Lundgren – more than suited my appearance.

Pulling on a thin white cotton shirt, I attached the shoulder epaulettes and clipped on the familiar black tie. 'Fuck's sake,' I exclaimed to the ARV skipper along the aisle, 'I haven't worn this for months. Do you find they shrink when hung up for long periods?'

He smiled.

I sucked in a deep breath and attempted to do up my trousers. Buckling the heavy-duty belt, I checked my reflection in the mirror and sighed. I'd definitely put on weight and no mistake. Wearing jeans and baggy sweat-shirts every day you don't really seem to notice it; now I was looking at something resembling the Michelin man. I shook my head, pulling at the throat of the tight collar. 'God,' I moaned. 'I've got more fucking chins than a Hong Kong phone book. Fuck the shooter – the way the buttons are straining I need a firearms certificate just to wear this shirt.'

The skipper pushed past opening the door. 'Cup of tea?' he asked, heading for the canteen.

I pushed open the canteen door. Sitting at a long table just inside was an eight-strong contingent from SO8, the flying squad. Since time immemorial a rivalry had existed between our two units. On the one hand there was us – the Force Firearms Unit, with enough skill, training and weaponry to take on all comers. Then there was the squad, whose shots were only allowed to carry a Smith & Wesson .38 Model 10 six-shot revolver. Hardly a match for a set of nostrils or something even heavier.

The squad resented SO19's involvement in their operations, whereas we resented the fact that they were allowed to carry guns at all. Many of them revelled in the old *Sweeney* image, having seen too many re-runs. Personally I didn't have too much time for the flying squad, and having seen them in action had formed the impression that they were trying to wear ten-gallon hats on two-pint heads. But for some unknown reason our own hierarchy (and that at the Yard) still allowed the squad priority over us when it came to robbery plot operations.

On this occasion they were standing by. 'All right?' I nodded to one of the squad drivers, whom I recognised from an infamous shooting incident that had followed a robbery. Apparently everything had gone to ratshit when the bandits had taken off, hotly pursued by the squad. During the ensuing gunfight – which took place at speed through the streets of London – the squad had managed to break most of the cardinal rules of engagement, including 'Never shoot at or from a moving vehicle'. In doing so they managed to wound a pram and a wardrobe, and to kill their own vehicle's wing-mirror.

The driver looked up at my shirt and, obviously playing to the crowd, said, 'Fucking hell. I didn't know you boys had to wear body armour all the time.'

'You do when fucking squad drivers are about,' I replied.

He huffed. 'Well, we're on a job and we've come to see the late-turn duty officer,' he said in a superior tone.

I smiled. 'Yeah. Well you've just seen him, so fuck off!'

'Dolph!' The shout had come from the top of the steps. Turning at the sound of the familiar voice I took in the balding head and lithe body of Brad, his trademark ever-present pipe jutting proudly from the side of his mouth. After having his foot crushed by an armoured Range Rover during a street ambush in Clapham, Brad had been off sick, then on recuperative instructional duties at Lippitts. Now he was back on ops, but prior to returning to the team had to undergo an attachment to the ARVs. Brad was also an ex-Regular paratrooper and extremely proud of it.

'Hello, mate,' I said, allowing him to catch up and patting him warmly on the back. 'How's the foot?'

He pulled on his pipe thoughtfully. 'Not too bad, Stevie,' he replied.

'Jesus,' I said. 'Are you still smoking the fucking camel shit?'

Brad smiled. 'Back with the team tomorrow, Big Boy.'

I nodded. 'Yeah, nice one. Just like old times.' Brad walked the last flight of stairs with me, then suddenly stopped, a look of abject horror filling his features, his mouth open and pipe hanging limply from his lips. I followed his gaze to one of the many Regimental and Police Service commemorative plaques that adorned the staircase walls. It was one of which Brad was particularly proud: his old mob, Second Battalion, the Parachute Regiment. Tacked on to the bottom of the plaque was a white label, altering the motto to read: 'SECOND BATTALION QUICK HIDE UNDER THE STAIRS IT'S WAR REGIMENT'.

Ripping the sticker sharply from the surface, Brad rolled it into a ball and flicked it down the stairs, then using the sleeve of his pullover, he carefully buffed the badge. 'Bastard,' he spat. 'I'll kill that fucking Billy.'

I laughed. Paras and Royal Marines were natural-born enemies. And now that Bill had been successful in his application to return to ops, he, like Brad, started back tomorrow. This would be interesting.

In the briefing room I aimlessly flicked through a well-thumbed copy of *Combat and Survival* magazine (or *Throat Slasher's Monthly*, as Bill preferred to call it). Previous readers had obviously ordered some piece of kit or another, as almost every page had a small section cut from it.

Seeing an article on special forces I immediately began to think of the forthcoming Remount. How could I make it more interesting? Suddenly it came to me, and I decided that in the run up to the exercise I'd task Bill and Brad with a cunning plan.

Next door the phone rang. 'Stevie!' called the baseman from behind his console.

'What?'

'Phone. Somebody wants tactical advice.'

I tossed the magazine on a chair for some other sad bastard to read and headed for the door. 'Cheers, Alf,' I said. Of course, Alf wasn't his real name, just a handle given to him by others. And it was obvious how he'd earned it – because he was indeed an Annoying Little Fucker.

As I took the phone from him I covered the mouthpiece with the flat of my hand and asked, 'Why didn't *you* talk to him?'

He raised his eyebrows. 'Because you're supposed to be the guvnor.' Alf was a team man who, like many others, was on attachment to the ARVs. It was a move calculated to inject the skill and experience of a team member into the ranks of the less-experienced ARV personnel, and it worked. But many of the older guys hated their tours, seeing them as a demotion of their status rather than anything positive.

'Duty Officer,' I answered.

'Hello, guv,' came the reply. 'Ricky Molloy, South East Regional Crime Squad.'

I knew Ricky, a tall, wiry, tough south-Londoner and a successful undercover operator. 'Ricky,' I said. 'Steve

Collins. I'm acting up for the day. What you got?'

'Hello, Steve!' His tone had changed. 'Need a bit of advice,' he said.

It turned out that, as part of an ongoing SERCS operation, a UC operator had arranged a meet with some bad guys in the car park of a large, well-known London hotel near Tower Bridge. As part of a goodwill gesture on the UC's part, there was to be a 'flash' and the villains would be shown a briefcase of used notes as part of the deception – in this case, twenty-five grand of the commissioner's readies. 'What I'd like to do, Steve, obviously with your consent,' Ricky explained, 'is have myself and one other AFO tooled up – purely in case of a rip-off and for the security of the UC.'

I thought for a moment, weighing up the pros and cons. 'If there's going to be any sort of exchange or a hit, Rick, you'll need a team there, you know that.'

'Steve,' he said seriously, 'stand on me, there's nothing like that. A flash only, I promise.'

I covered the mouthpiece. 'Alf,' I asked, 'who's the south car today?'

He looked up at the postings board. 'Brad.'

I nodded. 'OK, Ricky, I'll stick in a Tactical Advice Given form. But if there's any change of plan I need to know immediately. Trojan 504 is the south car, one of the team guys on board. I'll let them know so they stay clear of the plot. But if you need assistance you call for them on channel six – you got that?'

'Cheers, Steve,' he replied. 'But it won't get that far.'

Once I'd filled Brad in I felt a lot happier about the whole situation. The flying squad's earlier job had folded and they'd gone home, so at least now there was only one band of cowboys out on the ground. Settling back into my chair I sipped a hot cup of coffee and got down to some long neglected paperwork.

Three hours later, the phone rang.

'Stevie,' Alf's urgent voice called, 'something's just gone

down by Tower Bridge. Think you'd better look at it.'

Taking the stairs two at a time I reached the baseroom in record time, just as Alf was tearing the message from the teleprinter.

'Bollocks,' I said, looking at the bold, neat typescript. 'And they promised me it was only a fucking flash!'

Brad later recounted the story. Driving the powerful Rover 827 north across Tower Bridge, the three-man crew, call-sign Trojan 504, had nothing more on their minds than the finish of another boring shift. Much resembling a regular, uniformed traffic patrol car – set apart only by the yellow helicopter identification disc on its roof – the ARV was suddenly hailed by a pedestrian in the one-way system. Duty bound, they pulled over and bought the car to a stop.

Brad wound down the electric window with a faint mechanical hum. 'Yes, guv?' he asked.

He was confronted by a small, black leather wallet containing a battered colour photograph and a shiny silver Metropolitan Police coat of arms. 'SERCS,' the holder announced flatly. 'Do us a favour, fellas. There's a blue Sierra Estate down aways, three up. Can you give it a tug for us and make it look like a routine stop?'

Brad nodded and wound up the window as he gunned the accelerator and they took off. In seconds the high-powered police car was behind the Sierra. Brad looked about for any sign of the surveillance vehicles; if there were any, they were well deployed.

Flicking the dash-mounted switches, Brad illuminated the blue roof-mounted bar-light and momentarily activated the siren. As the wail cut off, the Sierra was already dutifully indicating and pulling slowly in towards the kerb.

Brad got out and made his way slowly towards the front seat passenger. To all intents and purposes he was just a normal plod. He doubted that even SERCS had realised that the crew were carrying. But after what happened next, it annoyed Brad to think that they'd actually fed them into a situation believing them not to be armed.

In accordance with the standing orders of the day (which were subsequently changed as unworkable), the two ARV guys had locked their sidearms in the vehicle's safe, along with the two Heckler & Koch MP5s. Brad, the wily old ex-para, was however wearing a high-rise 'pancake' holster tight to his kidneys, concealed under his baggy pullover. Inside was a seventeen-round nine-millimetre Glock self-loading pistol. Standard Team issue.

'Yes, Officer?' the front-seat passenger asked politely. 'Step out of the car for a moment, please . . .' Brad instructed.

'Sure,' the man replied, calmly opening the door. 'What's this all about?'

'Nothing to worry about,' said Brad. 'Just a routine stop check. Your car?'

'His,' replied the passenger, nodding to where the driver and back-seat occupant were being similarly questioned. Brad was suddenly at a loss. The CID guy had indicated they'd move in once the car had been stopped; now Brad was looking around for the fucking suits to show. But there was nobody in sight. He didn't want to blow a potential operation, so as they'd told him to make it look routine that's what he did.

'Your briefcase?' he asked, nodding to the small black attaché case on the back seat.

'Yeah,' the guy replied nervously.

Brad reached inside, pulling the case from the seat. 'What's in it?' he asked.

The man's body language was now telling Brad something was wrong. 'Nothing really,' he replied, looking at the ground in an effort to avoid eye-contact.

'Well . . . what, exactly?' Brad demanded firmly.

'Just . . . just some stones, that's all.'

Placing the case on the bonnet, Brad flipped the metal catch and cautiously lifted the lid.

'Stones,' Brad repeated, almost to himself, his senses now heightened. He looked the man square in the face: average height, slim build, snappy dresser. But most of all he had the type of face that said 'Been there, seen it, done it'. But then, so had Brad – only ten times over.

'Diamonds?' he asked inquisitively.

The man laughed, then added almost plausibly, 'Good God, no, officer. Cubic Zircona – diamond substitute. Totally worthless.'

Brad picked up a handful. 'Well you won't mind if I have a few then, will you?'

The man's face reddened as he blustered, 'No! No . . . I don't.'

Brad smiled and replaced the gems before picking out a large cut stone, holding it up to watch the light glinting spectacularly from its many hundreds of precisely cut surfaces. 'Looks like a diamond,' he said.

'No, no – honestly,' repeated the man who was fast becoming a suspect.

Nonchalantly Brad scored the stone down the windshield of the car, tracing a deep and ragged path. He looked at his handiwork. 'Cuts like a diamond,' he mentioned. 'Something you want to tell me?'

The suspect stood dumbstruck as Brad snapped shut the case.

'You got any ID on you?' Brad asked.

'No.' The man shook his head, eyes darting suspiciously towards the vehicle. 'I . . . I may have some in the glove compartment,' he quickly added, making a move towards the door.

Suddenly things started to make sense.

With lightning reactions born of many hundreds of dangerous operations, Brad made his move, eyes flicking towards the now visible self-loading pistol in the passenger footwell.

'Gun!' he screamed, as much for his own benefit as that of the rest of the crew, the sound of his own voice startling him into action. In one swift, practised movement he grabbed the suspect with his left hand, twisting him and throwing him flat across the bonnet. His right hand swept aside his pullover and emerged with the Glock gripped firmly in his fist. He pushed it menacingly in the small of the suspect's back. 'Armed police,' he announced, kicking the guy's legs apart before expertly running his hands down his body in search of concealed weapons.

Talking to the other suspects at the rear of the car, Brad's companions had seen him move, and taking his example had done likewise. All three were swiftly detained.

Suddenly, with the dirty work done, the suits appeared from nowhere and started to take over. Brad checked the self-loader and made it safe, and was amazed to find it had a full clip and one in the chamber. If they'd been a rat patrol (even fellow Metropolitan Police officers refer to traffic branch as the black rats), it could have been a very different story.

However, acts of extreme bravery within the department were commonplace.

Woodhatch, Surrey. If ever there was a one-horse town, then this was it. Situated eight miles north of Gatwick airport and two miles south of Reigate town centre, with the A217 running through its heart connecting the two.

It was 27 November 1990, and Woodhatch was about to get a wake-up call.

In the months preceding this day, the flying squad at Tower Bridge had been building a case against a team of old adversaries: a south-London firm hailing mainly from the Walworth area, graduates of the Bermondsey School of Armed Robbers.

The suspects were believed to have been involved in a number of armed robberies, and on separate occasions a security guard and a police officer had been shot.

For the past few weeks, teams of detectives – backed up by members of PT17 (SO19 prior to the internal reshuffle) – had been involved in a number of stake-outs across London and the south east.

On that November Tuesday, PT17 had been called in early to Kenley police station on the outskirts of Croydon. The Woodhatch area had come under scrutiny for the first time, and although nothing was said it was apparent that the flying squad really favoured this one; in fact they seemed almost sure an attempted hit was to go down.

The briefing was impressive, real I.I.M.A.C. stuff – straight down the line. The teams were shown a series of photographs. Although no names had ever been mentioned, quite a few of the lads recognised some of the faces, simply from working rough areas such as Lewisham and Deptford. These were not your run-of-the-mill slags, they were bad men – professional criminals as high as you could get in the local pecking order of crime – who didn't mess around. As the briefing progressed, it became obvious to the guys that they were dealing with real talent. Career villains.

There were believed to be a minimum of four, but for obvious reasons the squad couldn't take that as read.

Having seen the layout of the plot, the PT17 team quickly got down to business. As with all static operations the geography of the plot was very significant. At the heart of Woodhatch is a major set of crossroads; governed by traffic lights, they can be a major cause of congestion. At the north-east corner of the lights stands the Angel pub. On the north-west corner, amid a small parade of shops, is Barclays Bank, while to the south-west lies a large, covered petrol station – accessible from a slip-road off the main A217 – which also serves a small number of shops and, more importantly, the local café.

The information was that the Blue Box would always park up on the slip-road on the corner of the petrol station, where its crew would break for tea before recommencing their run. It was here the attack was supposedly going to take place.

On many previous operations like this, PT17 had opted to use the familiar Trojan horse ploy to gain covert access to the plot. And again, this was to be so in this case. It was decided that the main attack team would arrive on the plot from the south in a side opening panel van, pull up alongside the box, and take out the bad guys. To add to the fright factor and to ensure everybody knew who they were dealing with, the seven team members would all be in coveralls and full assault kit. As a contingency, two PT17 gunships would be parked in a remote location about a mile north of the plot, and a third would be plotted on a housing estate nearby. Their primary role was to take off and house the box should it for some reason break free of the main ambush. They would also have a supporting cut-off role. As on all occasions, they would be working in plain clothes.

During the early hours of the morning the gunships had swept the plot to get a feel for the ambush site. They completed with plenty of time to spare – the optimum time for the hit was believed to be between 9.30 and 10.30 – so some of the lads took the opportunity to book a wake-up call and get their heads down in the cars . . .

The two-man, one-woman rostered Securicor crew reported to the duty office. Checking the schedule, they found they were on the Gatwick (or 'Bullion') run. It was never common practice to know how much you carried on any one particular journey, but with around twenty-five grand contained in each bag, and with forty-four bags loaded, it was certainly well in excess of a million . . .

Because it was known what day the robbery would take place, PT17 had been called in to cover this job on several occasions, albeit at different locations. So today the team were mildly surprised when they started to get radio traffic. The squad's surveillance guys had apparently clocked some of the players leaving their home addresses. A couple of them had even stayed together overnight, which was quite a good sign. Even better was the fact that they appeared to have a 'happy bag' with them. Things were now beginning to shape up nicely, especially as they were heading through Streatham and Mitcham in a red pick-up – in the general direction of the plot.

But things started to go wrong, and surveillance lost them in Wallington.

As the following team frantically backtracked and covered new grid references, the officer in charge at Woodhatch had to make a decision. He sent a covert car to sweep the plot in an effort to pick them up.

The Arif gang: Mehmet, with a blackened face and curly wig, drove the pick-up; his companion, disguised in a Ronald Reagan mask, gangland figure 'Crazy' Kenny Baker. Inside were Mehmet's brother Denis in an old-man mask, and Anthony Downer, wearing glasses and a wig. The gang were well known on the streets of south London. Despite their comical appearance, there was nothing funny about their guns: two 9mm self-loading pistols, two .38 revolvers, and a shotgun. They even had a high tech jammer with them inside the van, enabling them to block out the vehicle's signal, so it couldn't be tracked.

Ten o'clock: fifth drop of the day. The first four had passed without incident – three at Gatwick itself and a fourth in the small town of Horley. Now the Securicor van was heading back north on the A23, taking the Woodhatch Road, which led them to the garage.

Parking in the access road on the bend outside the service station, directly overlooking the bank, the crew stopped for refreshments at the local café.

It was obviously something they'd done plenty of times in the past.

Like most armoured vehicles, the Securicor vehicles, with their familiar dark blue colouring and silver livery, do not come as standard: both driver and front passenger doors are welded shut. That means that, apart from emergency exits, the only way into or from the vehicle is via a door at the rear nearside, a door which operates on an air lock principle.

Leaving the keys in the ignition, the driver and female

custodian climbed through into the 'vault', the domain of the backman whose job it is to pass out the cash through a side chute at each drop. In order to exit, the driver and custodian had to open the inner door and pass into the 'air lock'. Only when the inner door was locked could access be gained to the outside world; and only then through a series of complicated manoeuvres: having locked the inner door, the guard in the 'air lock' had to unlock the outer door while, inside, the backman throws a switch which disengages the outer lock, permitting exit. To regain entry one simply had to carry out the same procedure in reverse.

With no apparent need for their protective helmets, both guards headed towards the café. As they walked, their attention was drawn by the powerful revving of a car's engine. Turning, they saw a red pick-up truck speeding down the service road in their direction, swerving from left to right.

Throwing the vehicle at an angle across the road, both driver and passenger leapt from the cabin brandishing guns.

Two things struck the guards immediately: first, that the guns were pointing in their direction; and second, that one of the raiders was wearing a latex old-man mask. Screaming obscenities, the men directed the terrified guards back to their van.

Unbelievably, the squad had been unaware of any of this going on up until now; nobody had put the villains or the pick-up on the plot. To all intents and purposes it had been lost in Wallington.

Apparently it was the blaggers intention to gain access to the van then take it away to a nearby 'slaughter' and transfer the load. On previous jobs with a similar MO, the guards would usually be left behind, tied up. Hammering on the side of the van, the screaming robbers demanded entry inside. Looking out through a porthole, the backman could see his two colleagues, and the guns pointed at their heads. One of them, via his personal radio, was begging the backman to open the door.

'Open the fucking door!' screamed one of the robbers, pulling at the handle. 'How do you get into this fucking thing?'

The backman threw the switch, disengaging the outer door, which swung open. Bundling the two guards inside the tiny four-by-two-and-a-half-foot air lock, the gunmen demanded access to the inner sanctum, oblivious to the fact that, with the outer door open, that was impossible.

The blaggers became extremely agitated, so much so that all the guards were in fear of getting shot. With a third raider now joining the duo, the frightened guard finally got through to them and explained that, in order to gain access to the vault, they needed to close the outer door and open the inner one with a key. And so they crammed in, slamming the door behind them, and entered the vault.

By the sheer nature of their armour, cash-in-transit vehicles are extremely cramped inside, almost like a tank. With two raiders and three crew inside, there was hardly room to move.

As luck would have it, in their haste to gain admittance to the vault, the raiders had left the driver and custodian in the air lock at the back . . .

'Attack! Attack! Attack!' boomed the radio.

There was no 'Standby', no build up; the team never got as much as 'India on the plot'. All they knew was that the box was suddenly there, then the attack went in. Hurtling down the hill from the north, the two gunships swept on to the plot. To the south, however, baulked by the heavy traffic at the lights, the slower horse was hardly making progress, so it was left to the four guys in the first two gunships to deal.

Certainly not part of the plan.

The first vehicle entered the forecourt, and chaos reigned. The lads inside didn't know anything about the pick-up at that stage, so everybody locked on to the box.

Rick, one of the guys in the second gunship, bailed out just as Downer, gun in hand, crawled from the vault of the van into the front seats.

'Armed police! Drop the gun!' Rick screamed. Then events around him spiralled rapidly out of control.

Crack! Crack!

Behind him Rick heard the sound of gunfire as the red pick-up, Mehmet still at the wheel, sped through the forecourt, squeezing between parked vehicles and the petrol pumps.

Pulling the passenger door open, one of the team found himself staring at the guns of Baker and Arif. No time to aim . . . *Crack!* From the hip, he delivered a shot with his MP5. Finding its mark the round struck Baker a vicious blow in the left side, killing him almost instantly.

Crack! The second operative, now covering on the front nearside, engaged Arif with his high-powered rifle, shattering the side window and showering the occupants with glass.

Rick, oblivious to all but the noise, continued his challenge. 'Armed police! Drop the gun!'

Crack! Crack! Crack!

With no response from Downer, Rick brought the MP5 into his shoulder and fired three quick rounds in succession.

Thump! Thump! Thump! The three soft-point rounds found their mark, penetrating the outer skin of the armoured door. But Downer failed to react.

Crack! Crack! A further pair shattered the toughened glass into a dazzling spiderweb. Releasing his grip on the weapon Downer threw his hands up in surrender.

Suddenly the air lock's outer door opened. The backman had seized the opportunity and, with a total disregard for his own safety, had thrown the switch inside, giving his colleagues the opportunity to escape, knowing full well it meant he would be trapped.

The team managed to get the guards out and into the safety of cover. By then the horse had arrived, and some of the guys had gone over to look at Baker.

'Fucking Hell!' Rick screamed, clocking Arif through the window. 'There's a second man!'

Clearly things were not over yet.

'Show me your hands!' he shouted as Downer pressed his empty palms against the windscreen. With the initial panic over, Rick was starting to take control. He knew there was one guard and at least two bad guys inside the box – at least, that was the information he gleaned from the custodian. The only problem was how to get them out. Rick had ordered Downer to turn off the engine, take out the keys and set the handbrake, so he knew the vehicle wasn't going anywhere. And the occupants were worried – but for how long? And how long would it take them to realise the implication of the fact that Rick's rounds hadn't penetrated the cab? To all intents and purposes they still had the upper hand. And the hostage.

Realising something had to be done quickly, the acting inspector, a tall, affable Scot, stepped forward and prepared to enter the vehicle. It is a common procedure, when dealing with besieged criminals, not to allow them access to anything that could be of use to them – for instance, firearms, ammunition, radios etc. Thus the inspector was doing everything by the book when he took off his Glock and gave it to one of the team. No point in giving them an extra weapon inside.

Rick, however, had other thoughts, and quickly advised that, with two armed men inside, and with room for only one SO19 man to enter, perhaps the guvnor should be carrying.

The inspector took the hint and went forward armed.

It was quite an anticlimax after all the action. After gaining entry, he handcuffed the two suspects, reporting later that they simply had no fight left in them.

In the end the only problem was how to get everybody out. An easy answer to this dilemma was provided when suddenly the escape hatch in the roof of the van flew open, accompanied by a harsh, recorded vocal alarm. As if the team didn't have enough on their plate – a hijack, a kidnapping, hostage rescue, shooting, one dead, large crowd – and now a metallic voice booming: *'Securicor vehicle under attack! Securicor vehicle under attack! . . .'* And to top it all they couldn't turn the fucking thing off.

Eventually everybody was brought up through the roof and passed down. Amid the excitement a robber had shit himself – and that's the one thing that really stuck in everybody's mind.

Mehmet and Denis, the leaders of the gang, subsequently received eighteen and twenty-two years respectively. In a strange twist, their brother was arrested on a plot by PT17 six months later, receiving six and a half years. It was strongly believed at the time that he was attempting to finance an escape bid for his brothers.

For all of their bravery, SO19 are probably one of the least recognised departments within the Met. To senior officers they represent a necessary evil, the unacceptable face of Policing.

To the Woodhatch boys we were a team of guys who rode into their manor, shot up the town, and rode off into the sunset. Nothing more than glory boys.

Rick summed it all up recounting the whole operation. 'So that was the Woodhatch job,' he said quietly. 'One bad guy died, and everybody went home.'

Amen to that!

6

The Return of the Arctic Fox

'The Arctic Fox returns!' Bill threw open the canteen door dramatically. I stood up and headed for the counter.

'Cup of tea?' I asked.

Bill nodded and patted his stomach. 'No sugar. I'm watching my figure.'

'Somebody has to,' Chris grunted. Chris, my number two, was a man of few words.

Billy ignored the jibe as I handed him the cup, and nodded towards the senior officers' canteen. 'Have a word?' I asked. 'You and Brad?'

'Sure,' said Bill. 'What's up?'

The door was open as we stepped inside the small, neat room, a long table down its centre. Quite why senior officers have to have their own canteen always amazes me. A throw-back to the officer class, perhaps? Or is it simply that their eating habits leave a lot to be desired?

'What's up, leader?' said Brad, sucking on his foul-smelling pipe and customarily ignoring the large, red NO SMOKING signs.

'Nothing,' I said, indicating a seat. 'But I've had an idea in relation to this fucking exercise later in the week.' Having seen the article in *Throat Slasher's Monthly* I'd managed to get hold of some military trip flares. I certainly had the makings of an idea on how I wanted to use them – but no

94

clue how the fuck they worked. And who better to show me than two old soldiers?

'We've come in here because I didn't want to say anything in front of the other teams. You know . . .' Friendly team rivalry was one thing, but at the time certain back-stabbers had been bitching about my methods and the methods used by Black team to get the job done. To me, this was nothing – rumours that we were somewhat maverick had always circulated – but I think certain people resented our closeness, our camaraderie, and our reputation with other agencies. But recently things had got worse, what with snide remarks being made about me going training. The reality of the situation was that I was my own worse enemy, doing nothing to dispel the rumours; even making up a few of my own.

'Are either of you familiar with trip flares?' I asked now.

Brad paused. Taking his pipe out of his mouth he blew thick smoke ceilingward, where it hung in a dark cloud. 'Dolph,' he said finally. 'Standard military issue.'

Bill nodded in agreement. 'Nothing new to the engineer of death,' he added. 'Huh! When I was in the Falklands . . .'

When Bill was in the Royal Marines he'd served as an armourer during the Falklands conflict, and didn't we all know it!

'Right,' I interrupted – 'then this is the plan.'

The exercise would be spread over two days, and was to take place in a large deserted hospital on the outskirts of Surrey. The whole purpose was to test the combined response of the police and the military to a large-scale terrorist hostage incident, along the lines of the Iranian Embassy siege. An exercise like this would normally start with the SAS Counter Revolutionary Warfare instructors playing the role of terrorists and taking a large number of people hostage within the grounds of the hospital. As with any armed incident, the initial response would be from normal uniformed officers, who in turn would request ARVs. The vehicles would arrive and the teams would quickly establish an armed containment and control, thus escalating the incident to the next phase, when senior officers, hostage negotiators and an SO19 team would respond – and the long, laborious task of negotiating and setting up a formal control would begin. Ultimately (as we all invariably knew in advance), the SAS special projects team would be contacted.

This particular exercise coincided with the new SP team coming in to take over from the outgoing lot – part of their ongoing operational cycle. So, having trained hard, this exercise would be the first real test of their calibre.

Black team was set to be the initial response (as per the senior officer's request). After the first night we would be relieved and hand over to a second team, so we wouldn't witness the dramatic end – but that suited me down to the ground. It was something akin to being Jimmy Greaves on the substitute bench of the World Cup final – watching everybody else have the glory you should have shared . . .

'You know how sneaky these Regiment bastards can be,' I said to Brad and Bill. 'They're just as likely to sneak out under cover of darkness and come round behind the containment. They'd like nothing better than to see Old Bill with egg on his face.' They nodded. 'What I'd like to do,' I added, 'is set up a cordon of trip flares around the strong-hold in case they do try to slip out.' I knew it was pretty unorthodox, but certainly felt it was worth a try . . . And so we agreed to take the team to Lippitts the next morning to practise the plan!

After a large fry up we set out in the battered white Obo van. I'd had a moan in the yard to Rod, the small, toothless, cockney garage hand, about the constant lack of decent motors. With hands deep in the pockets of his overalls he'd simply said, 'Well I can't fucking help it if you lot keep smashing the fuckers up, can I?' Of course he was right. On one recent ambush option the lads had steamed into the plot fast and, slamming the Range Rovers to a halt, one front-seat passenger had thrown the armoured door open. The momentum, coupled with the heavy steel plating, had ripped the door from its hinges. It was now held on with plasticuffs. We'd tried everything to get the fleet up to scratch, but always seemed to get knocked back at the first hurdle. The truth of the matter was that we just didn't treat our vehicles with respect. Once, a couple of the guys had returned with a gleaming new trophy; the Home Secretary's Jag – V12 engine, walnut interior with leather upholstery and bandit glass, the lot. The luxury car had been replaced with a newer model, and seemed ideal for our purposes; the only trouble was that everybody wanted to use it. Also, it had one major drawback, particularly on operations: with four young men cruising around, all in tatty jeans and T-shirts, we were constantly getting stopped by the Police!

Arriving at Lippitts Hill, I said, 'Get a cuppa, fellas, on the Banjo in fifteen. If we get time later we'll fit a shoot in.'

Strolling to the canteen with Chris and Joe, I was intercepted by a lone figure. 'Steve Collins?' he asked. I took in the training blues of the older man, his smooth features, the beret on his head barely covering the mop of greying hair, and his eyes seeming to smile with an intensity. That took me aback.

'Yeah,' I said.

He smiled. 'Pat Hodgson. I'm coming back to ops soon, and Black team's been mooted.'

I nodded. 'Heard something like that myself,' I replied.

'Well, nice meeting you,' he said, adjusting his beret. 'Don't see you up here much.'

'No,' I said to his back as he walked towards the range. 'I avoid this place like the fucking plague.'

'All right, Andy?' I asked, bumping into the guvnor on the way out.

'Yeah, not too bad, Steve. Up here for a management meeting.'

'Oh.' I nodded. 'Let us know if there are any new moans

about the team.'

He smiled. 'What you lot up to?'

'Nothing,' I replied. 'Just brought the lads up for a play on the Banjo. Might have a shoot later, if you're up for it . . .?'

He looked at his watch. 'Doubt I'll have time, Steve. Thanks anyway.'

'Oh, by the way,' I said, 'I've just bumped into Pat Hodgson. Said he may be coming on the team.'

'Yeah,' said Andy. 'A few of the instructors have put in to come back to ops, but nothing's been finalised.'

'OK,' I said, wandering off. 'Catch you later.'

As Bill held up the black, soup-tin-shaped device attached to a long green spike, Brad spoke to the gathered semi-circle. 'OK, chaps – military trip flare. The spike is pushed firmly into the ground, with another series trailing out at intervals.' He pulled out a roll of thin metallic thread. 'The trip-wire is attached to the device, then strung out through the others, holding the wire from the ground ideally at a height of six to eight inches. Once we are happy, the pin can be removed.'

He pointed to the top of the flare. 'This arm is held in place by the pin at the end of the wire. The operation is simple,' he added, taking a puff on his pipe. 'When the wire is tripped by foot, the pin is pulled out and the device ignites. The wire can of course be camouflaged if desired.'

'What's the effect when it explodes?' I asked.

'Much like a large ground-burst firework. Flames shoot up into the air, illuminating the surrounding area,' said Bill.

'Ideal for our purposes, then?' I asked.

Brad and Bill nodded in unison.

'OK. Let's have a look.'

Standing well to the rear, next to the perimeter fence, the team looked on enthralled as Brad and Bill went to work. My mind wandered off to the room across the Banjo, where the management meeting would have started. Were there any new complaints against us?

Pushing the long spikes into the soil in the prescribed manner, Bill was busy running the wire, while at the other end Brad was taking care of the 'bang box', a box containing the team's stun grenades, specialist shotgun and rifle ammunition, and pyrotechnic devices, which travelled everywhere with us when operational. This was a role he always threw himself into with gusto. I could only assume he was either stone deaf, or just liked blowing things to pieces.

'OK, mate,' said Bill, dropping beside Brad and handing him the end of the wire.

Brad inserted it gently into the flare.

Rising, Bill made his way swiftly to our location.

Brad looked back, puzzled. 'Know something I don't?'

Bill grinned, 'Yeah – never trust a para. Only two things drop out of the sky: birdshit and paratroopers.' He chuckled.

'Fucking cabbage-hat,' Brad retorted. 'Right . . .' He pulled a small pair of pliers from the leg pocket of his coveralls and pushed himself lower into the ground. 'As I said, simple operation – the only tricky part is removing . . .' He tugged gently at the pin with the pliers. 'The . . .'

Ping! It came loose.

Booooommmm!

The intense white light rocketed skyward. Shielding my eyes with my hand, the last thing I saw was a quick X-ray of the back of Brad's head as the flare erupted in a spectacular display of sound and vision. I removed my hand and blinked.

'Fucking hell!' I shouted, running to Brad's last known location and seeing his unmoving figure prone on the ground. 'You all right, mate?'

Brad rolled over, pipe clamped firmly between his teeth, face covered in soot and mud, his chin jutting out proudly. 'Leader, told you that was the tricky part,' he grinned.

In the small, stark room, the management meeting had gone

momentarily silent. Andy groaned as my words echoed in his brain: Just brought the lads up for a play on the Banjo . . . As if we weren't in enough shit already.

'As I was saying,' said the chief instructor, 'due to the injunction by local residents, a flag must be flown indicating the use of any pyrotechnic, and then only after consultation with me . . .'

'Got a couple of things I'd like to show the boys while we're here – if we've got time, Stevie?'

I looked at my watch. 'Sure. How about some distractions?'

'Course,' said Brad proudly, hoisting a large round tin from his box. 'Now, you've all seen the mothball before . . .' We had. This was the mothball distraction – electronically detonated, it produces a large explosion and thick black smoke which mushrooms into the sky and smells remarkably like mothballs. This type of device would be used to distract hostage-takers to one part of a building while an assault takes place in another, a classic Trojan-horse type ploy used by every major CRW unit in the world.

'Well . . .' Brad held up a small green device, not dissimilar to the flare. 'When coupled with one of these mini ground-bursts and a litre of petrol, it really gets their attention.'

I watched in fascination as Brad taped the devices together, partially buried them, then ran out his command wire. We all dived for cover behind the bunker as he bared the ends of the copper wire and connected them to a hand-held clacker. Anxiously we flattened ourselves against the rough concrete wall as Brad hit the button . . .

Booooommmm!

The door to the conference room burst open. 'Sir! Sir!' interrupted the duty sergeant excitedly, halting the meeting. The small group of senior officers looked up, irritated at the interruption. 'It's Black team, sir,' he grovelled. 'Up on the Banjo. They're—'

Boooommmm!

The building shook, rattling the ancient windows in their frames as the tremors rumbled like a mini earthquake beneath their feet.

All eyes were on Andy.

Boooommmm!

Out on the Banjo, the thick black cloud mushroomed heavenward then hung in the air like the aftermath of Hiroshima. A modest cheer rose as we admired Brad's handiwork.

I slapped him on the back. 'Fucking belting, mate! Now that's what I call a distraction.'

The fallout hung dramatically in the air as I heard the noise – faint at first, but getting louder . . . *Whappa whappa whappa* . . . Suddenly the white and red blur of a helicopter cleared the fence, the buzzing rotor-blades busily dispersing the smoke. We looked up at the small round heads of the crew as they peered down at us, strangely alien in their large round helmets. The machine set down on its pad some two hundred metres to the south.

I looked at Brad. 'Fucking hell, mate – two minutes earlier and we'd have shot down the paraffin parrot!'

The bollocking I later received was relatively minor. I pleaded ignorance to the flag rule, but as team leader it *was* my responsibility.

'What you got there?' Chris asked Sinex, putting down his newspaper.

'Thermos flask,' he replied in a somewhat superior tone. 'One of those new ones from Makro. Stainless steel. I can use it on exercises, keeps liquids hotter for longer.' He tapped the dull, cylindrical body. 'Robust, as well – you can do anything with them,' he added disappearing into the small kitchen.

I could hear him running water. 'You making the coffee then?' I called.

'Bollocks,' came the reply.

I looked at Chris and raised my eyebrows. 'I can see how

he got his name,' I said. 'When he gets up your nose he certainly lasts eight hours.'

'I heard that,' Sinex moaned from the kitchen.

Three minutes later he was back. 'You staying here?' he asked.

I nodded.

'Well I'm going out for a run. Don't let anyone nick my Thermos, it's filled with boiling water.'

I looked up, puzzled. 'What for?'

Sinex huffed, looking at me as if I were some sort of moron. 'Because I'm testing it out,' he said, somewhat irritated. 'If it does what it's supposed to do it'll still be piping hot by the end of the shift.'

I nodded and, picking up the remote, flicked through the TV channels.

'You ready?' Bill called as he bounded energetically into the room.

'He's playing with his flask,' I said, nodding towards the kitchen.

'Oh,' said Bill, bending down and touching his toes. 'You coming for a run?'

I looked up at him. 'Be serious . . .' In truth I'd always been quite a useful runner, but just recently I had begun to let my personal fitness slide, and the old spare tyre was getting bigger

Sinex jogged out of the kitchen.

I looked at his long white legs. 'D'you know you've got two pieces of string hanging out of your shorts?'

'Bollocks,' he replied, and they jogged out of the door.

Rising, Chris threw down the newspaper on an empty chair and strode into the kitchen.

'You making the coffee?' I called.

'Yeah, if you want one,' he replied, 'plenty of hot water.'

Following him out, I watched in amusement as he tipped the contents of Sinex's flask into two cups. He then poured the remainder down the sink before topping up the flask from the cold tap, securing the lid and replacing it in its original position on the draining board.

'Coffee,' he said as he passed me the steaming cup.

Getting all the kit together for a Remount was a major exercise in itself. Vehicles, firearms, radios, booster aerials, batteries and chargers, first aid equipment, pyrotechnics and breaking kit . . . Apart from this there was also the personnel's own equipment – sleeping bags, grub and reading material.

'We got enough guns?' I asked Dave Mate, the force armourer.

Short and fit, with a greying moustache and a cockney accent, Dave proudly displayed his name badge on his overalls – DAVE MATE. Needless to say his real name wasn't Mate – that was just what he called everybody, even if, as in my case, he'd known you for years. Dave was also a hero in his own right: while serving with the RAF during the Dhofar campaign in the early seventies he'd been awarded the British Empire Medal for gallantry in the field, having risked life and limb carrying out bomb disposal under fire.

'Steve, mate!' he said in response to my enquiry. 'You've got shit-loads.'

That was good enough for me.

The mood was jovial as we cut out for the exercise. The wagons were packed to the gunnels and I was wearing a felt International Rescue hat like a *Thunderbirds* puppet. When we arrived the ARVs had already responded to the initial call and were now in the throes of setting up a full-scale operation.

I looked at my watch. Twenty three hours to go.

The large, red-brick Victorian building sprawled out across an expanse of spacious grounds. Some sections of it lay derelict, their coppering and lead pipes long since removed. Driving in through the entrance gate, we were flagged down by a somewhat officious security guard.

I adjusted my hat and clambered off the coach, taking in the vast scale of the exercise. Special constables, drafted in at little cost, swarmed around the perimeter, aiding their regular colleagues with the security. Off to my left a strange mixture of SAS troopers and police patiently filed into the makeshift canteen. Directly ahead lay the site of the exercise proper.

I self-consciously removed my hat.

'All ammunition and explosives are to be handed in to the security building,' snapped the guard, eyeing me up and down.

'What we supposed to do then – point our fingers and shout bang?'

He huffed. 'No ammunition, including blanks, is allowed in the exercise area. Order of the Marshal.'

'Wyatt Earp?'

'No, me,' came a vaguely familiar voice from behind.

Turning, I was confronted by a face I knew well. 'Fuck me! How you doing, boss?' I asked the Chief Inspector with whom I had served when in the Surrey force.

'Not bad, Steve,' he replied. 'You're looking well.'

I smiled. 'When people say that it usually means they think I've put on weight . . . Not very realistic though, guv – having to give up the ammunition. Suppose something happens?'

'Safety,' he replied. 'And we all know how it'll end anyway.'

Dragging the kit from the vans, we quickly made our way to the gates and the cordon control officer – in this instance an older special constable with the flashes HAC – the Honourable Artillery Company – on his epaulettes. This is the oldest regiment in the British Army, whose territorial ranks are swelled predominantly by successful city businessmen and MPs, notably a certain ex-Prime Minister.

'Safety cards!' he barked.

'What?' asked Bill.

'Safety cards. Nobody goes through without handing in a Major Incident safety card,' explained the jobsworth.

Safety cards were certainly a new one on me, although I

vaguely remembered seeing one once – a small, blue, laminated card with name, warrant number and department printed on one side and the helpful mnemonic CHALET on the reverse, designed to aid the first officer on the scene at a major incident: Casualties, Hazards, Access routes, Location (exactly), Emergency services (required), Type (of incident). The logic behind the cards was that you were supposed to hand them over on the way in and retrieve them on the way out; thus a log of who was unaccounted for could be kept.

'Sorry, bud,' Chris growled menacingly. 'Don't apply to us – we're the firearms team.'

The special stood his ground. 'Well I've been told nobody enters without a card.'

'Oh yeah?' I smiled, brushing him aside. 'So stop us!'

Dumping down my bergen in the cavernous hangar, I quickly set about establishing my territory – home for the next twenty hours or so – not too near the large concertina doors, where it was draughty, but in a nice little corner out of the way.

Brad, who was obviously a firm believer in the 'why stand when you can sit, and why sit when you can lie down' attitude, made himself busy stringing up his small light-weight hammock, watched silently from across the hangar by the boys from the Regiment.

Shivering involuntarily against the mid-afternoon chill, I pulled on my coveralls, boots and body armour, then checked and holstered my empty Glock. Beside me, Andy struggled into his waterproof Goretex jacket.

'Best get down to control, Steve. See what's going on,' he said, adjusting his beret.

I nodded and dug into my pocket for the dark blue headgear. (Orders from above dictated that, when out and about, SO19 personnel would wear the outdated beret. The thinking behind it was that it made us look far more professional, and, as the inspector and sergeant, Andy and I had to set an example.)

As we moved out of the hangar, I felt rather than saw the Regiment's eyes burning into my back.

The control room was chaos, exactly what you would expect from a hastily thrown together mish-mash of personnel. Radios of all descriptions squawked unintelligible gibberish, while mobile phones and pagers played their own individual tunes.

'Fuck this,' I whispered to Andy. 'Where do you start?'

'Over there,' he said, nodding towards the worry of senior officers and negotiators gathered in the corner of the large, airy room.

The commander looked up, immaculate in his blue serge uniform. 'Ah, Inspector,' he said, taking in the embroidered pips on Andy's jacket. 'Where are your team?'

'In the hangar at the FHA, sir. We've only just arrived.'

'Well, I'd like them out, please,' he instructed arrogantly. 'Things are starting to hot up, what with the terrorists threatening the hostages.'

'I'll tell the men, sir,' I said, giving Andy the respect of his rank in front of the management. Then I added, 'It's getting dark. I'll have a couple of the boys kit up and get out on the plot with some PNGs. See what they can pick up.'

'Well, inspector,' said the commander with typical 'rank assumes knowledge' attitude. 'I want a full briefing from you in an hour so I can approve your plan.'

'What plan, sir?' asked Andy.

'Your plan for the storming of the building, of course!'

I laughed involuntarily; it just slipped out.

'What's funny?' he asked, shooting me a glance like I was something he'd stepped in, and acknowledging my presence for the first time.

'Well, the Regiment's here to do that,' I said. 'I thought it was the whole point of the exercise.'

'Regiment?' he asked.

'Yeah,' I replied. 'The SAS. That's why they've been here two days.'

Ignoring me totally he snapped at Andy, 'Well I'm in

charge here, not the SAS, and I may decide not to hand it over. *And* I want SO19's plan for the taking of that building.'

An uneasy silence hung in the air.

'Sir.' Andy nodded.

'One hour,' said the commander, looking at his watch.

It was dark outside as we headed for the canteen. 'He's having a fucking laugh,' I said to Andy. By now I'd formed the impression they couldn't organise a piss-up in a brewery. 'We've only just arrived, had all our kit taken from us, haven't even been afforded the courtesy of a recce – and he wants an emergency reaction in an hour! What we need is a fucking miracle worker.'

And then I heard one.

'Steve.'

I studied Roy's wiry frame as he took my hand in his vice-like grip. It never ceased to amaze me that the majority of these SAS guys looked outwardly like small, unassuming types, while inside they were actually coiled springs.

Roy and I had first met at Hereford when I was down there with a team for a week's training. A sergeant on the CRW training wing, he had been our liaison man – and during that hectic time had certainly put us through our paces. Since then we'd met occasionally for a beer when he was on 'business' in London. Now, I discovered, he was part of the Regiment's planning team for the exercise.

Over a cup of tea in the canteen, Andy and I filled him in on our predicament. Occasionally he'd interrupt to clarify one point or another, and nodded thoughtfully when I concluded, 'The problem is, Roy, that we haven't even got the time for a full recce, let alone enough to knock up a plan. Sure, in reality, if they started topping hostages, we'd go hell for leather, but that's not the point. This guy's just being an arsehole.'

'How many you got?' Roy asked.

'Twelve,' I replied, 'including me and the guvnor.'

He laughed. 'Do you know how many men we're planning to use on the final assault?'

'Well, I can imagine you'd probably use the whole squadron,' I said. 'But all we need to do is get this tosser off our backs and let you get on with it.'

'OK,' Roy replied. 'How can I help?'

I smiled. 'I know it's a fucking liberty, but by now you must be well on the way to fine-tuning your DA . . .'

'Yeah, we are,' he replied.

'Well,' I whispered, 'if we could have a quick glance at your ER we can prop it up as ours . . . But tell him we don't have enough men. There's no way they'll draft more in; he's bound to fall for it.'

Roy nodded. 'Come with me. I'll run it past our head-shed, see what they say.'

'You can't come in here without an incident safety card,' said the monotonous, now-familiar voice on the gate as we rounded the corner.

Standing before us was our old friend the special, and standing before him was the tall dark shape of a fully kitted SAS assaulter. The whites of his eyes glared out of the slits in his balaclava, the only part of his body visible, and PNGs hung limply from his neck beside his fully automatic Heckler & Koch machine-gun. On one thigh was fastened a Sig-Sauer P226 pistol, while on the other were his spare magazines. His black suede assault vest was dripping with multi-burst stun grenades, and high on his left shoulder was the abseil-line-cutting crew knife. It was obvious he'd been out on a recce.

Apparently a man of few words, he brushed the special aside with one swipe of his huge, gloved hand.

Recovering his composure, the special adjusted his hat, looked our way and raised his hand.

'Don't even think about it,' I said.

'This is highly irregular, you know,' said the young, rather pompous SAS rupert after Roy had given him the run-down.

By now we were attracting more than just the odd glance, and some of the Regiment lads had started strolling over to see what all the fuss was about.

'Besides,' the rupert added, 'we have to do the final assault. It's the whole point of the exercise.'

'Yes, sir. I know,' I said, affording him the privilege of his Queen's commission. 'But try telling him that. You know the ground rules as well as us – and the last thing we're trying to do is steal the glory – but at this time it's his exercise, and protocol dictates that the military can only intervene if he officially requests it in writing.'

'This is highly irregular,' he repeated, nodding to Roy.

'OK, guys, listen in.' Roy stepped up to the overhead plan. 'Our ER is simple. If the shit hits the fan we need to be in quick. We have frame charges already made up for blowing the windows. The Range Rovers will steam in to the FAP here . . .' He poked a finger at the rear aspect of the strong-hold. 'The rest of the team are standing to at an LUP . . .'

I scribbled furiously in my notebook. From the drawings I could see they had done their homework – but then they had been here two days, not two fucking minutes.

'Thanks, Roy,' I said. 'I owe you one.'

Covering the short distance to where the boys were happily making themselves at home, Andy and I quickly set about drawing up a set of plans that looked half-way feasible.

'I'm going for a cup of coffee,' Sinex bleated.

I looked at my watch. 'OK, mate, but don't be long, we may need a quick heads-down.' Looking across at Chris and Bill I called, 'Kit up, fellas. I at least want somebody on the ground. Take some PNGs – it's getting dark.'

I turned to Sinex. 'I thought you had one of them super-duper flasks?'

'Nah,' he moaned. 'Fucking thing was useless. I took it back and complained. The water got colder than it would if I'd left it in a cup.'

The commander nodded, satisfied. 'And you're sure you don't have enough men?' he asked, studying the plans.

'Absolutely, sir,' said Andy. 'We'd probably need the whole wing.'

'All right, I suppose we'll have to use the SAS if it becomes necessary.'

I looked at him. Becomes necessary? I thought. What colour's the fucking sky in your world?

Back in the hangar I said, 'Two of our guys are going out on a recce, Roy. White aspect. I know you've got men out there yourself and I'll let our snipers know. Are yours working with ours?'

'No, they're working under our sniper team commander, Chris Ryan,' he replied.

I shook my head. 'Don't know the name, but I may recognise the face. I'm sure he won't let one get away.'

The light snapped on suddenly, illuminating the men in their sleeping bags like large black maggots.

'Turn that fucking light out!' came a cry in the distance.

'Where's your Inspector?' shouted the chief instructor. 'I've been looking for him for hours.'

Beside me, Andy crawled from his grot.

'The commander wants you,' the instructor growled.

Andy nodded at me, but I was already half-way out of my bag.

'What's that truck?' bleated the Commander.

I squinted at the small video screen. The white vehicle was barely visible in the eerie white glow of the infra-red monitor. 'That's out of bounds of the exercise, sir,' I said, looking up. 'It belongs to the firm's technical guys. I saw them arrive earlier with all the surveillance equipment.'

'I don't care who it belongs to,' he said. 'If they decide to make a break for it they could steal the van and get away.'

'Well,' I started, 'I hardly think—'

'I don't want you to think, sergeant,' he snapped. 'I just want it immobilised.'

I nodded. 'OK, sir. I'll get it put on the incident log that, for the purpose of this exercise, the vehicle is nominally immobilised.'

His face visibly reddened, the stress of command obviously getting to him. 'I didn't say *nominally*, did I?' he screeched. 'Now get out there and immobilise it!'

Chris and Bill pulled on their hoods.

'Don't forget,' I said, 'immobilised he wants, immobilised he gets. No half measures.'

Bill nodded, staring into the eyepiece of the PNGs then disappeared into the night.

Wide awake now, unable to get back to sleep, I strolled across the hangar to where Roy was sitting alone. 'We're being relieved in the morning,' I said, checking my watch. 'What time's the final assault?'

'"Bout four, I would guess,' he replied. 'Normally happens about then so we have time to stow the gear and get back to Hereford.'

'Got much on?' I asked.

'No, not really – silly bits and pieces. How about you?'

'Rushed off our feet,' I said. 'We're totalling about three hundred ops a year.'

Roy whistled. 'Fucking hell! We'll have to see what we can do about getting a couple of the boys attached.'

I nodded – it had been in the pipeline for ages. 'The offer's always there,' I said. 'We constantly have guys on attachment from other forces, so why not the Regiment?'

'I'll look into it,' he promised.

'Trojan two-seven,' the call-sign blared urgently into my ear-shell. It was Billy.

'Two-seven,' I answered.

'Yeah,' he whispered from his prone position just yards from the stronghold. 'This is a brand new motor. It belongs to the job; it's not even part of the exercise.'

111

'I know,' I replied. 'I've already told him. But he wants it immobilised, so do it.'

By early light the hangar was a hive of activity. In the middle of the room the Regiment had marked out a life-size floor-plan of the stronghold, complete with doors and windows. They were now in the throes of choreographing their assault, running through the plan and getting to know the ground. In about ten hours they'd be doing it for real. As our relief arrived I bade Roy a friendly farewell and promised to keep in touch. Driving past the old special on the gate, I grinned and saluted, then, feeling the hair on the nape of my neck rise, I turned to look back at the old red-brick building and the unseen eyes of Chris Ryan's snipers.

We later heard that the exercise went off without a hitch. Specially adapted Range Rovers sped on to the plot, disgorging the black clad assaulters. The air was filled with smoke and cordite as the sounds of exploding frame charges reverberated from the buildings, accompanied by the high-pitched rattle of small-arms fire. In the air, troopers fast-roped from helicopters on to the roof, then disappeared from view . . .

Three days later I was summoned to the first floor. Knocking on the superintendent's open door, I entered.

Glancing up from an official-looking document, he nodded at the opposite chair. 'You were the initial team to respond to the Remount request – is that right?'

'Yep,' I answered.

He looked back at the letter. 'I've just had this through from the vehicle garage at Lambeth.'

'Oh?' I said.

'Yes,' he replied. 'Apparently, at the end of the exercise when the technicians packed up their van to leave, it was only as they attempted to drive off that they realised the entire wiring loom had been ripped out and all four tyres slashed. Apart from the inconvenience of alternative transport, the damage runs to thousands of pounds. I don't suppose you know anything about it?'

'No, sir,' I said.

The mood was jovial as Green team arrived back at base. A couple of weeks had passed since the Remount exercise, and with them had come the usual regularity of early-morning dig-outs, robbery plots and the odd rapid entry – things I'd always termed 'bread and butter' jobs for the department. The two SAS troopers who'd joined us, however, were more than impressed by the workload. Roy had been as good as his word and – with a few strings pulled here and there within the higher echelons of command authority – had finally been given permission for no more than two troopers to be attached at any one time. For obvious reasons, strict guidelines had been drawn up and had to be adhered to: they would for example be attached only to SFO teams, the idea being for them to attend as many incidents as possible, purely as observers to witness the way our teams dealt with day-to-day operations.

The troopers – whom I'll call Will and Jim – had at first appeared somewhat sceptical. What could the world-renowned hostage-rescue unit, 22 SAS, possibly learn from the tactical firearms unit SO19? A question posed on more than one occasion and one which I always attempted to explain.

We were in no way attempting to emulate the SAS, for we were professionals in our own right – and, for that matter, with a great deal of experience.

I'd once been training at Hereford with the team. We were sitting in the canteen, a queue had started to form, and a number of guys from the Regiment were strung out past our table. Noticing the not-dissimilar coveralls, one trooper had asked his colleagues in a loud voice, 'Who are those blokes?'

'Oh,' the other had replied for all to hear, 'they're those wankers from the Met who think they can do what we do.'

Downing my tea I'd asked just as loudly, 'I've done four hostage rescues this year – how about you?'

It was a minor incident, caused by one guy opening his mouth before putting his brain in gear.

In general, though, I'm happy to say that our rapport with the Regiment was good. I always try to make people fully aware that the Regiment trains for a vast variety of roles, including jungle and desert warfare, so their tour of the Special Projects team played only a small part in their operational sphere. With us, room combat and covert ops were our primary role, something we did every working day. With this in mind, secondments of this nature could only be healthy for all concerned.

Although unable to 'carry', Will and Jim both looked well capable of looking after themselves if the shit hit the fan. Short and muscular, Will had a perfectly groomed head of hair; Jim's was shorter and cut tight. Both were in their twenties and wearing the ubiquitous lumberjack shirts, jeans and desert wellies. They already fitted in well with the teams, and were starting to compare the camaraderie with that of the Regiment.

The telephone rang.

'Load up,' shouted Paul, the stocky, curly haired team leader, as he listened intently to the message. Paul had recently taken charge of the team and was as professional as they came. With the receiver grasped beneath his chin he scribbled furiously in his notepad, nodding occasionally and barking out commands. 'Bang box, distractions and hattons.'

'Fucking hell.' Pecky grinned at Will and Jim. 'Sounds like a good one.'

'Tiger kidnap,' Paul snapped, slamming down the phone. This was the expression for a situation where the victim is held by one part of the gang while the other part makes the demand. An example would be a bank manager getting a call at work saying his wife is being held hostage at home.

'Pecky, plot us a route to Wembley,' Paul added.

'No need,' Tony 'The Equaliser' called, though he would

be under threat of a hefty fine if he got it wrong. 'I know the way.'

And with blue lights flashing and two-tones blaring they left the yard, cutting a swathe through the early-afternoon traffic.

Arriving at Wembley the team immediately set about distributing the kit while Paul made his way swiftly to control. The small room was buzzing. Detectives from every conceivable unit of Scotland Yard sat huddled together, deep in discussion. As Paul entered, the talking stopped and all eyes in the room were quickly on him. The Glory Boys had arrived!

After a quick run-down on events from the organised crime branch and the surveillance team leader, Paul decided that with the little information there was to hand, the only thing they could do was keep it fluid, let it run and think on your feet until something concrete developed. In other words, the team didn't know what was going on. All they had been told was that a team of bad guys (numbers unknown) held a hostage, and wanted to make some sort of exchange in McDonald's.

With the rest of the team climbing into full kit, Paul immediately dispatched Pecky and Tony on a recce of the fast-food venue.

It was all very strange; they had the feeling that they weren't being told everything. Running through their options, FUPs, escape routes and communications, they decided that SO11 would take control, effectively having 'eyeball' on the surrounding area and putting out as many footies as they could while monitoring the restaurant from an OP opposite. In such a busy street this would prove to be difficult, particularly as – if the bosses were to be believed – there were no clues as to the identity of the hostage, or indeed the kidnappers.

Finally they were ready. Tony and Pecky pulled on the lightweight undershirt armour. They were to remain in plain clothes – giving them the option of a fast, covert move-up on foot should the need arise. However the rest of the lads carried stun grenades, breaking kit and a Hatton gun. (The sawn-off Remington 870 pump-action shotgun is an invaluable piece of equipment. Loaded with the powdered lead and wax Hatton round specially designed by the SAS, its original use had been for shooting off door hinges; now SO19 had found a new use for it: the ability to incapacitate a vehicle. Contrary to what Hollywood film directors would have us believe, unless you are extremely lucky a normal round simply bounces off if fired at a pneumatic tyre. Hatton rounds, on the other hand, work every time!) Still the team was severely stretched, and found itself short of a plain-clothes driver. It was a role for which both Will and Jim enthusiastically volunteered – and although bending the rules slightly, a grinning Jim sat at the helm when they left the yard.

As each vehicle self-plotted, they were able to contact each other. None the less, things soon began to go wrong.

Click, click, click.

'Oh shit,' said Tony. 'The fucking batteries are going down.'

Pecky reached for a spare, which he quickly fitted. He flicked the switch to on, and immediately it crackled, 'Tango one and Tango two in vehicle towards your location.' The targets had been spotted.

'Whose location?' asked Pecky.

After a few moments of confusion it was confirmed: he was towards McDonald's and the game was on.

With the life of a hostage at risk it was with nerves tingling and chests pounding that the team waited. This was the time that each man inevitably ran through his kit to keep himself alert. I've seen it hundreds of times in the past: hands run over weapons, checking the magazines are fully seated, magazines that have already been checked a dozen times; body armour is made secure and radios are tested. It's a strange ritual that precedes every operation.

'Stand by.'

Evening Standard

LONDON, TUESDAY, 17 OCTOBER, 1995   INCORPORATING THE EVENING NEWS   30p

Pc ACCUSED OF MURDER

Firearms unit man charged over London shooting

by SANDRA LAVILLE

A POLICE officer from Scotland Yard's firearms unit was today charged with the murder of an unarmed suspect who died after a shooting in west London.

Pc Patrick Hodgson, 48, is believed to be the first Metropolitan officer ever to be charged with murder in the course of his duty.

Officers from the Police Complaints Investigation Bureau, led by Detective Superintendent Aidan Thorne and supervised by the Police Complaints Authority, carried out an eight-month investigation into the shooting of David Ewin, 38, which happened as armed response officers carried out a routine patrol in Castlenau, Barnes on 28 February.

Papers were handed to the Crown Prosecution Service and today Hodgson, who was one of three

officers in the armed response unit vehicle, was charged with the murder of Mr Ewin and bailed to appear at Bow Street Magistrates' Court on 28 November.

Mr Ewin, a hardened criminal with more than 40 convictions for robbery, possessing guns, burglary, assault and car theft, died

in hospital 16 days after the incident. Listed on police records as "highly dangerous", he was on day release from prison and was working as a dispatch rider.

A spokesman for the Crown Prosecution Service said: "The CPS has decided to prosecute a Metropolitan Police officer for murder following the death of Mr

Ewin. Police constable Patrick Hodgson has been charged today and bailed to appear at Bow Street Magistrates Court on 28 November. Mr Ewin was shot twice in the Barnes area of west London on 28 February. He died on 16 March in hospital."

Mr Ewin was shot once in the stomach and once in the

arm after being spotted acting suspiciously in a stolen Toyota car with another man outside an off-licence.

An official inquiry was immediately launched by Commander Roy Ramm, head of Scotland Yard's armed response unit.

Earlier this year two Met officers were cleared of the manslaughter of illegal

immigrant Joy Gardner in Hornsey. But it is believed to be the first time an officer has been charged with murder while on duty.

Scotland Yard said Hodgson was a single man who was stationed at Old Street Police Station at the time. He was suspended during the inquiry and is still under suspension.

Unarmed suspect David Ewin is taken away from the scene of the shooting by stretcher to be airlifted to hospital. He died 16 days later

TV & RADIO GUIDE 46 & 47   BUSINESS DAY 33   EATING OUT 26   ENTERTAINMENT GUIDE 48   LETTERS 51   PATRIC WALKER 52

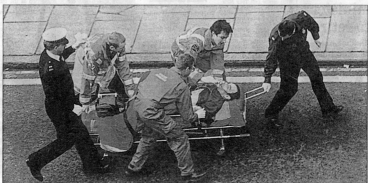

1. 'A sad day for all': SO19 officer Pat Hodgson becomes the first Metropolitan police officer to be charged with murder in the execution of duty, following the shooting of David Ewin.

2.'Scene of the crime': Marsh Lane, E10. Armed robbers would 'hit' a Securicor van parking outside the school on the left – under the watchful gaze of an SO19 sniper positioned on top of the tower to the right. © Author collection

3–7. Unique security camera footage captures the Marsh Lane robbery on film.

3. 'Stand by, stand by': as the Securicor van arrives SO19 deploy from the rear of the Trojan horse, pictured left.

4. Oblivious to police activity, Drakou walks through the plot.

5. 'Attack, attack, attack!' : the team move in.

6. Move up: the cut-off team in action.

7. Re-org: the cut-off team, aided by SO19 dogs, search for the missing robber.

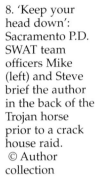

8. 'Keep your head down': Sacramento P.D. SWAT team officers Mike (left) and Steve brief the author in the back of the Trojan horse prior to a crack house raid. © Author collection

9. 'Go, go, go!' The hit is on; the team deploy from the vehicle. © Author

10. 'Bad guy down' - SWAT team members cuff a suspect. © Author

11. 'Recce': A typical aerial photograph used by SO19 during the planning of an assault. The arrows denote the route in, and the F.U.P. on the blind side of the stronghold is outlined in red. The occupant (a drug dealer) had a saucepan of acid ready for unwanted visitors. © Private collection

12. 'Attack, Attack!' This drawing, presented to the author on his leaving of the department, is by an SO19 artist and vividly portrays the deployment of a team from a Trojan horse. © Private collection

13. 'International rescue': Promotional photograph depicting various phases of SO19 operations, from plain clothes through ceremonial to full blown hostage rescue.© Private collection

14. 'All in a day's work': the author (front row, second left) poses with an SFO team on top of a London tower block. The ability to abseil down high buildings forms a crucial part of a team member's training. © Private collection

15. 'Kitted and ready': The author stands beside a Trojan horse prior to a rapid entry into a fortified drugs den.
© Author

16. 'Evening, all': the author (front right) poses with the team for a photograph. On this operation information had been received that armed raiders were to rob the house. The family were shipped out for the night, and an SO19 reception committee moved in.
© Author

17 and 18 (Middle).
SO19 (SFO) team
members training
with the new
Heckler & Koch
L104A1 riot gun
prior to the Notting
Hill Carnival.
© Author

19.'Chinese
parliament': the
author (green
helmet) and the team
discuss tactics; Pat
Hodgson stands in
the foreground
whilst Brad puffs on
his pipe. © Author

20. 'Stand by, Stand by...' SO19's Black team stack up at the back ready for a building assault. The man at the rear carries a Remington 870 pump-action shotgun. © Margaret Zakovicz

21. Meanwhile... a silent approach to the front of the stronghold gains vital seconds. © Margaret Zakovicz

22. 'Sunset in paradise'... two heavily armed members of St. Kitts S.S.U pose for the camera. © Private collection

23. 'All quiet on the Western front': the square in Basseterre, capital of St. Kitts, shortly before the prison break-out. © Private collection

24. 'Prison inferno': set ablaze by rioting inmates, the prison in Basseterre, St. Kitts, burns as the prisoners run amok. © Private collection

25. 'A bucketful of bullets': with MP5 slung over his shoulder, this member of the St. Kitts SSU displays the abysmal lack of equipment by stuffing his ageing .45 in the waistband of his trousers.
© Private collection

26. 'Fill your hands...' Jane Wayne demonstrates a quick draw. Training the local police 'paramilitaries' became a 'hearts and minds' exercise for SO19.
© Private collection

27. 'The wild bunch': SO19 and Scotland Yard officers pose with the S.S.U. during a short respite in the inquiry. © Private collection

28. 'Recovered': the rusting, burnt-out hulk of Seko's car found in a cane field weeks after his disappearance. © Private collection

29. 'Together in life, together in death...' The charred remains of Vincent 'Seko' Morris and Joan Walsh recovered from the boot of the burnt-out vehicle. © Private collection

30. 'Graveyard': during the inquiry the SSU HQ became filled with recovered vehicles. In the foreground stands Jude Matthew's bullet riddled four-wheel drive, behind which is the burnt-out wreck belonging to Seko; in the distance are the remains of Michael Glasford's taxi.
© Private collection

Police Press Release

This morning at about 0740 hours, Superintendent Jude Matthew, Head of the Special Branch of the Royal St. Christopher and Nevis Police Force was assassinated at Franklands, while he was driving his vehicle on his way to work.

Superintendent Matthew was in charge of the investigation into the disappearance of Vincent Morris and Joan Walsh on 1 October 1994.

He arrested and charged the following persons for conspiracy to murder Vincent Morris and Joan Walsh.

1. Glenroy Matthew alias 'Bobo'
2. Charles Miller alias 'Little Nut'
3. Noel Heath alias 'Zambo'
4. Michael Glasford alias 'Illa'
5. Kirt Hendrickson alias 'Ibo'
6. Clifford Henry

A suspect is in police custody and a firearm was found in his possession.

Officers from Scotland Yard are assisting the local police in their investigations.

Police Headquarters
13 October 1994

3 Of The 6 Accused

Noel Heath alias 'Zambo'

Charles Miller alias 'Little Nut'

Kirt Hendrickson alias 'Ibo'

THE OTHER 3 OF THE 6 ACCUSED

GLENROY MATTHEW ALIAS 'BOBO'

MICHAEL GLASFORD ALIAS 'ILLA'

CLIFFORD HENRY

31. Issued on the day Police Chief Superintendent Jude Matthew was assassinated, this press release shows the six held in connection with the disappearance of Vincent 'Seko' Morris and Joan Walsh.
© Private collection

32. In Memoriam: Superintendent Jude Matthew assassinated whilst in the execution of duty.
© Private collection

Jude Thaddeus Matthew

Funeral Service
at the Wesley Methodist Church
Monday October 24th 1994

at 2:00 pm

33–38. 'Aftermath': the Regent Street robbery captured on film.
© E.C. Images

33. (*Above*) 'Captured': one of the raiders lies face-down and cuffed.

34. (*Left*) 'Captor': Brad, MP5 at the ready, covers the suspect.

35. 'It's only a replica': the gun thrown by one of the raiders.

36. 'Smile, please': Brad and Chris shortly after the ambush.

37. (*Right*) 'Come quietly': Brad looks on as the author (brown shirt) leads the suspect away.

38. 'Job done': the author and Chris place the robber in a van for the short journey to Marylebone police station.

39. 'Nowhere to run to, nowhere to hide': St Martin's Close, Camden, scene of an SO19 ambush. © Author

40. 'First aid': tended by police officers, David Ewin lies bleeding in the gutter, cut down by an SO19 marksman. © London News Network

Suddenly there was another situation. One of the surveillance operatives had come out on to the street and taken off his coat. It was a pre-arranged danger signal: there was a problem inside.

Throwing open the doors of the vehicle, Tony and Pecky strode the ten yards to McDonald's; if the shit had hit the fan, best move up quickly and be ready to react.

It was only when he was in the queue and getting nearer to the till that Pecky realised he didn't have any money. So he was well relieved when a surveillance guy walked past and whispered in his ear that the hostage was upstairs with the Tango.

Scooping up a tray and some rubbish, Pecky and Tony took the stairs in an orderly fashion. It was important now to blend in with the large number of punters already in the restaurant; the last thing they needed now was to stand out like a pair of bulldog's bullocks.

Reaching the top step, Pecky scanned the interior of the room, and what he saw at the far end made his blood run cold. The hostage, a smartly dressed Asian man in his early thirties, was sitting by the toilets, accompanied by three large white males with broken noses and weathered faces. Outnumbered and probably out-gunned, Pecky now had to make a split-second decision, and one that would not only affect the life of the hostage but also the large number of men, women and children present. Taking the initiative, he moved forward under cover of a surveillance detective's back. Ten feet from the target, he drew his Glock and closed the distance.

At five feet he barged the detective unceremoniously out of the way, punched the handgun out in front, dropped his knees and screamed, '*Armed police! Get on the floor!*'

Surprise on the face of the Tango turned into shock.

'*On the fucking floor!*' called Pecky, grabbing the hostage with his free hand and throwing him to the ground. All around him pandemonium reigned. Tony, covering his back in the event of a third eye, scanned the sea of shocked faces, all eyes on the spectacle that unfolded in front of them.

Outside, the team were stuck in the heavy evening traffic. 'Fuck this,' muttered Will in his thick Northern accent. 'Hang on, boys.' He slammed down the accelerator and spun the wheel to the left. The van shuddered violently as the front wheels took the kerb at speed, shoppers diving for cover as the team hurtled along the pavement.

Pecky pulled on his baseball cap before pulling the plasticuffs from his jacket. By now you could have heard a pin drop in the place. Everybody had stopped eating; no doubt all they wanted to do was get out, but nobody moved.

Pecky holstered his Glock and held up his hands. 'It's OK. We're police officers,' he said calmly. 'Please carry on eating.'

Still no one budged, even when they heard heavy footfalls on the stairs and the team, fully kitted and with weapons drawn, finally dashed into the restaurant.

The drive back to Wembley was reasonably sedate. Laughing and joking as they came down from the inevitable rush of adrenalin, the team pulled Will's leg about his driving, asking him if he'd been in the tank regiment prior to the SAS. In the Yard of the local police station they pulled off the heavy kit and stowed their weapons for the run back to base, when they were suddenly interrupted by the shrill ring of Paul's mobile.

'Fuck me,' he mouthed, punching the cancel button as he finished the brief call. 'Get kitted, there's a second hostage in a Shogun with two more Tangos. They're headed for Notting Hill.'

Within minutes the convoy was stacked up and ready to leave. Snatching a fire axe and stun grenade from the boot of the hire car, Pecky dived into the passenger seat, joined a split second later by Tony.

Thumbs up all round, and they were ready to roll. '*Shit*,' moaned Tony, patting his pockets. 'Where's the fucking keys?' Pulling himself out of the driver's seat, he double-checked before heading for the boot. 'Oh fuck. Oh fuck,' he cursed, seeing the top of the fob sticking out an inch. The rest of the bunch was firmly wedged inside. Tony was revered for his professionalism, he simply didn't make mistakes. But now, with the convoy ready to leave, smiling faces peered out of the windows, revelling in his dilemma.

'Bollocks.' He reached into the car and grabbed Pecky's axe. Without hesitation or compunction he started to hack at the boot, levering at the lock until finally, miraculously, the keys dropped out.

'Ladbroke Grove, Ladbroke Grove,' came the cool, collected voice of the surveillance officer over the din of the two-tone horns. Then suddenly there it was, the Shogun, in the line of heavy traffic dead ahead. It was one of those flash jobs with blacked-out windows, which made the job even harder as they had no vision on the inside.

'Hard stop.' Paul gave the command with a no-nonsense approach, and the heavy armour-plated Range Rover moved out of the line of traffic and hurtled down the off side, followed by Tony and the van. It was a move practised many times over and was now almost second nature: box the vehicle, one in front, one behind, smash the windows, disorientate the occupants, do what you have to do. In a perfect move, the lead vehicle pulled up hard, ruling out any forward movement as Tony blocked the Shogun's retreat. Pecky was out, Glock in one hand and a stunnie in the other, when suddenly the Shogun's reversing lights came on. The Tango was going for it!

Pecky pulled the pin, and *Boom!* The grenade exploded beneath the vehicle. Shocked onlookers dived for cover. It was chaos. The ambush had taken place underneath a railway bridge, and the echo was enormous.

Closing in on the vehicle, Pecky raised the axe.

Bang! Suddenly he was aware of gunfire off to his left. It was one of the new guys on the team. Having seen what was happening, he'd started to blow out the tyres with the

Hatton. Now the car wasn't going anywhere. Pecky punched the axe through the rear window while other members of the team dragged the occupants from the vehicle and threw them to the floor . . .

There was no hostage. Having heard through the grapevine about the incident at McDonald's, the targets had dropped him off prior to the attack.

'How'd it go?' I asked a smiling Will and Jim, back at base.

'Great,' said Jim. 'But you shouldn't be doing things like that – that's what the Regiment's for.'

'Yeah,' I grinned, remembering the conversation in the canteen at Hereford. 'Two hostage rescues in one day can't be bad.'

'We're in the wrong fucking job,' moaned Will. 'The only difference is, we get to operate abroad.'

I shook my head. 'International crime knows no borders,' I said philosophically. 'It's a little-known fact that SO19 have become so successful in their own right that they've even been called in on specialist operations abroad.'

'Where?' asked Will.

'Small British dependencies mainly,' I said. 'Mainly in the Caribbean.'

7

A Bucketful of Bullets

On days when there are no current operations to attend to, SO19 teams are pretty much left to their own devices. This was one such day.

It was two in the afternoon and Phil, one of the Green team guys, found himself with a group of others honing their shooting skills at City Road range. Phil is a dedicated professional who prides himself on his physical fitness, and spends as many hours in the gym as he does on the range. Unlike many of the team guys, who like to wear the standard uniform fleecy jackets, jeans and hiking boots, Phil is more at home in Chinos and a blazer. And in deference to his past RAF police days, he sports a tightly clipped moustache.

Within minutes of their arrival at the range the telephone rang. Phil stopped shooting and looked at Chris, another member of the team. Call it a sixth sense, call it what you like – but somehow they both knew it was something more than just a routine job, and as Phil's eyes met Chris's they both ran for the door.

Phil reached the outer office slightly ahead of his rival and snatched up the phone. 'GD range,' he answered.

At first he thought it was a wind-up; the officer at the other end of the phone asked if he was currently on the training team. When Phil answered in the affirmative he was asked if he had a current passport – and would he be prepared to fly out on a job at six o'clock the next morning. Talk about bite his fucking hand off!

The short drive back to Old Street was somewhat harrowing. While Phil was desperate to get back to see what was happening, Chris, in a separate vehicle, was more intent on feeding him a line of traffic so he could get there first.

Having received the initial request for assistance the hierarchy at SO19 had, for once, put their arses into gear, and within the hour a team comprising one inspector, a sergeant and four PCs was assembled in the small office. Had they at that stage known the potential for violence the operation offered, the lads would have requested more men – but with the way these things are, and with the fag-packet briefing they were given, they only got the bare bones of the job.

Apparently the authorities on Grand Turk Island were holding a guy wanted by the American DEA. All SO19 had to do was ensure that no harm came to him pending his extradition.

It was as simple as that . . .

Just over an hour and a half's flight from Miami and lying south of the Bahamas is a small cluster of lush, green islands nestling in the azure blue ocean, their total population around fourteen thousand. A popular tourist location, the Turks and Caicos Islands remain a British crown colony, the easternmost island of Grand Turk being the administrative headquarters.

The rank and file of the police service here is made up mainly from local islanders; only the chief of police, his deputy, a superintendent and the lone Customs officer are British. Hence, things around these islands tend to run on 'Jamaican time'.

Pulling himself out of the plane, the tall, immaculately dressed European stretched his legs on the runway, his well-groomed, sandy hair hardly moving in the warm afternoon breeze.

For one reason or another, the Customs officer was unhappy with the plane – probably because the flight had originated in Bogota, Colombia. But after probing the aircraft he could find nothing out of the ordinary. And the passenger was absolutely charming; he told the officer he was simply a businessman on his way to meet up with his wife and children, who were on vacation in Mustique. His voice was extremely sophisticated and his manners impeccable; he was totally personable. Would have made an excellent hostage negotiator . . .

From his research, the Customs officer discovered that the small charter plane had, in accordance with CAA rules, filed a flight plan. Nothing sinister in that – small planes were a common feature around many of the smaller islands, far preferable to travelling by boat. A simple journey from Bogota to the beautiful Caribbean Island of Mustique, the millionaires playground . . . However, as it had reached the vicinity of Grand Turk, the small aircraft had experienced some difficulties and requested permission to land.

With little or nothing for these officials to do, anything out of the ordinary became an adventure – besides, the plane had set down on British territory. And the more the officer investigated, the greater his reaction that there was something about the man which didn't ring true. This prompted him to dig just a little deeper and, after numerous enquiries, he came up trumps on the passport: this mystery gentleman traveller was none other than John Paul Serri, a.k.a. Robert Serri, brother-in-law of the infamous Pablo Escobar, cocaine baron and ruthless head of the notorious Medellin cartel. Wanted in France and the US to face charges of smuggling six tons of cocaine, Serri was ranked number three in the DEA's top-ten most wanted list. Minus the porkpie hat, he was the original French Connection, and they had him!

But what the fuck were they going to do with him?

They contacted the Foreign Office in London, where the Americans immediately put in a bid for his extradition, and detained him.

In the week that followed everything seemed to be running smoothly. The Grand Turk authorities had, however, overlooked one important little detail. On the one hand, Serri was an extremely powerful and well-connected man who had, in the interests of justice, been allowed to contact a lawyer. On the other hand, to his brother-in-law Escobar, he was an extremely expensive commodity who knew everything about the organisation, and was now in the hands of the police. To assume Escobar was unaware of his whereabouts would have been extremely naive.

The prison building on Grand Turk Island is exactly what one would expect: a whitewashed building with thick walls of clay and a heavy palm roof, more accustomed to accommodating the island's drunks than international drug barons.

Serri was placed in isolation in the empty women's block, and within twelve hours had managed to escape through his cell's ceiling.

The manhunt was something the like of which the islanders had never before witnessed. Every nook and cranny was searched, no stone left unturned and Serri was soon found hiding in the loft of a derelict building.

Foolishly, nobody seemed to question why he'd escaped at all. Where could a distinctive European hide on such a small island – unless of course he was expecting help? And what had he said to the lawyer?

The simple answer was, nobody knew. But all of a sudden arses in high places on Grand Turk began to twitch.

Oddly enough, it was shortly after Serri's discovery in the loft that the sleek, unmistakable outline of a Bell UH1 'Huey' helicopter was spotted hammering inland from the south. Best remembered as the helicopter gunship used extensively by the Americans during the Vietnam war, the Huey is a versatile transporter favoured for the fast delivery of personnel from its huge side-opening doors.

Hovering low across the airfield, the distinctive American

voice requested permission to land – the chopper was low on gas and they needed to refuel.

Fearing some sort of rescue mission, Air Traffic Control refused. They had no fuel available; permission denied.

The Huey landed anyway. No sooner had the skids hit the runway when three men burst from the chopper and melted into the thick undergrowth. All were white, all young with tightly cropped hair: the stamp of the professional mercenary. Three hours later they were back, and airborne again.

It had obviously been a recce. Would there now be an attempt to spring Serri?

Realising the full implication and perhaps fearing all-out war, the governor of the island made an unprecedented plea to the Foreign Office, requiring military assistance.

Whether the recent SAS shooting incident in Gibraltar came into the equation is a matter of debate; perhaps it was simply protocol that dictated it should be a non-military option. Whatever the reason, the Foreign Secretary gave authority to call in the Yard. By way of a compromise, the Royal Navy frigate *Amazon* would stand by off the coast of the island.

For the team, everything happened fast. Apart from organising their families and their private lives, they still needed to get kit together – and time was running out. They'd been told to expect to be away from home for ten days or more.

After the inevitable Chinese parliament and working hard through the night, the team finally came up with a list of equipment to cover all eventualities. Apart from their personal Glock handguns they settled on three MP5 A3s and three MP5 Ks, extremely versatile and fully automatic machine-guns, ideal for concealment beneath a jacket. For a containment/sniper scenario they packed two Heckler & Koch 93 rifles with telescopic sights. Then came the stun grenades, respirators, belt rigs, body armour, first-aid kits, ceramic plates, batteries, radios and sun-tan lotion.

Not to mention ammunition: they quickly decided they'd need at least a slack handful – possibly even a shitload . . . But in the end they settled on a bucketful. This was SO19 speak: when ordering a specific number of rounds, fifty is a handful, two hundred and fifty a slack handful; a thousand is a shitload, and two thousand a bucketful. A 'few', for people who can't remember how many they wanted in the first place, is any random number between one and 200.

Starting out early the next day, the team was driven swiftly to the airport, only to experience the inevitable delay in 'Logging' the weapons: everything was checked – all serial numbers, rounds, and grenades. The amazing thing was that it was all eventually stowed in the hold with the rest of the luggage. If only the other passengers had realised they were sitting on a potential time bomb!

But if the passengers were unaware of their companions, the air crew fully understood who they were, and arrangements had been made for the weapons to be stored overnight in a Customs strongroom at Miami Airport, pending the connecting flight.

After check-in the lads were quickly ushered into the executive lounge. It was only then that they realised they were travelling club class. With everybody else dressed in suits, the team wore the standard T-shirts, jeans and boots, looking like a gang of soccer hooligans. They were told by staff to help themselves to drinks, but at first they were too conscious of their image to take advantage. However, because most of the boys had never travelled club class before, and because it's not the sort of perk our type usually gets, once on the plane they made the most of it!

Touching down at Miami International, the team passed into the lounge where security pinged them straight away, taking them aside and rushing them into a private holding area. From here, Phil looked down on the baggage reclaim area, and there among the rest of the luggage, were the guns and ammo. Going around the carousel. In the middle of the airport. Phil shook his head. 'Only in America . . .'

Amazingly, all of the equipment was accounted for and safely loaded on to trolleys to be stowed away for the evening.

The next morning the team were shattered, the long-haul flight taking its toll. Still, it was quite exciting, and Phil for one was looking forward to what lay ahead. Collecting the equipment, the travel-weary group made their way to the check-in desk for the connecting flight. No such rigmarole with the weapons this time; straight on to the plane. And what a plane! Phil had never been on a flight like it. If it could have taken chickens it would; talk about a let down after club class! The guy beside him had two car tyres on his lap, and the aisles were stacked high with cooking fat.

Arriving at Grand Turk, they were ushered through the small airport and taken on the scenic drive to the police headquarters where, once again, they checked the kit. Satisfied finally, they headed off to meet the chief, who turned out to be a diamond guy.

The lads had wondered how they would get around operating on the island, but that had already been planned. After taking an oath, they were signed on as special constables. It was all quite bizarre really, but Phil was just happy it wasn't a blood oath where he'd have to bite the head off a chicken.

In fact the chief was absolutely falling over himself, totally at SO19's disposal and more than happy to allow them a free rein; after all, they were the experts, the tacticians, and this was their field – even if it was slightly out of the ordinary. Showing the team around the relatively sparse police armoury, the chief announced, 'Take anything you want, if you think it may help.'

Ferreting through the piles of obsolete weaponry, the lads suddenly made an important discovery; they found a 'Gimpy' – or more correctly a GPMG, British Army general-purpose machine-gun. This extremely versatile weapon could well be used to fortify a position. With an effective range of about 1800 metres, it can fire its belt-fed 7.62 ammunition at a rate of around a thousand rounds a minute. For this reason alone, it is much favoured by four-man SAS patrols.

John, a wiry ex-Royal Marine who would later become my team inspector, immediately piped up that he knew how to use it; but the idea was quickly kicked into touch by the guvnor. Now they knew it was there, he said, they could come back should they need it later.

The briefing was given by the chief's deputy, a larger-than-life superintendent who reminded Phil of our own boss – a character nicknamed Fifty Fucks because of his frequent expletive outbursts. This guy, however, was more of a Jack the lad, a real-life Jack Regan, straight out of the *Sweeney*, with the vernacular to carry it off. The briefing was excellent. The superintendent certainly pulled no punches, laying all his cards on the table; because of the threat level it would have been foolhardy to do otherwise. It was only afterwards, when the full implications of the operation had sunk in, that some of the lads felt slightly downcast, because from that point it became apparent that, to carry out the job successfully, they may need more men.

The drive to the prison to meet their charge was a sombre occasion and Phil, a true professional, never one to overreact, took in the spectacular scenery on the way. It should have been a dream – everybody at Old Street had been falling over each other to get on this trip. One guy had even come to the airport to wave them off, probably waiting for a last-minute injury.

It was a beautiful sunny day. The azure sea lapped at the most incredible white sandy beach. Everything should have been perfect, but Phil felt ill at ease, a bad feeling . . .

Then the reality of it all struck home: suddenly he thought of his family. The island's medical conditions and the fucking crap hospital . . . OK, so there was a warship somewhere out there with a doctor, possibly even a surgeon on board, but suddenly, overwhelmingly, Phil vowed that he wouldn't die in this place.

The minibus swept into the courtyard. The prison was exactly as they'd imagined it: something out of Rourke's Drift. There was a long-house off to the left, and a vast open kitchen to the right. The only other construction of note was the water tower, easily defendable, and which at that moment Phil decided would be 'home'.

A further briefing was to follow, this time in the presence of the consul and the island's governor. It was short, sharp and to the point: they had heard of the reputation of Scotland Yard's SO19, and they knew that they were professional enough to engage a threat on their own terms and within their SOP. Thus the governor said he saw no reason to impose any additional sanctions or restrictions. If the team saw fit to open fire, the island authorities would back the decision to the hilt in any subsequent inquiry. This immediately put the lads at ease, as all of them had been wondering where they would stand legally should they have reason to slot any would-be aggressors.

After the statutory recce a plan was quickly formulated so the team could get down to work; after all, that was what they were there for! It was decided that they would operate in pairs on a shift system – eight hours on, four hours off, during which time they'd flop in a hotel room some four or five hundred yards from the prison.

Phil was paired up with Paul, a tall, extremely fit ex-Paratrooper, himself a veteran of an SO19 shootout which had bagged him the Queen's Commendation for brave conduct. Phil was more than happy with his partner.

While on duty, a pair would patrol the outside perimeter in a jeep, leaving a second pair to guard the yard. It was left up to each pair's discretion as to how they patrolled, but Phil and Paul quickly decided on one roving while the other covered from the relative security of the base of the water tower. Radio communications would be open at all times between the on-duty teams and those on down-time in the hotel.

It was difficult to know who to trust. They knew Serri was influential, and they guessed the mercs had already recced the prison. And with the type of corrupt official often found in this type of environment, they were more than a little worried. After all, money talks and bullshit walks – and Serri certainly had enough of both.

The prison housed around fifty inmates, incarcerated for a range of crimes, from petty theft through to assault and rape. For their own security, Phil drew an imaginary 'line of death' around the water tower which, if anybody invaded, they would be encroaching on his personal space. And anybody with balls enough to do that would be game on. There was a washing line just past the water tower where, every day without fail, the guys would witness the inmates getting closer and closer. One particular prisoner was huge and had a lot of bravado. He was the prison's Mr Big, and really did seem to want to push things to the limit, constantly showing off in front of the others, seeing just how far he could get without prompting a response. Although Phil knew it was unwise to make enemies of the prisoners, one day he felt he had to make an example. The guy was simply getting too cocky. Sticking a Kurtz up his hooter, Phil pointed to the invisible mark and told him, 'You cross that fucking line again and I'll shoot you.'

After a few days things for the team started to become unbearable. They were watching Serri around the clock with so few men that the lack of sleep was beginning to take its toll. That and the hot Caribbean sun, each man standing around in the heat wearing body armour and carrying a resi just in case . . .

Phil had long ago realised that, if the mercs were worth their salt, the first people they'd take out would be the back-up, those on down-time in the hotel. In fact he didn't really sleep in the time he was there, apart from the odd cat nap.

The team had two mopeds stashed away, in case they had to get out quick or respond to the prison in the event of an attack. For there was no back-up to rely on, just the six of them. Phil even rested with a Glock under his pillow and a Kurtz on the bedside table.

If the ship had a shore party or a detachment of Marines, then they didn't let on. This, after all, was a non-military operation, and they were there only to provide radar cover in case of incoming choppers. Besides, if the shit went down, by the time they got ashore the team would all be dead.

On one occasion when Phil did nod off, the balcony door slid open (there was no lock on it) and a figure stepped into the room. It was only the maid, coming round the back as he'd locked the front door, but Phil was up with the Kurtz in his hand before she'd even got both feet through the doorway.

Serri was housed in one of the old cell blocks in what can only be described as Spartan conditions. Only the basics were provided: a bed, a toilet and bare walls, with bars on the windows and door. The team had briefed him, and left him in no uncertain terms as to what would happen should there be an attempt at springing him. The tables would be turned and he would probably find himself being held hostage by them. And they certainly had the weaponry to do it.

It was the phone call he had been allowed to make that really bothered the team. They didn't know for certain that he hadn't simply called on a hit.

During the original brief it had been suggested that they should just stick him on the ship. After all, nobody is going to attack a fucking great Navy frigate. But for some reason the hierarchy wouldn't allow it. The boys guessed it had something to do with them not losing face; besides, they had SO19 to prevent any attempt at a rescue – so why worry?

Whenever Phil and Paul were on compound patrol they made random checks on Serri who, strangely, appeared to be building a new sense of purpose. Until, that is, his extradition came through.

With that, Serri's mood changed. The team knew now

that if there were to be any serious moves now would be the time to make them.

To general disbelief, Serri was allowed another phone call to a lawyer at this time, pending the Yanks' jacking up his escort. The call was monitored, but only by SO19, who had briefed Serri that if he lapsed out of English or gave a series of numbers or anything else they didn't like, they'd cut him off there and then. Serri was talking to the lawyer when he suddenly started spouting off a string of numbers. The boys cut him short, but from the smug look on his face they didn't think they had been quick enough.

During their down-time the team, for want of something better to do, had taken the opportunity to recce other locations on the island. The SO19 plan would have built into it certain contingencies in the event of part or all of the operation being compromised. One of these contingencies would have been a safe relocation for both themselves and the prisoner. On a small Caribbean Island, however, where the locals inevitably knew everything, the plan was compromised even before it was hatched.

By now the team hadn't slept for six days and were living in body armour and surviving on club sandwiches. Even when 'Jack Regan' and his wife invited Phil round to their house for dinner he turned up with his ever present 'briefcase'.

John, the team skipper, finally consulted with the boss. The prison was definitely compromised, he said, and with it so were the team and their ability to carry out the task. The prisoner had to be moved, and fast.

They settled on the police HQ for the prisoner's new accommodation. Handcuffed, Serri was placed in the back of a jeep for the short ride from the prison.

Phil and Paul were riding shotgun in a vehicle behind. As the lead car swept in through the gates they put in a block across the entrance. As they deployed, they heard the sound of a motor further down the road. Suddenly a large Jeep with blacked-out windows was screaming down the lane.

Quickly they took cover behind an ancient cannon that formed part of the entrance, wishing now that they had the Gimpy.

Without slowing, the Jeep did a handbrake turn in front of them, gunned the engine, and took off.

Fuck knows what that little demonstration was all about, but as far as they were concerned it was as near to a threat as they'd come.

As it transpired, the only available room in the police compound with a locking door was that of the armoury – as it was purely headquarters, there were no cells. So they put Serri where they could see him – and as things now appeared to be hotting up he was plasticuffed to a concrete pillar in the middle of the room.

All this time, Serri appeared to be extremely well switched on. I suppose you don't get to be an international drug baron without a little bit of nous.

After the Jeep incident the guys had a word with the guvnor, but he couldn't or wouldn't take the whole thing seriously. It was later, at team change-over time, that Phil was to hear something that made his blood boil.

'I know you,' Serri said to one of the outgoing team. 'I know you work in pairs, you and the other guy. Then there's your boss and the sergeant. They sleep a lot.' But try as he might he'd been able to glean nothing of Phil and Paul. It was obvious that he was gathering intelligence.

The following day he was taken to the airport by all of the team who were extremely eyes about. If it was going to kick off, now would be the time. First checking with air-traffic control, and monitored by the state-of-the-art radar system, the small DEA Lear jet requested permission to land.

With the runway secured by SO19, they landed and taxied to a stop. Serri was walked out and handed over. Plain and simple. No sooner had they shut the door than they took off again.

That's how seriously even the Americans considered it all.

*

Serri eventually stood trial in the US – the first ever successful extradition by the federal authorities from the Turks and Caicos Islands.

But it doesn't end there. It later transpired that, during that second phone call, Serri had imparted what was believed to be the details of a secret bank account, paying the lawyer he had managed to contact four hundred thousand dollars in cash to finance his rescue if the extradition looked like going ahead.

The threat was real enough, and always there; but as it turned out the lawyer had sticky fingers. Neither the lawyer nor the money has been seen or heard of since.

With Serri in gaol, Escobar's entire organisation came under threat. Other members of the cartel, perhaps sensing some small chink in his armour, showed themselves to have aspirations of their own – aspirations that didn't include him – and already vast shipments of cocaine were being sent to the United States via different routes. Events took a turn fast, and soon even the Colombian government, a government whose paramilitary troops were rumoured to be led by SAS advisors, were beginning to sit up and show an interest.

With so much in the way of opposition, it is hardly surprising that, months later, Escobar was gunned down and killed in a reputed dawn contact with government troops. Whether that was true – and whether the SAS were involved - is a matter for debate. That SO19 had played a small, albeit vital role in his demise is a matter of fact. Yes, we'd won the battle, but all around us the war was still raging.

Indeed, back home, while we revelled in our immediate success, none of us could possibly have been aware that already events were unfolding thousands of miles away on a small, beautiful sun-kissed Caribbean island – events that would fester and eventually shape the future of SO19.

*

Set apart from its smaller neighbour, Nevis, by a two-mile-wide channel, St Kitts nestles in the eastern Caribbean at the northern tip of the Leeward Islands. Covering an area of only sixty-eight square miles, its splendid scenery, dormant volcano and beautiful beaches are encompassed by dense, lush, green vegetation and sugar-cane plantations, making it a popular tourist attraction.

But St Kitts's ideal location within spitting distance of the United States has, over its chequered history, lent itself to all manner of dealings. During the late seventeenth and early eighteenth century, it had been used as a staging post for slave traders who, en route to the US, would land their unfortunate captives ashore before the final leg of their journey. Now, however, like many of these smaller islands, it was used to land cocaine.

In the summer of 1994, William Herbert – an extremely wealthy lawyer, banker, former ambassador to the United States and United Nations, and founder of the island's ruling party, the People's Action Movement – set sail with five friends on a fishing expedition. The weather and sea conditions were perfect. However, the twenty-four-foot oceangoing launch was never to be seen again. The boat and all its occupants seemed to have vanished off the face of the earth.

Initially there was a lot of speculation. Drug involvement was certainly a strong possibility. Despite his outwardly respectable appearance, Herbert's name had continually cropped up over the last ten years, following the impoundment of the Irish-registered freighter *Marita Ann*, loaded with several tons of weapons and ammunition, allegedly destined for the IRA. In the joint FBI/Scotland Yard investigation, Herbert was accused of laundering IRA drug money through a series of banks in the West Indies.

The disappearance of such an influential man – who by now was something of an island celebrity – prompted the government to act, and, being an ex-British colony, they turned to the Yard.

SO1 were alerted and responded at once, sending a detective superintendent and a sergeant from the laboratory to liaise with one of the island's top-ranking police officers, Superintendent Jude Matthew, head of CID and Special Branch.

That the six missing occupants of the boat were already dead I think there is little doubt; but rumour was rife, and the locals soon came up with a theory - that the boat and its occupants were all loaded into a large container and shipped off to Colombia.

The detectives went through the motions of taking statements and interviewing potential witnesses, but with a lack of any hard evidence they eventually had to call it a day. The boat was simply listed as 'missing'.

It wasn't long before the case faded from the public eye and the customary carnival atmosphere returned to the island. But it was to be dramatically shattered.

Barely two months had passed since Herbert's disappearance when Hugh Lowry, a local fisherman, was digging for turtle eggs on a beach near Cayon, just north of the island's capital, Basseterre. Purely by accident, Lowry stumbled across a hidden cache of five hundred kilos of cocaine which, with the aid of a friend called Shabba, he removed from the scene.

Now they had it, what were they going to do with it? And who did it belong to? They certainly didn't know; but they knew a man who would.

Taking the find to a nearby house (shared by the three sons of the island's Deputy Prime Minister, Sydney Morris), they showed them the haul. Of the three boys – David, Dean and Vincent (a.k.a. Seko) – it was Seko's opinion they particularly valued. He knew that two of the island's 'local faces', Clifford Henry and Glenroy Matthew (alias Bobo), were expecting a delivery; he also knew that they'd be none too happy if they realised it had been intercepted. And there he wasn't wrong.

In the five hectic days that followed the find, a number of

things were to happen. Seko would contact his brother Dean to inform him that Bobo knew they had the drugs. Seko in turn would be attacked and badly beaten by three Spanish-speaking males (presumably Colombians), who demanded the return of the coke. Now realising that they were seriously in the shit the brothers decided to offer a peace token: the return of seven boxes of cocaine.

Call it foolhardiness, call it greed, but Seko had somehow managed to secrete the remaining seven boxes, each weighing in at around fifty-five pounds. By doing so, he unwittingly sealed his own death warrant, plus that of his girlfriend and a hardworking cop!

Handing the boxes to a friend for safe-keeping, Seko and his girlfriend Joan Walsh hired a car for a trip to the north. At ten o'clock that evening an unhappy Bobo came to call, missing Seko by minutes.

At midnight, a friend reported seeing Seko speed past in a car. It was his last sighting alive.

During the early hours of the morning on the first of October, a worker on a remote sugar-cane plantation at the far end of the island heard what he believed to be an argument, closely followed by the sound of gunfire . . .

Two days passed before the burnt-out remains of a vehicle belonging to Michael Glasford (alias Illa), a close associate of Bobo, was found. Inside was a distinctive 'Malcom X' watch, similar to the one worn by Seko.

The young couple's disappearance prompted Superintendent Jude Matthew to act and, over the course of the next five days, he swept into action, rounding up and throwing into jail six prime suspects: Bobo, Henry and Illa, along with Noel Heath (alias Zambo), Charles Miller (alias Little Nut) and Kirt Hendrickson (alias Ibo). Before long, and even in the absence of any bodies, all six were charged with conspiring to murder Seko and Walsh.

Perhaps aware of his own limited resources, Matthew once again sought assistance from the Yard. Two days later the inquiry team, led by Detective Superintendent Alex

Ross, arrived. Ross had been the initial investigator on the Herbert case, so he knew Matthew and the islanders well.

On the morning of the thirteenth, Ross had arranged to meet Matthew at the Ocean Terrace hotel in Basseterre. It was a meeting that would never take place. Leaving his home at around seven-forty that morning, Jude Matthew climbed into the driving seat of his blue all-terrain vehicle and set off for the meet. Perhaps he was aware that even he may have been singled out for assassination, for about his person were a couple of handguns, while on the back seat of the vehicle lay a Kalashnikov AK47 assault rifle.

It was later alleged that as the vehicle hit a narrow track, whoever he was, the killer with devastating accuracy peppered the vehicle with a withering burst of machine-gun fire.

Mercifully, Jude Matthew died instantly. Arrested near the scene, David 'Grizzly' Lawrence, a local man, would three days later be charged with murder.

Deeply saddened by the death of his friend and colleague, and fearing now for the safety of his team, Alex Ross contacted the Yard; now they needed protection, something the locals couldn't provide. They needed SO19.

Back at Old Street, the telephone rang. The call was passed to the first floor and answered by the quality insurance inspector. He hadn't been on ops for years – apart from when he had been the guy in charge of Phil's team in the Turks – and obviously saw the opportunity for another little outing, so leapt at it for himself. Initially it was suggested that a small team of guys would be responsible for the training of the inquiry team, a sort of one-day basic defensive weapons course on the Smith & Wesson model ten revolver.

Then they were to leave the detectives to fend for themselves and spend the rest of the two weeks getting their knees brown. It was only when they arrived in St Kitts, however, that the inspector suddenly realised that he may have bitten off slightly more than he could chew. Apart from the training implications, he now realised the team's primary role would have to be one of close protection.

Soon the bodyguard team was bolstered with more men, complete with MP5s and a bucketful of bullets. The rank and file of the inquiry team were more than happy to have SO19 around, but on the face of it the lads didn't think the superintendent was too keen. He was old school, a career detective, and although he was deeply shocked and saddened by the death of Matthew, he kept on about 'Why do you need machine-guns?' and 'Why do you have to have a torch on the end?'

The St Kitts government now offered to fund the investigation – which had originally started as a missing person inquiry but had now become a tangled web of mystery, drugs, kidnapping and murder – a web that perhaps only Alex Ross and his team could unravel.

It was a strange situation for the SO19 boys to be in, and it became more entangled the deeper they became involved.

Take Jude Matthew, for example. He seemed on the surface to be the only hardworking guy on the island, and the team didn't doubt for one minute that he was a decent bloke. But they soon found out that, apart from being a police superintendent, he was a paid agent for the FBI and the DEA.

He was also hated by the opposition party. It appears that senior police posts on the smaller islands are almost political appointments. By taking out the six suspects, all of whom were from the opposition, Matthew had caused uproar. It was almost as if he was doing the government's bidding. On top of this, the Americans seemed to have a huge influence on the Island which was split into two distinct factions. The Government had won the election by a narrow majority. Drugs obviously featured high on the agenda with some politicians actually thought to be funded by the Colombians. Not only that, the relationship between the two parties was extremely incestuous with people constantly changing allegiances. At the time of his disappearance, even the Deputy Prime Minister's son Seko was working for the opposition.

With so much intelligence filtering in, sooner or later it was inevitable that SO19 would become involved in the inquiry. More surprising was the unprecedented fact that they soon became involved in an investigative role.

The amount of information the team received about drugs was phenomenal. At one stage the new evidence was threatening to bury the original inquiry; but they knew they had to keep the locals on their side to show that they were doing something about it. A sort of 'Hearts and Minds' approach. So, to free up the SO1 guys, SO19 eventually took on some of the caseload.

The weight of allegations snowballed. The team even received intelligence that one guy had forty kilos of coke stashed in his back garden. It was rife; there were drugs everywhere.

The team threw that one to the DEA, who were more than happy to get involved. They even brought in a female officer from a neighbouring island.

The team soon discovered that, a few months prior to his death, Jude Matthew was given a lap-top computer by the CIA. Could this possibly hold the key to the entire inquiry? Whatever the case, this particular lead soon became academic. Just prior to this information coming to light, agents had landed on the Island. Now the lap-top had conveniently and mysteriously disappeared.

The boys now found themselves in a bit of a predicament. They didn't really know whom they could trust. Some of the lads had become quite friendly with the guys from the Special Service Unit, the St Kitts paramilitary equivalent to SO19, and its inspector in particular. But even then they weren't telling them everything they knew. One of the guys had to take one island officer down to the beach just so he could talk to him. Even then the bloke was cagey. It had now got to the point where the team were using the local police as fucking informants!

Inevitably, a rumour soon spread that members of the inquiry team had contracts on their heads; in particular the bodyguards, for if you could reach out and take one of them you could set an example for the rest. As a result, the SSU were assigned to protect their hotel at night. Two of their guys would patrol the grounds dressed in DPMs and armed with M16s. In fact the SSU were armed with a mish-mash of different weapons which had been supplied by various US drug agencies. As such, many of the weapons were non-standard and varied from a Smith & Wesson six-inch Model 19 revolver, through World War Two .45s to Armalite rifles and Heckler & Koch G3 machine-guns. Needless to say, holsters were in short supply, so many of the team carried their weapons in a variety of ways, the favourite being stuffed into the waistband of the trousers. Indeed the whole attitude towards weapon handling was one of such indifference that in their down time the SO19 instructors took to training the SSU.

There was one woman among their squad. She was fucking brilliant, and put her heart and soul into her work. She was better than most of the men. She carried a large forty-five in an even larger holster strapped to her leg, and the boys called her Jane Wayne.

As the inquiry progressed the inevitable whisperings began, rumours once again fuelled by speculation: 'It's connected to the Herbert case,' said many. Others suggested Seko had also been 'crated up' and shipped abroad. That myth, however, was about to become dramatically shattered.

Although they'd been charged, it was soon apparent that whatever evidence Matthew had on the six accused had obviously died with him. Just as that side of the case was about to collapse, a detective mysteriously arrived on the island from Antigua. He was a guy SO19 had done jobs for in the past, who worked for the South East Regional Crime Squad. It transpired that one of the guys banged up was actually his snout, who not only had been keeping him up to speed on Herbert, but also had informed him on goings on in the US and the UK.

Things now appeared to be rapidly turning into a three-ring circus, in what must go down as one of the most complicated and bizarre operations SO19 has ever been involved in. Ross finally decided to act. Believing the Deputy Prime Minister's remaining two sons to be way in over their necks, he ordered a raid on their house – five weeks since the disappearance of Seko.

It turned out to be quite profitable. The team recovered fifty-seven kilos of the original haul, along with a firearm and ammunition. But little did they know they were about to set the cat among the pigeons.

Two days later, while the original suspects languished in gaol on what many now believed to be trumped-up charges, the Morris brothers were released on bail. Of course there was uproar. The opposition party screamed that it was political interference by the Deputy PM. Two days after that, some of the team found themselves taking a well-earned rest on a hillside overlooking Basseterre. From their vantage point they could see a glow on the horizon, and thick smoke . . . The bastards had set fire to the prison! For the whole evening the prison burned, set ablaze by the hundred or so inmates. The island had never witnessed anything like it.

Obviously SO19 couldn't get involved, and the SSU didn't have much of a heart for it. Like many of these small dependencies, St Kitts doesn't have an army - so they had to send in a detachment of the Caribbean Security Force from Barbados.

In the meantime, the whole island was going crazy. Prisoners were running around the streets and everybody was on the piss. Some of their families were passing them joints and taking them to restaurants for slap-up meals. Christ knows what the tourists thought of it all; they hadn't a clue what was going on behind the scenes, or what had caused it all!

Eventually, with the arrival of the CSF the near riot was quickly quelled. All but one of the prisoners were recaptured and housed in a makeshift gaol.

Ironically it was the next day, out on a plantation at the far end of the island, that three workers made a grim discovery: the burnt-out wreck of the car hired by Seko and Walsh.

That's when things started to get a little hairy. Everybody on the island is very superstitious; also they have this morbid fascination with death – they like to see nothing better than a stiff laid out in the street. Once they heard of the car's discovery they came from miles around.

But this wasn't like a normal death. There was nothing to see, because the bodies were locked in the boot – and that's what started things off.

The scene quickly turned ugly. The car had been found on the opposition's turf, and word was quickly circulated that the vehicle had been planted, that it was a mass conspiracy by the government and their Scotland Yard lackeys, a plan to discredit the opposition.

Consequently the area was soon alive with islanders coming in from every direction, and it was impossible to preserve the integrity of the crime scene.

Finally Superintendent Ross capitulated. It was something he hadn't wanted to do, but it had been raining heavily and much of the scene's vital evidence had now been lost. Now he had to work with what he had, he decided to take as much of it as he could to a sterile location: the headquarters of the SSU.

The local police refused to guard the scene that night, so SO19 had to try and get in and out by nightfall. They got hold of a low-loader, which they took up there with the SSU riding shotgun. The vehicles were up to their axles in mud when the lorry driver refused to go any closer. He considered the whole fucking scene 'juju'.

By the time they recovered the vehicle it was dark. The forensic team quickly went to work on the burnt-out car. By now the SSU compound was littered with wrecks, all of which in some way or another centred around the inquiry. Seko's car joined Illa's burnt-out van and Jude Matthew's bullet-riddled Jeep.

When they opened the boot they didn't find much remaining after the fire. There was a single bullet-hole in the boot's lid, and a gunshot wound to Seko's skull. It was a guess that they had been bundled inside, shot, and the vehicle set ablaze. The two skeletons recovered were practically fused together.

It was four days after this grim discovery that Deputy Prime Minister Sydney Morris resigned his post amid growing political pressure.

On Saturday 21 January 1995 the Scotland Yard team pulled out. With absolutely no evidence to support a conviction, the six defendants were released. The fact that they'd been inside for so long was a dark tribute to the archaic laws of these lands.

To date, the murders of the two young people, Vincent 'Seko' Morris and Joan Walsh, remain unsolved. Their murderers are still at large.

Their job done, all that the Yard men could offer was sympathy, experience, and a full and impartial investigation.

With the island now left to its own devices, David 'Grizzly' Lawrence was tried for the murder of Superintendent Jude Matthew. Moves had already been made to have him tried in the UK or even another impartial island, but that was not to be. At his subsequent trial he was acquitted of murder.

As the tourists continued to flood in, St Kitts returned to some semblance of order, but the shadow of the past stormy and violent days still hangs heavily over the island, grim testament to the power of a drug called cocaine and a man named Escobar.

8

Pandora's Box

'Steve, we've had a request for witness protection,' said Andy. 'Don't know much about it but they'd like somebody to attend a meeting with SIS this afternoon. Can you fill in for me? It's got something to do with a supergrass and a big-time villain. Couldn't say too much on the phone.'

'OK, boss,' I said. 'What time?'

'Three o'clock – ask for him.' Andy slipped me a scrap of paper.

'OK,' I said. 'I'll take Chris.'

The headquarters of the Special Intelligence Section is housed in a tall, grey, innocuous-looking, typical government building in the heart of Putney. Security here is tight – exactly what you'd expect from this secretive, shadowy department. Pulling up at the red and white striped barrier, Chris and I were immediately approached by the uniformed, clipboard-wielding security guard.

I don't know what it is with me, but I've always seemed to have a downer on security staff. Perhaps it was because I dreaded the day I left the job with no qualifications; maybe I actually saw part of myself in them. The only thing I'd be qualified to do is lift a barrier. I've always had a saying: 'Never upset anybody on the way up, because you never know who you're going to meet on the way down.' For security guards, though, I made an exception.

Tapping the driver's window with the corner of the

145

clipboard, the middle-aged man made a circular motion with his finger, indicating that he wanted the window down.

'I can't,' Chris mouthed, throwing up both hands and shrugging his shoulders. 'It's bullet-proof. They don't open.'

'What?' The guard moved closer, cupping his ear.

'I said . . .' Chris shouted, throwing open the Range Rover's heavy armour-plated door and knocking him backwards, 'I can't. It's bullet-proof.'

I leaned across him, holding up my warrant card. 'Sergeant Collins for SIS, mate.'

He eyed it carefully. 'So?' he said, running his finger down the list of names on his clipboard.

'So – we want to park in the basement.'

'Can't do that,' he said. 'Restricted parking. You'll have to leave it on the street.'

'No. Sorry mate, you don't understand. This is an SO19 motor. We are currently operational and could be called on at any minute.' I threw my thumb over my shoulder. 'There's guns in the back; we need a secure area where we can lock it and alarm it.'

He gave me a look before consulting the all-important board again. 'All right,' he said. 'Down in the basement – but don't tell anybody,' and he lifted the barrier.

Securing the Rangey, Chris set the alarm. Apart from our Glocks and spare mags which never left our side, the rest of the weapons were stowed out of sight. Leaving guns unattended in a vehicle is something of a taboo, but with the armoured vehicle alarmed and a bank of hidden cameras recording our every move, I was more than satisfied.

Taking the lift, we made our way to the appropriate floor and found the door we were looking for. We looked at its automatic lock and intercom system and reckoned even the filing cabinets had big fuck-off locks on them.

I jabbed at the button. 'Yes?' came a stern female voice.

'Sergeant Collins, SO19, to see the DI.'

Clunk. The lock disengaged and the door swung open.

Stepping inside was like entering a different world. The plush, sweet-smelling offices were a far cry from Old Street, with its peeling, paint-blistered walls.

'Coffee?' asked the petite, pretty blonde who greeted us.

'Love one. White, one sugar,' I said. Chris nodded likewise.

'The DI will be with you in a minute,' she said, ushering us into his office.

The DI nodded as he entered a few minutes later, throwing a sheaf of papers on to his desk as he slumped down in the chair opposite. 'Thanks for coming, guys,' he said, leaning across the desk, hand outstretched.

I took it. 'Steve Collins, skipper, SO19. That's Chris.'

Chris nodded. 'Guv.'

'Dave Newberry,' the DI introduced himself. 'Do you mind if I bring in a couple of the lads? One of them used to be our man's handler; they'll be in on the job with you.' When a villain decides to turn informant, the officer that 'turned' him is known as a handler. Only he, his co-handler and the detective chief inspector is aware of the informant's true identity, as they are always given a pseudonym or code name.

I shook my head and smiled at the blonde as the coffee arrived. 'No, not at all boss. Be our guest.'

A tall, long-haired guy in a threadbare jacket nodded as he entered and introduced himself as Baz. He was followed into the room by a man called Ron, who the DI told us was the handler. Dark-skinned and thinning on top, Ron had a slightly Mediterranean look about him, with an accent to match. It transpired that Ron was a City of London detective seconded to the SIS.

Introductions over, the DI began. He held up a photograph. Joey Pyle, he explained, was a well-known south London 'face', a past associate of both the Richardson gang and the Krays. Intelligence had come to light that Joey was strongly believed to be now involved in drug racketeering. Efforts had been made for a considerable number of years, but no convictions had yet been obtained. Finally the Yard had decided to pass the dossier to SIS for immediate action. Unbeknown to Joey, he had become a target. Over the next few months his every move had been logged by the SIS watchers.

Outwardly, it seemed, Pyle was a normal type of guy, a neat if not flashy dresser, with a nice house and a certain air of respectability about him. He even had his own production company based at Pinewood Studios. So this was somewhere SIS could bug. A man had recently been arrested, the DI told us, whose name was Richard Green. Green was in deep shit with Joey, owing him a lot of wedge, and was consequently shit-scared; Joey was a powerful man who'd been using Green as his right hand to add an air of legitimacy to his business deals. Green knew Joey was in possession of a large shipment of heroin, because he'd asked Green to scout about for a buyer. Arrested for fraud, Green had offered the police a deal. In respect of Joey, and from that moment on Green had been given the code name 'Pandora'.

On top of the bug, a UC officer had been quickly installed at Pinewood Studios. Given the pseudonym 'Lucy', this experienced female operative had taken up a post as secretary in an adjoining office. There she'd had to befriend Pyle and report back on his associates and movements. This was a lonely and dangerous task, often performed without close back-up. While this was going on, and much to Joey's delight, Pandora had come up with a 'buyer', another UC named 'Steve'.

Green had agreed to do the intro to Joey. It would be dangerous, as Steve, like Lucy, would be on his own a lot of the time. But if Joey liked him and Green added the 'cred', they knew that they could deal.

With the initial introduction a success, Joey had begun to meet with Steve on a regular basis. Like most villains, UCs operate under the same procedure, almost like a courtship:

cautiously moving in, breaking down the barriers and building up a rapport. Some UCs had even come to like the people they would eventually set up, but never allow this relationship to cloud their judgement.

It was about this time that Pandora was sent down for a minimal sentence, which helped, as it happened, to avoid suspicion. Now it was make-or-break time: did Joey trust Steve sufficiently to deal with him and him alone?

Joey had continued to meet Steve, setting up a deal to give him a little tester first, to see what happens. Villains hardly ever 'shag' on the first date; the full consignment is never handed over, just in case they lose the entire shipment. Contrary to popular folklore there is no honour among thieves. If heroin is the deal, then they'll offer you a little sample of Amphetamine or something else, just to see if you have the cash without compromising the main stash.

Steve had been offered just over seven thousand Omnopon capsules for fourteen grand. This is an analgesic narcotic, widely abused by addicts. Its euphoric effects are similar to morphine or heroin. The main buy had been set up in a hotel car park near Heathrow, even though most of the meetings prior to this had taken place in the Black Bear pub near Surrey.

By coincidence the Black Bear was my local boozer, and was spitting distance from my house. I shook my head. You never know what's going on, even on your own doorstep. Although I didn't know it at the time, this coincidence would have some bearing on the operation ahead.

The meet had gone ahead as planned. Steve's car was laid down in the car park of the Sheraton Skyline Hotel near Heathrow. Joey and Steve had kept obo from a nearby window, while Joey's accomplice had reversed his own vehicle up to Steve's car, where he opened both boots and transferred the drugs (in large black dustbin liners) from one vehicle to the other.

Handing over the dosh Steve had shaken Joe's hand. Deal done, Joey left the hotel – and was nicked outside.

In the months that followed, there were three trials in all, mainly because of alleged attempts to get at the jury and knobble witnesses. Eventually Joey had got nine years, and he wasn't fucking happy.

'Great, guv,' I said. 'Sounds like you got a right result from a good job. So why are we here?'

The DI glanced at Baz and nodded. 'After the job we found about forty kilos of horse in a lock-up. We sat on it, believing it was part of Joey's stash, but it was never collected. Joey has appealed. We need to win that appeal, so Pandora has to give evidence. He's now got a new ID and been relocated . . . you don't need to know where.'

'Fine,' I said. 'I don't want to know. But where do we fit in?'

'Twenty-four-hour protection,' said the DI. 'Around the clock.'

'OK,' I said. 'But if we accept this operation, can I have what I need?'

The DI nodded. 'Sure – within reason.'

'All right,' I said, looking to Chris for support. 'How long do we have?'

'Ten days,' the DI replied.

'Great,' I said. 'I'll have a draft operational order for the big house by the end of the week. Anything else?' I asked, pulling back my chair. There was an uneasy silence as the detectives made eye contact.

'Just one,' said Ron, pulling out another photograph. 'We think he's been contracted.'

I sat back down, sighed, and pulled out my notepad. I took the photograph and studied the rough, pock-marked face, taking in the short-cropped steel-grey hair and the ice-cold 'been there, seen it, done it' eyes. I passed it to Chris, who looked at it with contempt. 'Scared of no man, me!' was his motto, and one he certainly lived by.

'OK,' I said. 'We've said we'll do the job.'

'Can we keep this?' asked Chris, already putting the photo in his notebook.

'Sure,' said Ron.

'What's his background?' I asked.

'Rhodesian SAS,' said Ron. 'A real pro.' Originally formed by Major 'Mad Mike' Calvert in the early 1950s to fight in the Malaya Campaign, the Rhodesian SAS had been disbanded in the 60s, only to be reformed after British rule. In 1978 the unit had officially become known as the Special Air Service Regiment 'Rhodesia'. Well versed in guerilla and counter-insurgency warfare, they would later conduct cross-border raids into Mozambique and neighbouring countries in search of rebels. After black majority rule in 1980, many had left to join the South African Defence Force or gone on to become mercenaries in their own right.

The drive back to base was fast and furious; there were lots of things I needed to get jacked up PDQ. 'Fucking hell, mate,' I said. 'No wonder it's out of SO10's remit.' SO10 was the department responsible for witness protection and relocation, even to foreign countries if deemed necessary – all at the taxpayer's expense, of course, but in many cases considered a necessary evil. SO10 were, however, purely administrative, and had no access to firearms. Thus, in cases such as this, SO19 were called in.

With only four days to go before I had to come up with the draft operational order, where did I start? Back at base I decided that we'd need twelve men and two of our vehicles. Pulling out my dog-eared notebook, I turned to a clean page and quickly inscribed the familiar mnemonic I.I.M.A.C.: Information, Intention, Method, Admin, Comms.

Information. We had the background on Pandora; the supposed 'contractor' however, was a different story. We did not need to concern ourselves with who might have hired him, but we did need his background.

Intention. That part was easy. The intention was for SO19 to keep Pandora alive, providing him with twenty-four-hour protection and armed, low-key escorts to and from court in order to hand him over unharmed at the conclusion of the hearing.

I closed the notebook. Method, Admin and Comms I'd have to work at later, but first I had to see Andy. After all, it was he who propped up the job.

'Sounds good,' said Andy after I'd quickly run through the bare bones of the plan. 'I'll leave the planning to you, then run through the Op Order.'

'It needs polishing,' I said, 'but I also need my team, three additional men from the spare team, and another skipper. Can I take Stevie?'

Andy nodded in agreement. 'Yeah, good choice.' Stevie I knew had been earmarked to eventually take over the team. He was a great guy and it would be good for him to see how the team performed – and besides, we needed two supervisors, one for days, one for nights.

'Do you remember we spoke about Pat Hodgson?' Andy asked.

I nodded. 'Yeah.'

'Well he starts with the team in a couple of weeks, OK?'

'No problems here, boss,' I said.

'Guvnor,' I said as the local DCI who had been put in charge of the case answered the phone. I'd been up most of the night, pen in hand and with Jill supplying endless cups of coffee. 'Steve Collins, SO19. I've got a shopping list for you. Do you have a pen?'

'Go ahead,' he replied not knowing what was about to land in his lap.

I rattled off the contents. 'I need a hotel. Somewhere suburban but within striking distance of Woolwich Crown Court. Four rooms – first floor, no balconies, and at the end of a corridor near to an emergency exit that we can control. Two rooms each side of the corridor, with an empty, sterile room between each and any other residents. That's six in all if you can swing it!'

He whistled. 'That's a tall order,' he replied, somewhat exasperated.

'I haven't finished,' I said. 'I need the technical boys from Lambeth down there. We'll need covert pin-hole cameras covering the corridor and emergency exit – fisheye will do – also one to cover Pandora's room. I need an alarm system and probably a panic button, but I'll let you know after you've found a venue and we've had a look-see.'

I paused – silence the other end, so I continued: 'I'll need to speak to the manager. The staff will have an idea something's going on as the rooms will be unavailable for cleaning, so that all needs to be squared away.'

'Anything else?' he asked sarcastically.

'Yeah, I want two high-performance hire cars for the duration – clean, not the firm's. They need to be four door, and not white or red – they stick out like a bulldog's bollocks. There's shit-loads more, but I think I can supply most of it. It's the venue I'm really sweating on.'

'I've got an idea,' the DCI said. 'Can I page you in say . . . thirty minutes?'

'No probs,' I replied. 'I'm not going anywhere.'

It was now down to the boss. Although we had a rough plan, we were unable to finalise it until we knew where we'd be operating from, and that would need a thorough recce. All we could do now was wait.

Beep, beep . . . Impatiently I cut off the pager midstream. It had been over an hour since our conversation and I was beginning to get worried. I dialled the number with trepidation.

'DCI,' he snapped.

'Guv – Steve,' I said.

'Hello, mate.' His voice was cheery now. 'How does the Richmond Hill Hotel sound?'

'Very nice,' I replied. 'I'm not familiar with it, but the location sounds good. What about availability?'

'I don't think it'll be a problem,' he replied. 'I know one of the managing directors. When can you go down for a look-see?'

With a great deal left to do, time was stacked against us. 'How about now?'

'OK,' he replied. 'I'll tell them to expect you in an hour. Ask for the duty manager, he'll show you the layout.'

Grabbing hold of Stevie and Chris, I thumbed through the *Geographia*. 'We've got a possible,' I said. 'BL 46 75. Richmond Hill Hotel.' I flicked to the appropriate page. 'That'll do nicely.'

The location was ideal. West of Richmond Park with its multiple routes into London, the medium-sized, plush-fronted hotel offered a variety of options. Once inside, we were shown around by the slightly bewildered duty manager – and the layout far exceeded my wildest expectations. A high-walled, 'corral'-style courtyard at the rear with just one entrance from the spacious front car park made surveillance easy. What's more, we could dominate the area from the relative safety of a room. The multiple entrances at the front offered excellent opportunities to come and go with our principal, while the first-floor, end-of-corridor location couldn't have been better.

'Great! We'll take these three, and these three,' I said to the manager. Now we could plan!

'Guvnor.'

'Yes, Steve?' sighed the DCI.

'Excellent choice. But I need some more from the technical lads.'

'Go ahead,' he said.

'Right. Apart from the three cameras and monitors, I need a panic alarm, a pressure-pad alarm and two non-audible door alarms. Oh – and by the way,' I added as an afterthought, 'one of the cameras needs to be infra-red – we need to control the stairwell.'

Now it was time to call the team together for a heads-down. Apart from Stevie and my own boys I'd taken the two Phils from Green team; both were extremely professional and, after his spell in the Turks, Phil One was well versed in close protection.

I outlined the information as we had it. 'OK, guys, what I need to do is divide us up into teams with responsibilities.'

Stevie, Chris and Dave – a tall, quick-witted, fast-talking Essex boy who had recently joined us from training – volunteered for nights with one of the other lads. As monotonous as it may seem, the night shift was probably the most dangerous time. During the early hours they would need to remain alert while at a natural low ebb, constantly watching the monitors and checking any movement indicated by the silent alarms. I guessed that if there was going to be any kind of hit, then that would be the time to do it – either then or during the daytime run to court, which was the other vulnerable time. But that, I decided, was to be my responsibility.

The drivers would kit out their respective vehicles. I wanted each to contain a minimum of: one *Geographia*, first-aid kit, stun and smoke grenades, MP5s, body armour (although we'd all be wearing covert gear for the run), portable blue lights, two-tones and main-set radios (for the hire cars), and route maps. This is where Paul came in.

'OK, Paul, what I need you to do is plot me three separate routes from here to Woolwich Crown Court. Each route needs to be driven to ensure it's not hampered by roadworks, width restrictions or any other obstacles.'

Paul nodded, writing furiously, and I knew I could rely on him.

'I want the maps sectionalised, with safe houses or police stations highlighted at intervals so we can divert to the nearest one in the event of an attack. Also hospitals – but make sure they've got an A & E. You know what state the Health Service is in.'

Paul laughed.

'The routes on the map are to be highlighted yellow, blue and pink. Every day the principal will be moved out of the hotel by a different entrance. Our own control inside will be manned by two men twenty-four hours a day. Each morning I and I alone will pick a coloured route depending on traffic, roadwork reports or whatever side I get out of bed.'

A chuckle ran through the room; the boys were keen.

'Again the route back will be at my discretion, and our control will inform the Central Command Complex Information Room at New Scotland Yard of the route. He in turn will inform India 99 [the Air Support Unit helicopter] that we are running, with a general location just in case.'

I looked around the assembled faces. 'Chris, can you get full layout and blueprints of the hotel, and as much background on our contractor?' Chris nodded. 'Phil and Rick – technical side. Make sure the equipment's where we want it and that it's up and running.' I turned to Stevie. 'Steve, can you sort out the Admin? We'll finalise it later, but I envisage the weapons being stored in control and handed over, so we need a written record of what's what. Also we need comms – mobile phones, radios, pager numbers, batteries and chargers.'

'Done,' Stevie replied.

We were almost there. After a morning's sheer hard work – much of it on Stevie's part, typing up the operational order on a word processor (I'm completely computer illiterate) – we were almost ready to go.

Numbered copies of the order were distributed, containing instructions for safe routes in, call-signs and details of the operation for the duty officer. The Team was given a sealed copy, to be held in the baseroom at Old Street with strict instructions that they were to be opened only should they receive the radio or telephone message: 'Pandora is compromised.'

Dress was to be casual but smart, in keeping with the status of the hotel. Coming and going would be kept to a minimum, with a change-over every twelve hours (plus travelling). Radios and spare batteries were to be taken home at the end of each shift, enabling the team to communicate with control when checking in the following day. Nobody was to enter the hotel at change-over without the express authority of the controller. This was in case the duty team were running an incident or perhaps had somebody suspicious on the cameras; the last thing they would need was the change-over team blundering into the area.

Paul had worked wonders with the routes, and we could now work out our convoy running-order and strategy. During the court run, Dick, an SO19 veteran and ex-Royal Marine, was nominated as Pandora's close-protection officer. He would on each journey be riding shotgun – literally, for beneath his long coat would be a sawn-off Remington 870 pump-action shotgun, secured around his shoulders by a quick-release strap. Our firepower was awesome.

Brad and Paul volunteered as drivers, Brad, having just passed his anti-hijack driving course, was dying to put his new-found skills to the test.

Finally the day of reckoning arrived, and by now I was quite pleased with the set-up. It was as water-tight as it would ever be – and, in true Glory Boy fashion, I secretly hoped somebody would put us to the test.

Arriving at the hotel early in the morning, the cover vehicles that had been laid down the night before to reserve our spaces were moved and replaced by the gunships. The control was beautifully set up and running like a dream: apart from a hand-held rocket attack, we had catered for every eventuality.

With tea and coffee laid on, we met up with Baz and Ron, who would be Pandora's handlers for the duration. This suited me, as apparently Pandora was known to be sulky on occasions. Baz and Ron would cater for his welfare and act as a buffer between him and the team. This would free me up to make the operational decisions, but did mean that we now had three unarmed guys to watch.

Prior to the operation I had sat down with Ron and Baz to give them the facts of life: if the shit did hit the fan we'd do everything we could for them, but our main concern was the protection of the principal. Much as it left a bad taste in everybody's mouth that we had to put some scrote's life above that of two police officers, it was the number-one rule of bodyguarding. Both Ron and Baz understood.

Stevie and I had recced the court building early on during the proceedings. Apart from their own armed unit (some of them ex-SO19 ARV men) within the complex, there was a secure tunnel running beneath the court and the adjoining Belmarsh Prison, specifically designed for this type of occasion as the prison housed many terrorist and Category A maximum-security prisoners.

I don't think Stevie would be too unhappy if I described him as a 'kit nut'. That boy does love the latest gadgets and bits of kit, so much so that he has to wear two coats – his normal jacket, and on top of that what I termed his 'kit coat'! A coat of many pockets. It was a habit that had long ago earned him the nickname 'Stevie Two Coats'. On the day of the recce, he and I had pitched up at the court's reception and introduced ourselves. The meeting had already been arranged, so all we needed was access to the building – but that's where the 'jobsworth' factor had come into play. Greeted by a pimply twenty-year-old in a uniform he'd probably grow into given another twenty or thirty years, we had announced our intention.

'You'll have to go through the metal detector,' he'd said, indicating a portal similar to that found in airports.

'Not much point in that,' I had joked. 'We're carrying.' He'd looked puzzled. 'Carrying,' I'd repeated, patting the Glock on my hip through my jacket. 'We're SO19; we're armed.'

'I need to see it,' the youth had replied.

'Look,' I said, 'I've told you we're armed, you've seen my warrant card, and we have an appointment. There's no reason on earth why you need to see the gun.'

'I need to see it or I can't let you through,' the little snot had insisted.

'OK,' I'd said, turning my back so only he could see. 'Have a look.' I opened up my jacket. 'Satisfied?'

He had nodded. 'But you'll have to take it off and then step through the metal detector.'

I'd banged my forehead with my fist. 'I'm losing something in the interpretation,' I said. 'Run this by me again, cos I think I'm fucking thick or something. You want me to take off my gun, right?' The lad had nodded. 'You then want me to step through the metal detector where I can collect my gun on the other side?' Again a nod. 'Then why do I have to go through the detector?'

'To see if you have anything metallic on you,' he'd said as if I were some sort of moron.

'Like what? Another fucking gun? I've already told you I've got one – so why wouldn't I tell you if I've got two? What difference does it make?'

He'd shrugged.

'Bollocks,' I had said, looking over his shoulder and seeing the security section Sergeant. 'Skip!' I'd called. He'd sauntered over and I explained our predicament; there was simply no reason for us to start unholstering and waving our guns about in public.

'Sorry, mate,' the sergeant had said. 'Private security. They report directly to the clerk of the court. We have no jurisdiction over them, what they say goes.' I shook my head in disbelief. 'But we're the fucking police. Does that count for nothing any more?'

'Apparently not,' he'd replied.

What a state of affairs, I'd thought, shaping up to smack the fucking pair of them. But there was no way I was going to give that little prick the satisfaction. 'Right. Come on, Stevie,' I said. 'Let's go.'

Stepping outside I was furious, and began ranting about everything I was going to do to my new-found friend – well, everything involving his bollocks anyway. Before these type of private firms had taken over it was always the job of the police to provide security for the courts and the escort of prisoners – and I'm sure we'd never 'lost' as many prisoners in a decade as had been lost in the first few weeks of private enterprise!

Finding our car, Stevie and I had unloaded, leaving our guns with a bewildered Paul. Striding back to the court, I was more than happy for a confrontation. But I hadn't gambled on Stevie's coat.

Whee-whaa whee whaa! I had groaned as the alarm stopped everybody in their tracks.

By the time we'd turned back to the desk my friend had vanished, to be replaced by an older, more cynical model. Having emptied the contents of my pockets into a small plastic tray, I had walked through the detector without further ado.

I'd eyed the guard with disdain as Stevie had dug deeper into his cavernous pockets. *Clunk!* A spare magazine had hit the tray, spilling its already overflowing contents across the counter-top. This had been quickly followed by numerous coins, three penknives of varying description, a martial-arts-style keyring baton, and an alloy extendable baton. I'd smiled in disbelief. Stevie's coat was like a fucking Tardis.

He'd tried again. *Whee whaa whee whaa . . .*

The guard had stepped forward. 'Look mate,' I'd interjected, 'you know who we are. Can we just stop this fucking around? It really is bang out of order.'

The guard had sighed, looking at the growing pile and probably expecting to be there all day. 'OK,' he'd said. Then, by way of a compromise, 'Take your coat off.' Stevie removed the garment, the guard shook it, and it rattled.

Fuck knows what he still had in it. As Stevie walked through the metal detector, his coat had gone through the X-ray machine.

'For Christ's sake,' I'd said as he replaced the contents and struggled into his second skin. 'That thing must be bullet-proof. It weighs about two stone . . . what else you got in there?'

Stevie had grinned as I held up my hand. 'No. Don't tell me. I don't want to know.'

Ron's mobile rang. 'Yeah?' He looked up and nodded. 'Yeah.' Pushing down the aerial, he said, 'The lobby in five. SO10 are bringing him in.'

'Phil, Paul, Brad – let's mingle,' I said.

Thinning out one at a time and taking different exits, the lads slowly converged on the lobby, picking up newspapers and ordering tea like any other punter.

Security was tight, even though it was unlikely any would-be assassin knew Pandora's whereabouts. No, the real trouble would come the day after tomorrow, once the guy had been to court where any villain could attempt to follow the convoy. I considered that a direct attack on the court was out of the question, unless of course they were equipped with a Sherman Tank.

Sitting in the hotel's lounge I sipped my coffee and chatted aimlessly to Baz. The rest of the lads had blended in well. I realised that if I hadn't have known them I wouldn't have sussed them . . .

Outside, a car door slammed. I didn't look up. Play it cool, I thought. You're a normal businessman waiting to meet some colleagues.

Baz looked up and nodded at the SO10 handler standing before us, beside him our charge – medium height and build, greying hair, slightly tanned and wearing glasses. Certainly not what one would expect confronting an informer – but then again, it seldom is.

Baz led the way as we headed upstairs.

Once we were in Pandora's room, the other lads started to filter in. 'Boys,' Ron announced, 'this is the guy you'll be looking after. Take a good look at him.'

'Pandora' smiled and nodded all around the room. 'All right?' he said in a slightly polished south London accent (if there is such a thing). 'Richard Green . . .'

I looked heavenward. Fuck's sake, I thought. Talk about operational security!

After the lads had left the room it was down to business. 'I'll pick him up after all this is over,' explained the SO10 handler. 'Take him back to where he came from.' Judging by Pandora's complexion he apparently came from sunnier climes – but of course that was none of my business. 'OK, son, I'll be on my way then,' said the detective, slipping Pandora a wedge (wad of notes). 'Bit of spending.' He added.

The weekend dragged by – a few false alarms and the evening handover to Stevie and his team being the only highlights. I'd decided for OPSEC reasons that the lads would travel direct to the hotel from their home addresses, keeping us totally unconnected to the base at Old Street. Stevie would make contact with the SO19 duty officer every evening, and if there were any urgent messages or correspondence for us he'd arrange a meet at another nick to pick them up. My reasoning for this caution was threefold: first, if somebody wanted to pick us up for surveillance, then the base would be a good place to start; second, we'd need transport, and I wanted to keep the two hire cars sterile; third, travelling to and from their home address would keep the lads on their toes. Not wanting any would-be tail to know where they lived, they'd practise a bit of anti-surveillance along the way.

I was happy. Everything, including the court runs, ran smoothly, crisply and exactly to plan. But by the end of the first week Pandora still hadn't been called to give evidence – and the tantrums had already started to occur.

'I don't believe it!' said Ron. 'He's only phoned his fucking missus and told her where he is! He's even given her the number of his room.'

'How could he?' I asked. 'I had his phone cut off for outgoing calls, and his room searched for a mobile when we were at court.'

'He had it reconnected. Don't know how,' Ron replied.

I exploded: 'For fuck's sake! You're supposed to be the one looking after that side of it. How secure is she?' I demanded, but already my mind was running through the compromise contingency. The last thing I wanted to do was up and move the entire operation to the alternative location, especially as this one was running so well. But the plain fact was that we were compromised; this could only be a damage limitation exercise. I discussed it with the lads and decided to hold off making a decision until I could speak to Stevie later.

'He wants us to go out,' said Baz.

'Out?' I asked. 'Out where?'

'Fuck knows. He's just being an arsehole. He wants to get out of here for a walk and something to drink.'

'Whoa,' I said. 'No way. No fucking pubs. He does know they're after him, doesn't he?' I asked.

Baz nodded. 'Oh yeah. But at the end of the day he's not in custody, and he's threatening not to give evidence. You know what this case means to us, how much money the firm's invested in him. Simple fact is, we need to keep him sweet.'

I looked at my watch: ninety minutes to change-over time. I could see Baz's point; besides, hanging around all day in a small room with him bleating in my ear had certainly taken its toll. 'Give me ten,' I said.

Picking Phil and Brad as the two most experienced bodyguards, I posted one as CPO and one at point. The rest of us would merge into the background as back-up and third eyes watching their backs. Out on the street would be awkward – the last thing we wanted to do was draw attention to ourselves – but seven guys are hard to lose, particularly in the early evening.

After a few minutes' walk, Pandora complained of being bored. He'd flexed his muscles and got what he wanted, but I guess he must inwardly have felt quite exposed and slightly uncomfortable; after all he was walking around with a price on his head, and even with us around, a sniper could quite easily put a bullet in his swede.

Finding a small back-street Mexican restaurant, we went to ground – and for the next fifty minutes or so we listened to him moaning about everything from his room to the food.

Back at the hotel I briefed Stevie on the day's events. 'I don't propose a move yet,' I said. 'Baz has got some feelers out – apparently he knows Green's old lady – and he'll get back to us in the morning.'

Stevie agreed in his usual relaxed style, poured himself a coffee and told me to fuck off home and stop worrying. He was right. The day shift, with its court runs, decision making and travelling, was beginning to take its toll.

I smiled. 'It's all right for you, but I swear: another day of his moaning and I'll fucking top him myself.'

That evening I drove wearily home, checking my rear mirror for any signs of a tail, taking the odd cul-de-sac, and staying once on a roundabout for a couple of circuits. Satisfied, I arrived home, parked the car, poured a large drink and slumped in an armchair. 'I'm getting too old for this,' I said to Jill.

She smiled. 'What about training?'

'Don't you start!' I laughed. 'I've had enough of that with the guvnors.' The truth was, I'd never really asked Jill's opinion on what I did for a living. It wasn't that we didn't talk – far from it; it was important that she was part of everything I did – I think it was just that I thought, perhaps rather arrogantly, that she simply took it for granted.

Dinner was a somewhat sombre affair, the day's events weighing heavily on my mind as I pushed the food aimlessly around the plate. Outside the wind howled relentlessly and the rain struck the windows with enough force to rattle the glass. 'Foul night,' I said. Then something outside caught my eye. I couldn't tell what it was, but it seemed as though something in the garden was out of place. In the kitchen our three German shepherds suddenly started going crazy and the intruder light in the back garden burst into life.

I peered out into the storm and my blood froze. Standing in the middle of the lawn, soaked to the skin, a man was staring at the house, his hood and dark clothing sticking to his body, his hands encased in black gloves. Momentarily our eyes met, his just discernible through the slits in his balaclava. It was enough to spark me into action.

Pushing back the chair, I darted through to the adjoining kitchen door, Jill's eyes widening as she realised what was going on. Like most good coppers, I kept something heavy by the front and back doors – in this instance a large truncheon subscribed, 'A Gift From Menorca'. Snatching it from its hook I opened the door to release the dogs. I was going to have this fucker!

The door blew back on its hinges. 'Get him!' I shouted as the target turned to run. Chan, the largest dog and leader of the pack, stopped barking, stuck his nose out into the night, then retreated into the warmth of the kitchen followed by his firm. Great, I thought, hurling myself across the patio.

'I'll kill you, you bastard!' I screamed at the intruder's disappearing back as I splashed through the mud in my slippers. Then I stopped. He was gone, and there was no way I was going to follow him into the undergrowth beyond the back fence, having no torch and no way of knowing if he was tooled up.

That night I lay awake, staring at the ceiling. To me this had always been a game, even since the day I joined – a violent game for sure, but still a game. One where you pitted your wits against another. But the game was on only at work. Funnily enough, in my experience most villains seem to respect that – and if they do happen to see you out shopping with your family or in a restaurant it's very rare that they'll say anything. It seemed to be the unwritten law: 'Don't fuck with me and I won't fuck with you' – a sort of gentlemen's agreement.

When your family did become involved, however, the gloves came off.

The thing I had to ascertain was whether the guy in the garden was involved in the Pandora case and was making a statement: 'We know where you live.' It wasn't, I decided, beyond the bounds of possibility, even though I had taken all the usual precautions travelling to and from the plot. That sparked a second question: if they knew where I was, did they know where Pandora was? After all, there seemed to be attempts to get at the jury and the witnesses during the first trials, and Joey Pyle was no stranger to this manor. I must think rationally for a moment, I told myself. Surely this could just be a coincidence. The guy could simply have been a prowler, or even somebody with a grudge from a previous operation . . .

I had managed to placate Jill by dismissing him as a harmless peeping Tom but I knew she didn't believe me. Peeping Toms don't go to so much trouble

The next morning I was in no mood for Pandora. The previous night's events weighed heavily on my mind, even though in the cold light of day Jill had all but dismissed the incident – whether for my benefit or her own I didn't know.

When it came to breakfast I sent two of the lads down to the restaurant. I had the arse, and they all knew it.

The rest of the week passed much like the previous one. Once again Pandora had not been called to give evidence. I'd hoped it would all have been done with by now, that we could have wound it all down, but now I had to consider the weekend and the possibility of yet another week.

That evening I found out that, despite all my efforts, Pandora had contacted his wife again. I exploded. 'What the fuck are we doing, going out of our way to protect this wanker who couldn't give a fuck about his own personal security?' I yelled. 'Don't get me wrong, I couldn't give a fuck if somebody topped him!'

'He wants to go out,' Ron said apologetically.

I looked at my watch and thought of Jill at home alone. 'Well he can't,' I said. 'It's too close to change-over time, I'll speak to Stevie when he gets here.'

The camera alarm sounded, and I looked up at the screen. Leaving his room was Pandora. I followed his progress on the monitor until I was looking down at the top of his head. Snatching open the door to our room before he could knock, I pushed him back out into the hall, jabbing my finger at his chest. 'You fucking listen to me, dicksplash,' I snarled. 'You are getting right up my fucking arse, understand?'

He looked down at my shoulder holster and nodded.

'Good. Now you go out when we say, and not before. Now get back in your room and stop bleating!'

'Shall we do something this weekend?' Phil asked when I returned.

'Like what?' I replied.

'Anything. Get him out. Better than hanging around here.'

I nodded. 'Yeah, that's a good idea. Sleep on it, Phil, see what you come up with.'

'OK,' he replied, and went back to cleaning his five.

'Do you like rugby?' I asked Pandora the following morning.

'Dunno, don't really follow it,' he replied. 'Why?'

'Because we're going to a rugby match,' I said, 'so I don't really give a toss whether you like it or not.'

With Pandora in tow we mounted up and drove to Twickenham. Apart from playing in the occasional local league, I wasn't really a rugby nut, but the other lads liked to watch, and it was somewhere relatively safe where I could think. The chances were that Pandora would give evidence on Monday and that would be the end of it. Since the phone call to his wife, the lads had been extremely eyes about, but still nothing seemed to be out of the ordinary.

The game passed without incident, a pretty uneventful match as I recall. 'I don't know if you know the score,' Baz whispered on the drive home, 'but his old lady isn't the one he's been relocated with.'

I looked at him, slightly puzzled by this information. 'What do you mean?'

'Well,' Baz started. 'His old lady, the one he keeps phoning, still lives in his old manor. She knows everybody involved . . .'

'Let me get this right,' I said. 'He's split from his missus, but she still lives in the same area and associates with his old cronies. Now she's the one he's phoned and told her where he is. Is that right?'

Baz nodded.

'Is he some kind of wanker or something? I only ask because he doesn't appear to be playing with a full fucking deck. Do you think she'll grass?'

Baz shrugged. 'Dunno. Hell hath no fury and all that old shit.'

'I'm not happy,' I said. 'I am not fucking happy at all. I think we'll have to move him.' Baz shook his head. 'It's your call, but I don't think it'll solve anything. We've only got – what? Two days to go?'

I nodded.

'Why not keep on the move?'

I thought about this and nodded. 'OK. Done.'

'You have been.' Baz smiled, patting my back.

I was slightly happier by the time I arrived home that evening. Jill was fine, and the incident with the garden intruder now seemed nothing more than a bad dream. Although sleep didn't come easily that night, I awoke in the morning feeling remarkably refreshed and with a new sense of purpose. After all, tomorrow and it would all be over.

After breakfast I had a heads down with Phil. 'What do you reckon, mate?' I asked.

'Well,' he said, 'if somebody's going to hit us, he wants to hurry up. He must know that time's running out, so it's got to be today or tomorrow.'

I nodded. 'Yeah. You're right, I guess. Where shall we go today?'

Phil smiled. 'Bowling,' he said.

The large, impressive bowling alley on the outskirts of Guildford proved the ideal place. As we entered the glass-fronted reception area the lads thinned out to check for escape routes and emergency exits. The alley, part of a leisure centre, wasn't really that busy for a Sunday lunchtime. Any self-respecting bloke would be down the pub for a few beers prior to going home for a Sunday roast and a kip in front of the telly. Still, that was fine by us, and I booked the two lanes at the far end of the building, next to the toilets and emergency exit. Swapping our footwear for red, white and blue bowling shoes, I smiled to myself; if we did suddenly have to have it away on our 'dancers' we'd certainly be able to recognise each other.

'Who knows how to score?' I asked as we strolled towards the lanes.

'Yeah, I'll do it,' said Phil.

It was only when we reached the far side that it suddenly dawned on me: our cover was one of a group of guys out for a good game of bowling. But with all but two of us wearing shoulder holsters it was going to be nigh on impossible to bowl properly in a jacket. Even with our Glocks clipped into their holsters, we still ran the risk of them flying out and disappearing down the highly polished lanes. So we took it in turns to disappear into the toilets nearby, removing our holsters and folding them loosely into our jackets, which were then placed in easy reach on a nearby chair. Now we were ready.

'*Aaarrrrgh!*'

My heart missed several beats as behind me Pandora cried out in pain. Fucking hell, he's been hit, my brain screamed as I spun round, scanning the area.

Lying half-way down the second lane was Pandora, eyes screwed up in obvious pain, bowling ball still attached to his right hand.

'Silly Fucker!' said Baz. 'You're supposed to let go of the ball.'

169

'I can't,' he whined. 'My fingers are stuck.'

I shook my head. 'Jesus,' I muttered. 'Who is this? Fred Carno – and where's his fucking circus?'

After stopping off for a bite to eat, we arrived back at the hotel shortly after change-over time. Stevie was busy calculating the amount of overtime we'd earned that week, and seemed quite happy and relaxed. Nothing seemed to faze him.

I brought him up to speed on the day's events. 'With luck,' I concluded, 'you can have tomorrow night off.'

'Great,' he replied. 'How's Jill taking it?'

'OK,' I said. 'You know how we're supposed to think we can take on the world - how stress is a dirty word, something we're far too macho to suffer from. But I tell you, this has really brought the pains on. You know, in a moment of madness I even thought about going training.'

'Nice one,' Stevie replied. 'Let me know when and I'll move into your locker.'

Monday morning: the day I'd been waiting for. Arriving at the hotel early, I thought it would be a gesture of good will to let Stevie go home early. Pulling up in the car park, I pulled out my radio as the engine died. A faint mist hung in the air and nothing stirred. What a beautiful morning, I thought.

'Control. Two-seven,' I called into the net.

Silence.

I checked the battery. 'Control. Trojan two-seven,' I called again. Silence. Getting out of the car, I looked up at the front of the hotel – nothing out of the ordinary there. I checked the channel selector and scanned the waves. The lads couldn't have been running an incident because there was nothing but static, not even the telltale three clicks for yes, two for no if they were unable to speak.

Odd, I thought, giving it one more try. 'Control. Control . . . Trojan two-seven,' I called, and once again there was no response.

I walked towards the lobby, pushed open the door and entered. Deserted. The *Marie Celeste* of the hotel world. No receptionist, no porter, no manager . . . nothing stirred but the butterflies in the pit of my stomach. Reaching over the desk, expecting to see the remains of the receptionist, I pulled out the telephone and dialled our room number. No answer. Gathering my thoughts I ran through the options open to me, but came up with only two that were half-way viable. I could ring the base and speak to the duty officer, or even phone the local plod – but I quickly dismissed that one; after all, I was supposedly in charge of a secret operation and I could end up with egg on my face. The second option was far simpler, and was eventually the one I plumped for. Breaking all the rules, I decided I'd have to check it out myself and hope that I didn't stumble across anything I couldn't deal with.

Turning off the radio I began to climb the stairs.

Creak . . . Bollocks! Perhaps it was just the adrenalin heightening my senses, but to my mind the creak had sounded like a herd of elephants out on the piss. I could even hear my heart . . . which stopped the moment I reached the top and peered around the corner.

Blue and white police incident tape hung loosely from the door handles, having been ripped in half. The corridor resembled a battlefield, with red-stained field dressings and bandages littering the carpet. Silently I came up on to the landing. Pulling my pager from my belt, I pushed the 'read' button. 'No messages,' came the silent reply. A million questions ran through my brain: why hadn't I been informed? Was it recent? How are the lads?

In the back of my mind, however, I knew something wasn't quite right. What was it? Of course. Why wasn't this place swarming with plod? Unless . . . unless this was nothing more than an elaborate 'Got you, you bastard' hoax. As if he'd read my thoughts, Chris grabbed my shoulder from behind. 'Dead around here,' he said casually.

'But the bandages . . .' I said.

'Old ones,' he replied. 'Found them in the bottom of the bag when I was checking my kit. The rest is just ketchup.' He grinned. 'What do you reckon?'

'I reckon you're a fucking sick bastard,' I said striding down the hall.

Although the day team had a good old laugh about it, my heart was still pounding ten minutes later.

'You're on.' Baz gave Pandora the nod half-way through the afternoon. It was comical really, but after more than a week's close protection, Pandora was allowed to stroll into court unescorted and in full view of the public gallery. Judges seldom allow firearms into the court, even if carried covertly. I thought what a pathetic, dishevelled-looking specimen Pandora made as he shuffled in to earn his thirty pieces of silver. Joey apparently had the same high opinion, and did nothing but sit in the dock growling throughout the entire testimony.

The only fly in the ointment was that court packed up early and we were on for another day.

Joey never did get the result he wanted, and returned to finish his sentence. On Tuesday afternoon SO10 pitched up at the hotel to whisk Pandora away to whatever hole he had crawled out of. Leering to the last, he insisted on shaking everybody's hand and telling them what wonderful company they had been. I was glad when he'd gone.

Paging Stevie and the rest of the night team, I told them it was a wrap and they could have a couple of beers – I'd see them at base in the morning. Brad, Phil, Paul and I stowed the gear, loading it into the motors, and left one of the other guys to mind the technical gear until the blokes from Lambeth arrived. Thanking the hotel manager, we departed.

Arriving home early that evening, I poured a drink and had a soak in the bath, pondering on the events of the week. It had never dawned on me before, but people looking in from the outside were right – we did have a stressful job, and whether we wanted to face it or not, it did take its toll.

Downstairs the dogs started barking and I heard the door bell. Towelling myself off, I listened at the bathroom door to the muffled conversation in the hall. 'Steve,' Jill called after a minute. 'Can you come down?'

Pulling on a track suit I made my way downstairs. 'Hi!' I said to our neighbour, who sat cradling a cup of coffee at the kitchen table.

'Sue wants to tell you something,' said Jill.

Sue nodded. 'Sorry to be a nuisance,' she said, 'but as you know, our garden backs on to yours . . .'

'Yeah,' I replied.

'Well it all seems rather silly now . . . but last night I was washing up in my kitchen when the intruder light went on in the garden . . .' I felt the hackles on my neck rise. 'I went outside and thought I heard a noise at the back, but it was too dark to see anything.'

'Probably a fox,' I replied knowing that some of the neighbours kept chickens. She sipped the coffee. 'When I went out this morning I found this,' she replied, dipping into her bag and producing a brand-new, stainless steel axe, complete with price tag. 'I have to admit, I'm a bit worried.'

I swallowed hard. 'You've just had a new brick patio laid, haven't you?' I asked.

'Yes, last week,' she replied.

'Well there you are then,' I said not too convincingly, eyeing up the evil weapon. 'They were probably after digging it up.'

'Do you think so?' Sue asked hopefully.

'Sure.' I nodded.

I reported the matter to the local police. There was nothing they could do, of course, apart from improve their response time should I call. I never did get to the bottom of it. I suppose the only positive thing to come from it all was the fact that I finally realised I was fallible. I had a chink in my armour. I vowed from that day on that nobody must be allowed to exploit it again!

9

It's Only a Replica

Booom! Booom! The door imploded, its hinges shattered beyond recognition by the powerful force of the specially adapted Hatton rounds. I kicked it hard, knocking it into the hall with a resounding thud, and with the MP5 hard in my shoulder I entered the stronghold. Turning to the right I took on the largest threat, the man with the shotgun. I pressed the trigger twice in quick succession . . .

Crack click. That ominous sound of a misfire, metal on metal, the dead man's call. The normally reliable MP5 had jammed.

But there was no time to dwell on the subject, and without thinking I went into combat mode, an action that had been drummed into me over the past five years with the department. Slinging the carbine to one side I dropped to the kneeling position, making myself a smaller target and allowing my number two to cover. 'Stoppage! Support!' I screamed, clawing at my thigh holster to release the Glock. The first stoppage drill: ditch your primary weapon – which in this case had become nothing more than a useless lump of metal – and draw your secondary weapon, the Glock.

Suddenly the air left my lungs as a knee struck me sharply in the back. It was Pat, coming in over my head. *Crack! Crack!* The suspect dropped.

Holstering up while Pat covered, I quickly racked back the cocking lever on my MP5 and cleared the jammed round, letting the action snap back with a loud metallic click as it stripped the top round from the magazine and placed it firmly in the breach. Happy, I reached back and tapped Pat's leg, letting him know I was back in business and ready to go. Had I merely stood up, he may, in the process of engaging another threat, have put a bullet in the back of my swede. Not recommended – but one of the risks you take when training with live ammunition.

'End-ex! End-ex!' shouted the staff instructor. The building was clear, our objective achieved.

'Nice one, Pat!' I said, pulling the balaclava from my head. Pat had just joined the team, and this was our first training session together, the ideal opportunity for the team to assess how he worked and if he would be able to slot in – and from what I'd already seen I didn't think we'd have a problem there.

It really was the ideal situation – whenever an instructor came from Lippitts on to a team he joined during their training week – a gentle introduction. Although he would have already passed the Back to Ops course, different teams adopted different SOPs and had their own way of doing things, so it was nice for the new man to ease his way in before the roller-coaster ops week.

'We've got a rapid next week, Pat,' I said. 'I'll stick you up front if you're happy, in at the sharp end. Don't let the lads trip over your tail, though.'

Lippitts Hill was jokingly referred to by the ops team as Jurassic Park, the instructors being the dinosaurs. Department folklore had it that as soon as you went training you grew a tail, and the longer you were there the bigger it got . . . and Pat had been there some time.

The operation in question had been propped up by Walworth police and centred around a housing estate in south-east London. I'd been to the briefing with Chris, and what I'd heard still made my blood run cold.

A well-known Jamaican crack dealer was supplying gear from his address, a ground-floor flat on the outskirts of

Kennington. The estate was known to be extremely Zulu, which made the prospect of a recce somewhat difficult.

Back at Old Street we had a communal wardrobe. Over the years the guys had collected a number of different costumes and props, which would disguise them as anything from ambulance personnel to punk rockers. On one occasion Brad and I had dressed up as postmen to recce a fortified address at the end of a cul-de-sac. Filling our postie bags with junk mail (and, of course, Glocks), we set off – only to bump into the real postman doing his rounds. Although we'd managed to bluff our way out of it by telling him we were new and learning the area, it had certainly been close. But the most audacious recce I'd ever heard of had been at a hostage incident, where one of the team had donned a pair of sunglasses, nicked a cane out of a nearby garden and 'borrowed' a police dog. Pretending to be blind, he'd tapped his way past the stronghold gaining vital intelligence! Chris and I had even dressed as council workers for one operation, complete with paint-splattered overalls and donkey jackets.

The target lived on the top floor of a particularly rough estate, and the door we were planning to put in the next morning was covered by a metal grille and protected by dogs. With a few tins of paint and a couple of brushes, we set out. Climbing the stairs to the top undetected had been relatively easy, but as we reached the final flight a pit-bull terrier had appeared behind me and attached itself to my trousers.

'Fuck it,' Chris hissed, 'slot the bastard.'

'What, and blow the fucking job?' I moaned. But things were turning ugly. I was in a dilemma: I had a Glock in one pocket and a four-inch paintbrush in the other. Selecting the paintbrush, I'd started slapping the slavering beast around the nut until finally he'd let go.

He was lucky. On another team job, the front door was blown off its hinges and smashed to the floor in the hall. The suspect at the address was known to have a particularly nasty dog, which everybody looked out for as they thudded across the fallen door and into the house. The suspect was being dragged from his bed when he asked, 'Has anybody seen my dog?'

'No,' the team replied, dragging him over the flattened door and out of his shattered entrance. The dog was found eventually, but not until they picked up the front door!

In this case the dealer was believed to be armed. No problem there – that was what we were there for. The twist was that he kept a vat of hydrochloric acid on his cooker. Our informants told us that the purposes of this were twofold: if he was raided by the police he could throw his stash into the powerful chemical, destroying the evidence; far more sinister was the fact that it could be used as a weapon to throw into the face of anybody unwelcome who came through the door – in this instance us! It was a powerful deterrent indeed and, we learnt, a weapon much favoured by Yardies. Having witnessed acid burns in the past, I certainly didn't relish having them on any part of my anatomy, so I turned to the London Ambulance Service for advice in relation to first aid. Although it was my intention to have a paramedic ambulance on scene in this case, there was always the possibility of having injured personnel at a scene we were unable to secure. In that scenario I would never allow the presence of unarmed civilians, be they paramedics or otherwise; thus it was imperative that our team medics knew how to deal. I would have thought that the best way to deal with acid burns would be to take plenty of water and irrigate the area thoroughly. That idea was swiftly kicked into touch when I was advised by the ambulance people that, apart from inviting infection, water may well transport the acid over a wider area. As they informed me, the simplest treatment is to cover the wound with a non-fluffy dressing such as clingfilm, to keep the wound sterile and free from infection pending removal for specialist treatment. A drug called Nubain, a powerful pain killer, could be administered by the ambulance crew if required. Knowing this, I was happier: clingfilm is carried by the team medics as a matter of course, in case of burns from flashbangs.

The next step was the recce – and with the target address not half a mile from Jill's mum's house, that's where I'd start.

Collecting Jill one afternoon, we headed off to the estate. I've always been a firm believer that a man and woman don't promote as much interest as two men or even one on his own, and as a result I had used Jill as a 'Prop' on a number of occasions. This estate was no different; and a man and woman wandering around hand in hand didn't look at all out of place. In no time I'd located the position of the flat and made a mental note of its entrances and exits. I could draw up the plan later. Pulling out a penknife, I quickly jiggled the lock on the communal door, breaking its internal mechanism.

With the recce completed safely, I turned to the ASU for help in obtaining aerial phots. Drawings are all well and good, but a photograph gives you a feel of the area, and as such plays a vital part in the planning phase.

I'd already decided this would be a two-team job. Red team were spare, so I pencilled them in for the op.

Now all we had to do was wait. We'd been given a specific day and a rough time – early evening. Though the cover of darkness is an added bonus, the tecs in this case needed the intelligence to ensure the drugs would be there before they could act.

'OK, fellas, this is the plan . . .'

The briefing room was still. I'd already outlined the information and intention; now it was down to the method – how we would achieve our goal.

'We'll be using two Trojan horses to deliver us on to the plot. They're both Luton vans with shutters, and each has been supplied with a local driver. When we get the "go" we'll take a circular route from the nick, back up to the

Elephant, left into Newington Butts, then left again into Kennington Park.' I paused. 'There's speed ramps down this stretch, so make sure you hang on tight. From here it's left into Hillingdon Street then right into the FUP on the blind side of the building.' I pointed to one of the many photos pinned to the wall before continuing: 'Team Alpha will be Red team. You'll be in the first horse. Myself and Black team will follow you up as Bravo. I can't stress enough how quiet we must be when debussing at the FUP. Even the locals and ambulance will not come in until well after our approach.' I pointed back to the photograph. 'As can be seen here, the target backs on to John Ruskin Street. There's an alleyway leading from the FUP along the side of the address, which is at the end of this block.' I indicated the path with a ruler. 'Half-way along the end of the block is an entrance into the communal hallway. The front door we want is the first on the left as we enter.'

Joe raised his hand. 'Is there a door on the hallway entrance? And if so, is it locked and which way does it open?'

Joe and Chris were the nominated MOE men. Joe's was a valid point; if the door should open outwards they'd require a Hooley bar.

'There is a door,' I replied, 'but I've already fucked the lock. It's on rising butts, so it opens either way.'

Joe nodded, obviously satisfied. 'There are no windows in the corridor,' I said. 'Just a spyhole in the door. Can you deal with that as we move up, Chris?'

'No probs,' he replied. I knew Chris would simply take a sticky target patch with him to place over the peephole. That way, should the suspect hear anything untoward and look through the door, he wouldn't see anything. After that there was a good chance he'd open the door to peer outside. That would be where we'd be 'Job done, thank you very much.' It had certainly worked in the past.

'Team Alpha,' I said, looking at the Red team's skipper, 'will go past the corridor and stack up on the rear of the flat. As it's ground floor it has a small garden and double-glazed patio doors and windows. In fact the whole of the rear is glass!' I smiled, knowing the flat would be totally air conditioned in a couple of hours. 'By the time you've reached the rear, Bravo team will be ready at the front. Andy will be link man,' I said, indicating the guvnor. 'When he gives the go we'll hit front and back simultaneously, although Alpha's role will be that of a limited-entry smash and cover, dominate the area.'

The skipper looked happy with that.

'When we take the door off, Bravo's primary role will be as the entry team. I figure that when our man hears the windows going in at the back he'll make a bolt for the door.'

'Oh – is he a metal-worker?' asked Chris.

'The old ones are the best,' I laughed, 'But I want him out of the game fast.'

I studied my notes. 'Dress, guys,' I said. 'I know we hate wearing them, but respirators and full protective kit are the order of the day. At least they'll provide some sort of protection for your face and eyes . . . Any questions?'

Silence.

'Andy?' I asked.

Andy took the chair. 'As Steve said, speed is of the essence. We need to get in fast and close this guy down. Good luck.'

Happy with the plan, the lads thinned out to collect their kit as I packed away the plans and notes ready for the next phase of the operation – the briefing at Walworth nick.

'Stand by. Left, left, left into Kennington Park,' the voice crackled in my earpiece as we hit the sleeping policeman at speed.

'Oi! Oi! A bit of fucking passenger consideration!' shouted Chris, his voice strangely muffled in the suffocating claustrophobia of the respirator.

'All right, mate?' I asked, tapping Pat on the shoulder. He nodded. Things must certainly have changed since his day; to him this must have seemed like a whole new world.

I looked at the luminous dial on my watch: five past seven. We'd actually been quite lucky; no sooner had we pitched up at Walworth and gone through the briefing when we'd been given the green light. The target was home, and a 'loose' OP, mounted from a car parked along the street, had been established on the address – which meant that from now until we reached the FUP the operation could be aborted at any time, should the suspect leave. At the FUP, however, we'd reach the point of no return.

From inside the lead vehicle Andy kept up a running commentary – which proved to be a great help as we were effectively blind, cut off from the outside world. 'Left, left, left, Hillingdon . . .'

I tapped the base of the magazine on the MP5 as the van slowed. I could almost hear the butterflies in my stomach.

'FUP ten seconds. That's ten seconds to FUP,' Andy called. 'Stand by, Stand by,' and the van juddered to a halt, the rear man throwing up the shutters almost before the engine had died.

Hitting the tarmac I quickly orientated myself before turning right and latching on to the back of Alpha team's rear marker as he disappeared into the alley.

The lock on the corridor door hadn't been fixed, and with a slight creak it opened inwards. With my right hand on the pistol grip, I pushed the five deep into my shoulder, enabling me to fire one-handed should the need arise.

I covered the danger area ahead. With my left hand I pointed to the door as I stared down the sights. As planned, Pat stacked on the hinge side, the rest of the team behind him. As I went right, Chris was already taping the spyhole. The initial information had been that the door was fortified; during the recce I hadn't seen any additional locks, but obviously I couldn't see what was on the other side. Whatever the case, with both Chris and Big Joe playing a tune on it with two Enforcers, I knew it would be no problem.

'Team Alpha, are you in position?' Andy whispered

through his resi.

Click, click, click. The almost silent affirmative response.

'Team Bravo, in position?'

I hit the PTT button three times.

'Both teams in position,' called Andy. 'Stand by . . .'

Joe and Chris stepped back from the door, raising the heavy rams.

'Stand by . . .'

I made eye contact with Pat and nodded, the butterflies now gone.

'Go! Go! Go!' The rams hit the door in unison, their kinetic energy of four and a half tons each sending the flimsy construction flying. Even through the tight confines of my resi I could hear the tremendous noise at the rear as the double glazing erupted, followed by the shouts of 'Armed police! On the fucking floor!' I thought Pat was about to enter – my intention was to be at his shoulder but he didn't move. Seeing the open door I went for it just as he finally made his approach. We collided in the doorway and I sent him flying as I stormed across the shattered wooden remains of the door, MP5 held high, making the living room in a second – where the occupant stood.

The man was transfixed. Glass littered the living-room floor and Red team hung through the shattered remains of the windows brandishing guns. The very sight of me apparently sparked the target into action. As he made for the kitchen I hit him hard and high, keeping the weapon raised and striking him in the face with my right elbow, sending him spiralling backwards.

Pat was on him as I entered the kitchen in search of other players. 'Room Clear,' I called, looking down at the colourless, innocuous looking liquid on the stove.

'Sorry about that,' Pat said apologetically. 'Everything was happening so fast.'

I shrugged. 'Shit happens. Don't worry about it, you did everything right by not allowing me into a room on my own. If anybody it was me who broke the cardinal rule. Anyway, I knew you weren't going anywhere in a hurry.'

'Why not?' he asked.

I grinned. 'Because I was standing on your tail!'

As usual the flying squad office at Barnes was a heaving mass of activity. Stressed-out detectives hurriedly answered telephones while others waded through the endless mounds of paperwork. To think that I nearly took that route, I thought to myself as I sought out the DI.

Early on in my career I'd been on CID for a while, and at one stage was convinced that my work should follow that path. Now, I was glad to say, I was nothing more than a support service with absolutely nothing to do with investigations or the associated paperwork.

'Be with you in a minute boys,' the DI called from across the room. 'Grab some tea and toast from the kitchen.'

We filed into the small room at the end of the hall, and were assailed by the appetising smells of coffee and freshly toasted bread. It was 6.30 a.m. The one thing I liked about the squad at Barnes was that they were so damned civilised.

After ten minutes or so the guys began to filter in with the usual jokey remarks about 'greedy SO19 bastards nicking all the bread and milk'.

'OK, boys, listen in,' called the DI after a few minutes. 'We're a bit low on the ground today with regards to the squad. Unusually for a Monday we have some long-term jobs running, and this one is fairly low key . . .'

Yeah, I thought. And we've only been brought in to make the numbers up. Casual remarks like this really did grip my shit. You could bet your bottom dollar that the other jobs were quality blags, kept back because the squad were trying to collar the glory for themselves. We reckoned that whenever we were offered a squad job it was only because they didn't have enough guys to do it. Throw the woodies a scrap and keep them happy. Things didn't always work that way, however, and although I'd certainly never wish a fellow Police Officer ill, sooner or later the bubble was bound to burst.

And burst it did.

On one such occasion the flying squad were behind a gang of armed robbers. Folklore suggests they had received intelligence that at least one of the gang was armed with a re-activated machine gun, but for reasons best known only to themselves SO19 were never informed. During the ensuing gunbattle a friend of mine from the squad at Tower Bridge, DS Micky Stubbs, was shot in the head. Luckily he survived. When the shit really hit the fan and they found themselves outgunned, who did they call on to bail them out? You guessed it. SO-fucking-19. The Glory Boys.

You'd have thought that little incident would start alarm bells ringing in somebody's head, that policies would be altered. Were they? Were they bollocks!

The smartly dressed female detective sergeant who had been sitting in the corner rose to speak. She was the OIC in this case and had pieced the intelligence together to prop up the job.

One of the DCs began handing out intelligence sheets along with photocopied street maps and hand-drawn plans.

The flying squad were distinct from any other agencies for whom we worked, police or otherwise. All its detective inspectors were obliged to attend a Tactical Advisors course at Jurassic Park. Two weeks in length, the course involved mainly tabletop exercises and debriefs on past operations, and at the end the inspectors passed out fully fledged 'tactical advisors', with the authority to plan and advise on this type of operation. It was great when they were using their own guys, who quite frankly didn't know any better, but to my mind they should never have been allowed to dictate tactics to SO19. Although I was relatively happy with this particular plan, being a tactical advisor in my own right, I felt justified in putting my oar in – after all, it was going to be my guys out there on the street.

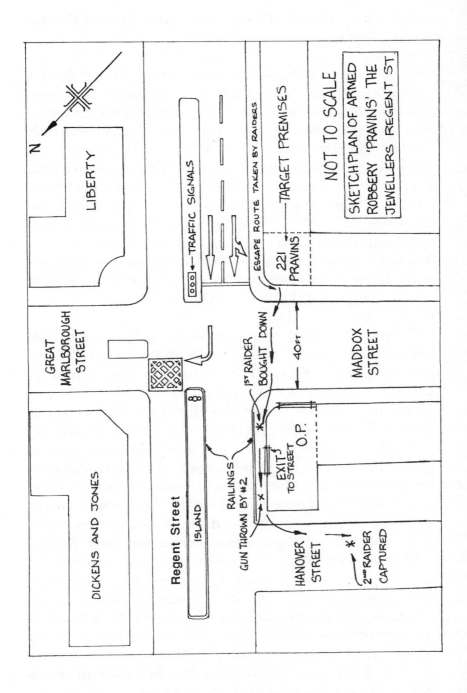

NOT TO SCALE

SKETCH PLAN OF ARMED ROBBERY 'PRAVINS' THE JEWELLERS REGENT ST

'Before we start, guv,' I asked the DI, 'are any of your guys carrying, even for their own protection?'

He shook his head. 'No. We know you don't like joint operations, so it's just your lads.'

I nodded. Well at least that was something. And he was right – I considered it taboo to work two units of totally different capabilities together. After all, we were marksmen on every team weapon, whereas their AFOs were required to achieve only the minimum standard of accuracy on the model ten, and a number of them couldn't even maintain that! A paltry seventy per cent was the target – in ideal range conditions and with an unmoving paper object that didn't shoot back. What, I wondered, would they be like in a crowded street on a wet afternoon with rounds coming back at them from a fast-moving suspect? It was an old chestnut, but in my opinion they were detectives and they should detect. Nothing more.

'Pravin's the jewellers,' started the DS. 'High class, and situated on the corner of Maddox Street and Regent Street, opposite Liberty's. More intelligence may yet come in, but at this stage all we know is that two black males intend to rob the shop sometime today. Because their identities are unknown, unless we see them loitering outside with guns, our intention will be to take them on the way out.'

I nodded. That at least made sense: no point in charging into the jeweller's after them and giving them ample opportunity to take a member of staff or a customer hostage. In these scenarios it was simpler to take them on the way out when, hopefully, the guns would be holstered and their hands would be full.

'Do we know what weapons they'll be using?' I asked.

She shook her head. 'No. Handguns, we think—'

'But don't worry,' interrupted the DI, 'they're replicas.'

I looked puzzled. 'Pardon?'

'Replicas,' he said. 'The guns aren't real.'

I stood to leave. 'I'm sorry then, guv. There's no point in us being here, is there?'

'What do you mean?' the DI asked.

'I mean, if they're replicas and you *know* that, then we can't consider them to be armed so it doesn't come into SO19's remit. Which poses the question, how did you get authority to use us?'

'Oh,' he blustered. 'Well, we don't know for sure – we just *think* they may be replicas.'

I sat down. 'So, by the same token they could be real?' I asked.

He nodded.

'Thank you,' I said. 'Please don't ever tell me or my blokes anything like that again. A firearm is a firearm and should be dealt with as such.'

'The OP,' said the DS in an effort to restore order, 'is situated in an empty office directly opposite, and has a clear view not only of the street but also the jeweller's front door. I'll be in the OP, which has access directly into Regent Street. We propose to cover the rest with gunships . . . if you can nominate your crews?'

'OK,' I said, still slightly angry. 'Myself and Chris will be in the OP with one of our small sets. I can control the move up from there. Brad and Rick,' I said, looking at the map, 'get your driver to self plot somewhere in the vicinity of Poland Street. That's off Great Marlborough, east of the plot. I want another pair in Maddox Street but at the far end, with the last pair at the south end of Regent Street in the flow of traffic. With myself and Chris on foot from the north end of the street, we have every avenue covered. I want everybody well off the plot just in case they sweep it first. Remember, we don't have the luxury of knowing what they look like – but sure as eggs is eggs, if they see us they'll ping us.'

With the postings complete, I quickly ran through the method of attack, which was relatively simple: as soon as the blaggers entered the shop we'd call on the attack. I guessed we'd have about two minutes to get to the jewellers and stack up outside, ready to take them down as they left. With a pair of us coming in from each point of the compass it couldn't have been sweeter.

The DS certainly wasn't wrong. The OP was perfect – and the comfy chairs were a bonus. Apart from the three of us there was also the job photographer, ready to capture the evidence on film. Chris and I had decided simply to go in with Glocks and lightweight undershirt body armour, leaving the gunships to bring up the heavy artillery. Once established, we quickly got the comms up and running. We were using two sets on this occasion: the squad's encripted Cougars – which were covertly plumbed into the gunships and, apart from being secure from scanners, offered a far greater range – and our own hand-held seventy-five sets. Although not encripted, these worked on UHF, which I had been told were harder to scan and provided an ideal back-to-back set for close-quarter work.

Now we were set, all we could do was wait. The DI had promised to review the situation at midday. I looked at my watch – it was 8 a.m.

Over the course of the next hour we witnessed the arrival of the staff and the increasingly fast-swelling crowd of shoppers. 'I hope the gunships can make it with all this traffic,' I said to Chris.

'Yeah. Well, there's only two of them, so it don't really matter,' he replied. He was right – I suppose from past experience I always reckoned on fifty per cent of the gunships not making the plot at the optimum time.

'How about them?' I called after a while, pointing to two males on the opposite side of the road.

'No, I don't think so,' replied the DS. 'They've just walked past without even looking at the jewellers.'

It was now 9.30, and for the past half-hour I'd been playing 'Spot the Blagger' – not easy in the heaving crowd.

'Hello,' the DS suddenly said, pointing up the street. 'They look promising. 'It's the second time they've been past and they're definitely eyes about.'

I sat up in my chair and studied the pair with interest,

willing them to enter.

Five minutes passed. Then suddenly they reappeared.

'Yesss,' I hissed as the photographer 'smudged' them. 'This is shaping up nicely.'

The DS shook her head. 'No . . . I don't think so. They're walking past.'

But suddenly and at the very last minute, they altered course, taking us all by surprise. Spinning on their heels they disappeared from view into the jeweller's. It was 10 a.m.

'OP. OP,' I called into the small set. 'Suspects into premises. Attack, attack, attack.'

Beside me the DS quickly relayed descriptions: 'Two black males, short-cropped hair; one in dark clothing, the other in white shirt and jeans. A handgun has been seen.'

Pulling on my HVC I drew my Glock and fell in behind Chris, who was taking the stairs to the street two at a time.

'Hand over the money!' Inside the shop pandemonium ruled as the raiders pointed their weapons at the staff. 'Hand over the jewels!' they screamed.

The plucky young assistant picked up a fire extinguisher and, striking the button, soaked both raiders.

Panicked by this sudden display of bravado they fled empty-handed. Well – not quite empty, for they still had the guns.

By the time they made the door, of the squad's estimated two minutes inside, a hundred seconds still remained.

Throwing open the door, Chris and I hit the street, knocking aside startled shoppers. Totally unaware of what had been going on in the shop, I was suddenly struck by two things: the first was that there was a large black man in a white shirt holding a gun not twenty-five feet away from me and gaining fast; the second was the amount of people between us. Caught off-guard, I barely had time to bring the Glock up and shout, 'Armed police . . .'

In that very nanosecond two things happened: I took up

the slack on the trigger, my brain suddenly screaming that it was only a replica, and at the same time he threw the piece to the ground and hit me with the force of a charging rhino.

'Fuck!' I clawed at his clothing as the Glock spiralled through the air before landing and skittering across the pavement. Suddenly I was aware of screams all around me and a parting of the crowd, desperate to distance themselves. To my left, Chris and the man in black appeared to be dancing with both arms raised. Snatching up the fallen gun I ran, turning left into Hanover Street.

One suspect was down, a detective sitting astride him. I threw him some cuffs. Witnessing my incident and seeing the robber throw down his gun, the unarmed surveillance officer had brought him down with a rugby tackle Will Carling would have been proud of.

'Shit!' I suddenly thought of Chris.

Sprinting back into Regent Street I was greeted by a grinning Chris, who had now been joined by Brad and Rick. Lying at their feet was the second suspect.

Already the press had gathered, much to my surprise and annoyance. Quickly clearing the street, I was again surprised at the speed with which the locals arrived in the station van. I pointed out the robber's discarded firearm to the SOCO, it was photographed in situ then retrieved.

'What happened?' I asked Chris, nodding at the face-down blagger.

'Fuck knows,' he replied. 'Saw him running at me. I just had time to draw on him when he was on me. He had a gun in his right hand, same as me. He grabbed mine with his left, so I did the same. We started to wrestle and I thought about kneeing him in the bollocks, but instead I stuck the nut on him.'

I chuckled.

'Don't laugh!' Chris said. 'It fucking hurt. I nutted him really hard and we both stood there looking at each other. I was seeing stars, when suddenly his eyes rolled up into his head and he fell down.'

Apart from the robber, the only casualty was a little old lady, a tourist from Australia who had a weak heart. She was taken to hospital and later released with a clean bill of health.

Rubbing my shoulder, I knocked on the office door.

'Come in, Steve,' said the DI. 'Well done. We recovered the two guns. One was a replica, the other a starting pistol.'

'That's why I'm here, guv,' I said, taking a seat. 'Today we were put in danger, and I'm here to say don't ever do it again. As I said before, to get authority for us you need to convince the commander that there are *real* firearms involved. I've never hesitated on an operation before – and I hate myself for it – yet I can live with it. But if I'd have slotted that guy having already been told he had a replica I'd be in the shit up to my neck. So I'm happy I made the right decision – but please tell your team not to put us in this position again.'

To this day I have no idea how the press arrived so quickly – something to do with the England cricket team being in the vicinity, I'm told. All I know is that, when the guvnors at Old Street saw the next day's papers, there was hell to pay. Because plastered across the front pages like some latter-day big-game hunters stood Chris and Brad, guns drawn, huge grins on their faces, their trussed-up trophy lying at their feet.

10

A Fearsome Set of Nostrils

Two weeks had passed since the Pravin's operation, and by now Pat was settling in well. Preparations were well under way for the forthcoming Notting Hill Carnival, and all of the teams had been summoned to the Public Order Training School at Hounslow for further training and deployment in the event of serious disorder. In those circumstances, SO19 would play a dual role. The first was the deployment of a team should shots be fired. Under these circumstances we'd use fully armoured Land Rovers and have a TSG team in full riot gear watching our backs. Our secondary role would be that of deploying with baton guns (large plastic bullets about the size and shape of a small aerosol canister), should they ever be authorised. To my mind, having the things was a total waste of time. During the large-scale Tottenham riots, where PC Keith Blakelock was hacked to death, SO19 riflemen were behind the scenes with baton rounds ready to deploy. The only problem then had been the senior officers. You see, no matter how many shops and cars are burnt out, no matter how many people are murdered, no senior officer to date has had the balls to authorise the use of baton rounds. The reason for this is simple: he or she doesn't want to be branded as the first senior officer to deploy these weapons on mainland Britain – after all, if somebody should get seriously injured, think of the repercussions on one's career! For my part, I felt sure that, once they'd been authorised on that first occasion, the next time would be easy; it was just getting over that initial hurdle.

The lads didn't mind going through the motions at all; besides, the firm had just taken delivery of some new baton guns: the Heckler & Koch L104A1 37mm riot gun, which had been brought in to replace the obsolete (and never used in anger) L67 baton gun. The training was great fun, if a little smoky, spent shooting hundreds of rounds at stacked-up tyres from various distances in a converted warehouse that served as a range. The day was only slightly marred when Pat stood on an empty casing and went arse over bollocks damaging his arm.

While we were tending his wound, none of us could possibly have known that just months later in a series of tragic events which would change his life for ever, Pat would be wrenched from the team, suspended from duty, and ultimately charged with murder.

Parking my car in the small side-street, I set the alarm and walked off towards the grimy red-brick building that housed the base.

Recently some guy had been clocked writing down the registration numbers of our vehicles as team members had left the yard. A quick check on his number had revealed him to be a south London villain with a string of previous convictions. Although our own numbers were blocked – so that even if a police officer innocently or corruptly attempted to check the details on the computer he would be automatically referred to the baseman at Old Street – this scare had made me sit up and take notice of my own personal security, something which up to now I had taken for granted. Why the guy wanted the details nobody knew. The incident was reported, but as always the management thought it easier to sit back and do fuck all than mess with the status quo. However, a couple of the guys had taken offence, and were actively looking out for him. If he did happen to return I think he would find himself answering a few unpleasant questions.

The heavy gate to the yard swung with a loud unoiled creak on its rusted hinges and slammed shut. I headed for the hustle and bustle of the briefing room. It was three in the afternoon – and little did I know that in less than twelve hours I was to make one of the most monumental decisions of my career.

'OK, fellas, listen in,' said Gary quietly. Gary was the Blue team skipper who'd been with us on the skip job. Now, due to staff shortages, he was acting guvnor. A veteran of many high-profile operations, Gary was extremely professional in his planning and approach – he had to be in this op, because as well as Black team, Green team were to be involved.

The general banter died as Gary surveyed the twenty-odd bodies packed into the cramped briefing room, some slouched in armchairs, others standing, while the majority (Chris, Joe and myself included) sat uncomfortably on the floor.

'This job really has got an international flavour, and it will hopefully be going down some time this evening,' Gary said. 'Information has been received by SERCS that a posse of up to four Yardies are going to hit a Turkish restaurant in Camden Town sometime this evening. The gang believe a dealer carrying drugs and cash will be eating at the restaurant tonight. Their objective is to rob him of his drugs, as well as any cash present at the venue. It has also been mooted that they may rob any other customers that happen to be there, so the potential for a hostage rescue is high.'

Gary paused. 'The restaurant stays open until the early hours, and we know a sawn-off is to be used . . .'

'Fucking great,' I muttered to Chris. 'A set of fucking nostrils.' I hated sawn-off shotguns (lovingly called 'nostrils' by the teams because when you stare at the receiving end that's exactly what they resemble). If somebody tells you you're going up against a thirty-eight, forty-five or nine mil, you know what you're up against. With a shotgun that's simply not the case. Because of the

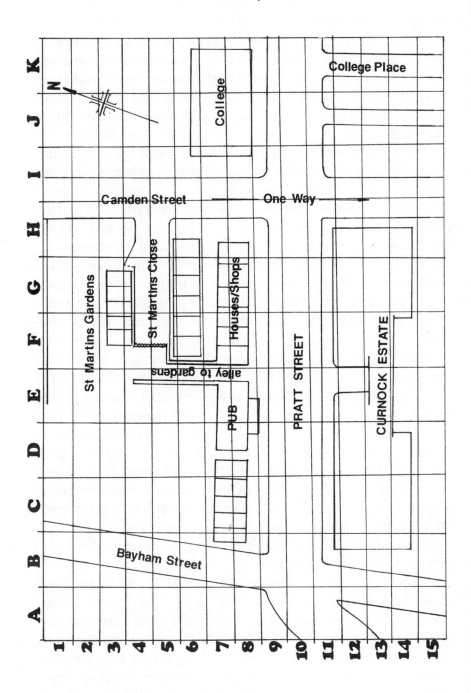

range of ammunition available, they are phenomenally versatile weapons. You could be up against a rifled slug (a solid lead projectile), a Privot (an optically ground stainless-steel ball which will cut through a car's engine block like a knife through butter), an SG (a number of large lead balls in one cartridge), or even birdshot (hundreds of tiny lead pellets). So you never knew what a shotgun was loaded with and what would be coming your way. Unnervingly, in the majority of cases neither did the shooter.

Gary pulled out a sheaf of papers and handed one to each man.

I studied the neat, hand-drawn plan which from memory looked something like the one on the previous page.

Laid over the top of the plan was a grid – which would later prove useful, and which made me marvel at Gary's ingenuity. And stapled to the back was a photocopied page from the London *Geographia* showing the surrounding area, the plot highlighted in blue (Gary had even gone as far as to think a yellow highlighter wouldn't show up under the orange glow of the sodium street lighting – such was the thought and care put into planning an operation).

After thirty seconds or so of flicking through the pages and studying the plot, Gary continued with the geography.

Pratt Street, NW1. Situated deep in the heart of Camden Town, just off the high street. The restaurant was located on the north side of the street. Fronted by huge plate-glass windows it nestled between Bayham Street to the west and Camden Street to the east, the whole area controlled by a system of traffic signals and one-way streets. Directly opposite and overlooking the plot from the south side were two large open-plan blocks of flats – Mexborough House and Warmsworth House – which comprised part of the Curnock Estate, and between them was an underground car park. An OP had been set up on the estate, Gary explained, with a commanding view of the whole area. For reasons of security (should it later be brought out in court), we were never told of the exact location – it was something we simply didn't need to know. What we *did* need to know, however, was that directly opposite the OP and to the east of the target was a large local pub, the St Martin's Tavern. If the attack happened to be called on around closing time, it would be chaos – with the whole area swarming with people.

With the plot firmly fixed in our minds (assisted by some Polaroid shots taken by Gary), we were happy with the geography. Now it was down to the nitty-gritty.

'Intention.' Gary cleared his throat. 'The intention of this operation is quite clear. SO19 will establish an OP on the target premises at dusk. When the suspects are sighted we take them out, hopefully before they enter the restaurant. This will negate any need for a hostage rescue. At the same time the restaurant itself will be hit by way of a rapid entry to secure evidence of drugs. It will be a two-pronged attack, fellas.'

I raised my hand.

'Steve?' Gary nodded.

'Yeah, just one point. How will we know it's the bad boys on the plot? Do we have photos?'

'No,' Gary answered. 'Good point – but I'll be calling it on at my discretion. I hope it'll be early morning, when four guys in a group will stand out. We're also banking on the fact they'll turn up for a look-see first, or sweep the plot.'

I nodded. Because of the complexities of taking two plots simultaneously, the method that followed was a little more involved than normal – but once Gary had started I could see the significance of the map grid.

'After grub we'll leave here, go to the local nick for a further briefing and to kit up,' Gary continued. 'Ground assigned under cover of darkness. I'll move out first with the SERCS boss and a radio man, and we'll establish the OP and comms. Once in position, I want Steve and Black team to self plot well to the east.' Chris jabbed his finger at the area on my map. 'Somewhere down by the college would be good. You'll be in two Rangies. Take the black ones if you can.'

I ticked vehicles off on my checklist.

'Green team will be in a horse with a plain-clothes driver. Again I want you to self plot on the west side, but watch out for those one-way streets.'

Now I made a mental note of Green team's position.

'There are two things we don't know for certain,' said Gary. 'The first is how they'll arrive on the plot – they may be hoofing it or in a motor. The second is which way they'll approach – east or west.'

A small murmur ran round the room as each man had his own theory on how to play it. But, much as we often found Chinese parliaments healthy, Gary obviously had this one covered. He raised his hand and, holding up his copy of the map, pointed to the approximate location of the OP. 'From here I can see both ends of the street. We know that they'll at least have a look through the window before they make their move, and that should give us time to react. All I'll do is give a grid reference over the net. If they are spotted east of eight echo, for example, then Black team will take them out and it will be Green team's responsibility to get on the plot and hit the restaurant. On the other hand, if they appear west of eight echo the roles will be reversed.

'As always, everybody will be plasticuffed in situ. I've devised a handover sheet to be filled in by each of the team leaders, it gives the prisoners' description, the detaining officer from SO19 and the arresting officer from SERCS. It should also help out when we do our notes.'

It was a good idea. In the confusion of a hit where a number of detainees were concerned, you often forgot who you'd put down – and anything that would make life easier when it came to court was fine by me.

'Nearly there, guys,' called Gary. 'Admin. The motors are all in the yard, and each team leader is to nominate his own drivers. Because of the fact that either team may have to do the rapid, I want both to carry their own breaking kit. You'll all be wearing full gear with respirators and helmets. I don't want any casualties from broken glass.' Surprisingly, the majority of injuries the teams suffered generally weren't from gunshots but from broken glass. When you're hacking away at double-glazing or a plate-glass window, the shards are razor sharp and potentially lethal.

Joe sighed. 'For fuck's sake . . .' Much to the chagrin of the other team members, Joe hated wearing the bulky Kevlar helmet and cumbersome S6 respirator which cut down your peripheral vision by about fifty per cent. No, for his part Joe always favoured the casual approach, a high-visibility baseball cap and face veil. On one occasion he smashed down a suspect's door and was greeted by the startled occupant, who took one look at Joe's unorthodox get-up and uttered, 'Who the fuck are you? Andy McNab?'

'No exceptions,' Gary added sternly. 'Casualties to be treated as per the SOP – medics to stabilise the bad guys as best they can, then ambulance to a designated hospital. There will be an India ambulance in the area. If one of the team goes down, it's straight in the lead Rangey and down to UCH. The route is highlighted on the team leaders' maps.'

I traced the line with my finger and nodded.

Gary continued: 'In the event of an incident I'll take control, securing the scene with SERCS, and hand over to the SI0.

'Comms,' Gary concluded. 'Channel seventy-five, National Firearms Frequency. Channel seven on the big set – and at the end I'll exchange Voda numbers with the skippers. We'll keep the call-signs simple: I'm OP one. Green is one-oh-two, and Black one-oh-five. Any questions?' He looked around the room, but there were none.

By the end of the briefing it was already five o'clock, and Gary advised everybody to get some grub – it could well be a long night. By seven we were to be at the local nick to link up with the SERCS guys, see if there was an update, and receive yet another briefing. It was imperative that the unarmed units working with us were under no illusions as to what would be required of them if the shit hit the fan. In some ways it would have been easier for them to attend our initial briefing, but that was the time when we would iron out any glaring difficulties and fine-tune our strategy. At the more formal briefing later we would have it all off pat.

I struggled from the locker room with my heavy bergen. I'd decided to spend the down-time sorting out my kit for the evening.

'I'm off to Brick Lane for a bucket of shit. Anyone want anything?' announced Eddie, one of the Green team guys.

'No thanks, Ed,' I answered, fiddling with a helmet strap on the floor.

Chris shook his head. 'Got me own.'

Joe merely added, 'Fuck off, I'm going down the chippy.'

Brick Lane, a stone's throw from the base, stands in the heart of London's Bangladeshi community. Its large number of ethnic cafés (that stay open virtually all night) and its take-aways were extremely reasonable – even if the meat was highly suspect, which gave rise to the now common phrase, 'a bucket of shit'. It wasn't the fact that I didn't like the thought of a spicy Indian meal or the fact that I'd go home to Jill smelling highly offensive, it was more the fact that I liked to remain awake. I knew, if I ate a huge meal, that as soon as we got to the plot I'd settle down in the motor and sleep it off like some sort of human snake. No, an empty stomach somehow gave me the edge, kept me alert.

'Crazy, innit?' I said to Chris, checking the action on my Glock before inserting it into the drop leg holster.

'What?' he replied.

'The number of fucking jobs we get involving drugs. Not only that, every other bastard's a Yardie.'

'Hadn't given it much thought,' said Chris. 'Suppose it's because there's so much of it about.'

'Exactly!' I added. 'And there's another one tomorrow. It just seems that now every fucker's got a shooter, it's almost as if we're an armed drug squad.'

Chris shrugged matter-of-factly. 'Job's a job,' he said.

The previous year, Black team had been involved in a long-term drugs operation run jointly by SERCS and Customs. Codenamed Emerge, it had centred on the importation of over a tonne of pure cocaine, shipped up the River Thames. In a co-ordinated hit involving SBS Commandos, we had successfully seized the haul (the largest ever), bringing the total seizures for that year to two and a half tonnes. Drugs and drug-related crime were definitely on the increase, and I sometimes wondered if even SO19 could hold back the tide that threatened to engulf us all.

The briefing with the local nick was relatively simple. No further update had been received from their snout, who for some reason had now mysteriously disappeared and was uncontactable. The squad, however, were happy to stand by the original information and were relatively happy that the op would kick off this evening.

'Fuck, it's hot,' Joe moaned, pulling his heavy flameproof coveralls over his track-suit trousers and vest. It was a beautiful summer's evening and, although the temperature had soared during the day, it had now settled down to a respectable sixty-five. Despite the fact that we'd be self plotting in a side-street away from the premises, I nevertheless decided that we'd still be in full view of the public, and as a result should wear our black waterproof Goretex anoraks over the top of our coveralls and body armour. It was the lesser of two evils; although we'd still stand out, it wouldn't be as bad.

Although we were well used to discomfort, the decision was about as popular as a fart in a space suit. I looked at Joe as he struggled into his heavyweight body armour. 'We'll keep the resis and helmets close at hand,' I said trying to wind him up. 'Put them on at the last minute as the attack goes in, just in case we show out by wearing them.'

Joe stopped and looked at me in amazement, then shook

his head. 'Sick Bastard!' he groaned.

Although I was the sergeant with ultimate responsibility for the team, the unit was somewhat unique in terms of discipline. Other squads had commented on the apparent disregard for the rank structure, the use of first-name terms and the banter, but the fact of the matter was, however, that the team was under no illusions regarding where the buck stopped. I was in charge, and I didn't have to remind them. There are two types of supervisor: one that commands respect, and the other, who demands respect. I considered myself the former – even when I did make unpopular decisions.

With the air conditioning at full blast we left the nick under cover of darkness, splitting the convoy so each vehicle took a different route in, to avoid suspicion. I'd nominated Chris as my driver; Joe sat in the back seat with the breaking kit, resi and helmet beside him. Having studied the map at length and committed it to memory, I'd decided to meet up with the rest of the team in the vicinity of College Place. This seemed far enough away from any villain's possible route for sweeping the plot, but near enough to move up quickly should the need arise. As we drove slowly down the long, residential street, I saw a spot that seemed as good a place as any. I would have preferred to be off the road, tucked up somewhere in an industrial or commercial unit, but there was none nearby – and besides, I for one didn't fancy the idea of explaining to some jobsworth security guard who we were or what we were doing.

'Alpha. Bravo.'

I picked up the mike on the big set. 'Bravo.'

The radio crackled again. 'Yeah, Alpha. You just passed us parked on the offside. We've left enough room in front for you to park up. Can you spin around? Over.'

I responded: 'Bravo received. Alpha out.'

Spinning the power-assisted wheel with ease, Chris executed a perfect U-turn before slowly cruising back down the road and slipping into the kerb in front of Bravo.

'Cheers, boys,' I called into the set, then delved into one of the many pockets on my coveralls for the small set.

Finding it, I called up Gary. 'OP one, OP one. Trojan one-oh-five. Over.'

'One-oh-five,' his faint reply.

I tweaked the volume control. 'One-oh-five. Alpha and Bravo in position east of the plot at eleven kilo.'

'One-oh-five received,' came Gary's flat reply. 'OP established. One-oh-two is in position. No movement target premises, but the pub's heaving.'

It was eight thirty.

The next three hours passed with the usual monotony; apart from the odd person passing by or taking the dog for a piss, nothing stirred. Occasionally Gary would call up with, 'No change, no change,' just to keep us informed and ensure the radios were still working.

I smiled the unnatural yellow wash of the street lamps. 'Old Billy's a boy,' I said.

'What's he done now?' asked Chris, somewhat bored.

'Nothing,' I said. 'But I was up at Lippitts with him the other day, there was this woman sergeant, and somebody made a joke about her figure.'

In the back Joe shifted, leaning forward to listen in.

I continued, '"Do you mind?" she shouted. "Only the other day a man told me I had the body of an eighteen-year-old." "Oh yeah?" piped up Bill. "Where do you keep that, then? At home in the freezer?"'

Joe's large frame sent the Range Rover rocking on its springs. Then the jokes came thick and fast.

'What animal's got a cunt halfway up its back?' asked Joe.

'Dunno,' I replied.

'A police horse!' he grinned.

I laughed politely; I'd heard it before, every fucker had heard it before!

'When I was on the miners' strike . . .' I said.

'Oh bollocks!' interrupted Chris, 'You and the fucking

miners' strike.'

Having been in a county force prior to joining the Met I had formed part of a PSU (Police Support Unit) drafted during the year-long strike to the north, to assist in quelling any public disorder. Now, much like Billy in the Falklands, the stories of my thirty-five weeks of conflict were legendary. I feigned a hurt look before continuing. 'Anyway,' I started, 'When I was on the miners' strike I happened to be at Orgreave coking plant, you know, the place where we had the big riot?' Chris nodded. 'The missiles were raining thick and fast, and all some of the lads had for protection were dustbin lids.' I added, setting the scene. 'The rioters were being chased in all directions by the arrest squads, it was totally knackering. During a momentary lull in the fighting we'd stopped to chat to a plonk (female police office) on horseback when a hand-cuffed prisoner was led past.' I imitated in my best northern accent. '"Aye, luv, do you know your horse is foaming at the mouth?" the miner asked. The plonk looked down at him and stared him straight in the eye. "Aye" she said, "And so would you be if you'd been between my legs for eight hours".'

At eleven-thirty the pub emptied without incident. After a whole even the jokes and banter in the vehicles died off, with each man sitting, head back, deep in his own thoughts. Before long we'd all settled back into an uneasy silence.

At one o'clock the radio crackled into life. 'No change, no change. All units, there's hardly anybody at the target now. Looks like he's about to close shop soon. Stand by for a stand-down.'

'One-oh-five,' I acknowledged. Tearing at the thick Velcro straps on my body armour, I breathed a sigh of relief as my guts expanded. The coveralls beneath were soaking. 'Well, that's another fucking ten hours wasted,' I moaned. 'Surely they must have guessed the job would blow out the minute the snout had it away on his dancers?' I checked my watch and mentally ran through my timetable: stand-down, one-thirty; back to base by two; de-kit, towel off (fuck the shower), and in my 'Grot' by two-thirty. Four hours overtime for sitting around doing sod-all – a nice result. Thank you very much.

My train of thought was suddenly interrupted by a whispered voice over the big set. 'Alpha. Bravo. Don't move. Repeat, do not move. Bandit vehicle your offside.'

'Fucking hell,' Chris hissed from the driver's seat. Then, without turning my head I slowly strained my eyes to the right.

Double parked directly beside us sat a light-coloured saloon. Barely inches separated the two vehicles, the four young black males in the saloon staring intently ahead. Surely, I thought, these can't be our men. Right colour, right age . . . but if they were and they looked slightly to their left, then we'd be blown . . .

Inside the vehicle the four men appeared to be deep in conversation. Sweat ran in rivulets down my face as the tension mounted. With my right hand out of sight I carefully and slowly inched it towards the grip of my MP5, tucked safely away in the footwell. The seconds seemed like hours as still nobody moved. They must have pinged us, I thought frantically, as the exhaust plumes rose steadily from their gently idling exhaust. They must have . . .

But what happened next was incredible.

Pulling on black knitted balaclavas, they checked their weapons. Then, as quickly as they'd arrived, they were gone!

'Fuck that!' I breathed a sigh of relief as I saw the brake-lights flicker in the distance as the vehicle manoeuvred left. Pulling my body armour tight, I flung my anorak on to the back seat and grabbed the radio.

'Stand by, Stand by. OP, permission? One-oh-five.' I called, using the correct radio procedure.

'One-oh-five. Go, go!' came the reply.

'One-oh-five. Light coloured saloon,' I called, reeling off the registration number from memory. 'Four suspects on board. Location eleven kilo in ten seconds, west towards your location. They are carrying. Repeat, they are carrying.'

'One-oh-five,' Gary's calm acknowledgement.

'One-oh-two, received.' Green team had also heard the transmission.

'OP, OP. All units, I have eyeball. Four now on foot.'

'Shit, they've ditched the motor,' I said, pulling on the resi.

Then, 'OP, OP. One-oh-five?'

I hit the PTT. 'Go, Go.'

'One-oh-five, they have now stopped eight echo. Standing in the pub entrance by the alley, tucked into the corner of the pub.'

'Yes, yes,' I called as Gary uttered the words I'd been waiting to hear. Having consulted with the SERCS guvnor in the OP it had been decided that SO19 could now deal.

'OP. I have control. Stand by,' said Gary.

I snapped the stud closed on my helmet strap, breathing now laboured through the filter of the resi, adrenalin born of excitement coursing through every vein in my body, the ultimate drug. I placed the five across my knees, ready to bail out as Chris inched the Range Rover out of the line of parked cars.

Then, 'One-oh-five, I put them east of eight echo.' I now knew the suspects were ours, the secondary site (the restaurant) going to Green team.

I pulled off the resi. 'All units, go, go, go!'

Gunning the powerful four-litre engine, we took off at speed, Bravo close on our tail. The early-morning traffic presented us with no problem as we hurtled through the Camden Street one-way system and on to the plot, lighting up the four huddled suspects with our powerful beams.

Trapped like rabbits in the glare of a poacher's lamp, the startled youths looked towards the screaming Rangies.

Slewing us at an angle across the road, Chris slammed on the brakes. Bracing myself with knees locked against the dashboard, I had one hand on the door handle, straining at the leash and ready to go. A hundred yards to my left Green team were already spilling out of the van and shattering the early-morning calm by hurling sledgehammers through the plate-glass window of the restaurant.

Throwing the door open, I hit the tarmac at a sprint – but already they were starting to react, and that made them dangerous! Pulling off his mask and throwing it to the floor, a tall, athletic member of the gang was starting to run, a long, dark, shiny object gripped tightly in his right hand. Gun? I thought.

Over my shoulder, Joe had bailed out and was heading for the trio that still stood transfixed and huddled in the pub entrance. 'Armed police!' he bellowed through the confines of the resi he'd not been quick enough to remove. (I later bollocked him for being obstinate – the guy that most hated resis being the only one on the plot wearing one, apart from Green team who needed them. 'It was an order,' came his flippant reply.)

'Armed police – stand still!' I shouted at the lone runner, who by now was making distance and just drawing parallel with our parked vehicle.

Supported by the crew from Bravo, Joe looked an awesome sight, dressed from head to toe in black, MP5 raised. Any thought of retaliation the suspects may have harboured was instantly lost. Throwing their hands in the air, the trio dropped a sawn-off shotgun, a baseball bat and a three-foot kebab knife as if they were electrified.

'On the floor! Down, down, down!' yelled Joe.

Meanwhile, I was more than occupied. 'Armed police! Stand still!' I shouted again – but with a quick glance over his shoulder the runner was off.

Bollocks, I thought. Straight towards the unarmed officers. And my head told me he was armed. It was decision time. Stopping momentarily, I bought the MP5 to bear. One last chance! 'Stand still!'

No reaction!

Finger already on the trigger, I used my thumb to flick the

safety to 'fire' in one practised movement. Then, lighting up his broad back with the built in torch-mount, I checked my sight picture and pulled up the slack on the trigger, waiting for the bang . . .

But in almost the same instant he threw a heavy object which struck the door of a parked vehicle.

'Shit!' I flicked the safety back and took off up the street like Linford Christie. 'Support, support,' I called into the radio as I ran. 'One adrift, eight echo, towards eight india.'

Having stopped the Rangey, Chris had seen what was happening. Snatching up his five he was close on my tail as the suspect disappeared from view.

'Lost eyeball,' I called. 'Suspect eight india, left, left towards one india.' By now I was getting out of breath, but kept up the pursuit.

Although we had trained in all the kit and trained hard, wearing up to four stone extra made you no match for a guy in a T-shirt and trainers.

Reaching the last house in the block, I instinctively stopped and peered cautiously round the corner. The street was deserted!

It had nothing at all to do with fear; the adrenalin overrode that. No, it was more to do with self-preservation – and once bitten, twice shy.

When I had been a normal plod many moons before, I'd been patrolling alone in a Panda when I stopped a guy I knew. A quick search had revealed a pocketful of LSD. As I was in the throes of feeling his collar he stuck the nut on me, breaking my nose. Then, turning on his heel, he had it away on his toes into a local council estate. Naturally, despite my nose pissing blood, I gave chase – but the vicious little shit had other ideas. Not content with getting one over on Mr Plod, he wanted to have his cake and eat it. As I had rounded a building he had bushwhacked me, hitting my already tender hooter with a length of four by two that he'd found in a bin.

I won't bore you with details, but suffice to say that by the time assistance arrived I was in the process of doing a Mexican hat dance on his nut.

Sometime later the guy would die in the most extraordinary of circumstances. Having been found naked in the woods, he was taken to hospital where he was declared dead and put in cold storage pending a post-mortem, it was only later, when they came to identify him, that he was found to be still alive (something to do with the fact that he was still breathing). Needless to say, that short spell with Jack Frost had been enough, and he popped his clogs shortly after.

My mind raced as I ran north along Camden Street. It was well-lit, and there was no way he could run *that* fast – so the only possibility was that he had turned left into St Martin's Close, and that was a dead end.

St Martin's Close, I remembered, was at map reference five hotel, one hundred and fifty yards long, with parked cars on both sides. None of the terraced houses had a front garden, but at the top right corner was the garden-gate access to St Martin's Gardens. At the far end of the close was a fifteen-foot-high wrought-iron fence, and the whole area was dimly lit.

By now I could hear over the radio that things the other end were winding down; Green team was secure, and Joe and the guys were cuffing up their posse. Only this end did things seem strangely unreal.

On the corner I did another snap inspection around the building line, and the street was deserted.

'Two-seven,' I whispered into the set, reverting to my own personal call-sign.

Gary answered immediately, knowing it was still all to play for: 'All units hold. Two-seven, go ahead.'

'Two-seven. I'm at six hotel. I need to clear towards five foxtrot.'

A quick look at his map told Gary that I was at the junction of Camden Street and St Martin's Close and that I wanted to move west.

'Two-seven received. Support, please,' he called.

I felt a light tap at my shoulder. 'Two-seven. I now have Chris at my location commencing the search. Over.'

'Two-seven,' Gary acknowledged.

Our luck was in. A glance across the road told me what I wanted to know: the gate to the gardens was padlocked.

'How do you want to play this?' whispered Chris.

'One each side,' I replied. 'Cover each other's arcs. A slow, methodical search. He could be between any of these motors.'

Chris nodded and tapped my back.

Bringing the MP5 up into my shoulder I covered down the quiet cul-de-sac. As Chris sprinted across the open expanse before disappearing from view in the shadows on the opposite side.

Breaking cover, I held my MP5 combat ready and covered across the street slightly in front of Chris's now advancing figure. In a similar fashion he in turn covered me. We were about half-way down, and you could hear a pin drop when the familiar roar of a Range Rover filled the night. Suddenly the whole close was lit up like a Christmas tree as the vehicle approached.

Momentarily Chris and I stood out like a pair of tits before we dived for cover between two parked cars.

Jumping into our abandoned Rangey, the squad man had thought he could help – the vehicle was armoured so he'd be safe, and he could give us a hand by lighting up the scene while we searched. His thoughts were of strictly good intention; however, he hadn't considered the tactical side one little bit.

'Two-seven,' I called over the net. 'Tell that Rangey to fuck off.' I was furious – and we were well on offer.

Then it occurred to me that we might just be able to turn it to our advantage. 'Cancel, cancel!' I said. 'Get him to come half-way down the street and stop.'

Pulling up at my location, the red-faced driver blustered an apology as I pulled open the heavy passenger door. I held up my hand. 'It's OK. Now this is the plan. . .'

With Chris at the driver's door, we advanced down the narrow close, MP5s covering through the half-open door jambs. As we neared the end my heart missed a beat as the suspect suddenly broke from cover. Thank God I hadn't lost him!

For the second time that morning he found himself trapped in the harsh glare of the headlamps, for the second time he ignored our commands. This time it would be different.

'Armed police! Stand still!' Chris shouted from behind cover as he made a futile attempt at clearing the fence. 'Get your hands in the air!' Oblivious, the villain tried once again in vain to run. Rushing forward, I took hold of him with my free hand, MP5 at chest height. Joined by Chris, I hooked his legs and took him to the ground. Once cuffed, a quick pat down turned up no weapons (something that didn't surprise me as he'd obviously thrown it earlier). Chris pulled him to his feet and led him off to the Rangey.

I was later to learn that he'd just flown in from Miami.

As the adrenalin waned I made my way back towards Camden Street. Already the curtains were beginning to twitch as unseen faces peered through the nets. Suddenly a door to my right banged open and an old lady stood silhouetted in the hall, all curlers and dressing gown. She took in my menacing appearance, eyes coming to rest on the MP5. 'Oh my god!' she gawped through toothless gums. 'What on earth had he done?'

I smiled wearily. 'Go back to bed, love. Nothing serious – no TV licence, that's all!'

Arriving back at the scene of the hit I realised that less than ten minutes had passed since the attack. It felt more like ten hours.

With the torch mount of my MP5 I frantically scoured the pavement, looking for any sign of the discarded weapon.

'Here it is,' Chris announced, stooping between two parked cars and holding up a rounders bat.

A shiver ran through my spine as I looked at the relatively harmless object. 'Fucking Hell!' I suddenly felt quite sick. 'Don't tell me I was a fag paper away from slotting a geezer with a stick!' I thought back to the sight picture between his shoulder blades and the feel of the trigger, then shuddered. No. There was no way I would have mistaken a bat for a shooter, no way. Not even in this light. I racked my brains, summoning all my memories of the action.

I mentally replayed the scene: he apparently had a gun in his right hand, I'd lined up the five on his back – then there was that distinct body swerve as he tossed the object before disappearing from view . . . I concluded that whatever he'd thrown had been with his left hand. 'You sure he had nothing else on him?' I asked Chris, somewhat puzzled.

'No, mate, nothing. Patted him right down. But now the SERCS boys have sealed off the street.'

Staying over at the base, sleep didn't come easy that night, tired as I was. Maybe it was the heat, the noise of the ever-moving traffic, or the sirens as yet another ARV left the Yard. Whatever it was, I felt like shit when I surfaced in the morning.

Showering off, I got dressed and made my way to the base room.

Seeing me enter, the baseman shouted, 'There's a couple of notes in your tray, Sarge.'

'Yeah, cheers,' I called. Pulling open the thin metal drawer of the grey filing cabinet, I retrieved the scraps of paper. One was a court warning. The other was slightly more interesting. It was from SERCS, and I had to read it twice just to make sure. It said: 'WELL DONE. SEARCH OF ST MARTIN'S CLOSE REVEALED A 9MM SELF LOADING PISTOL HIDDEN IN THE UNDERGROWTH.'

'So I was right all along,' I said out loud. I would have been justified in slotting him. The search of the cul-de-sac had left Chris and I well on offer, that was a fact . . . and suddenly I felt very old. Maybe they were right; maybe I *had* been on ops too long. Perhaps I should go training . . .

However, the choice was not to be mine. The decision had already been made – and just two months later I suddenly found myself wrenched from the team.

My days on ops were over.

Pulling on my training blues, I adjusted my beret at a jaunty angle and picked up the clipboard. Striding purposefully from the instructors' block at Lippitts Hill, I passed the parked team call-out van and stopped momentarily to check my reflection in its blacked-out windows.

Satisfied, I smiled.

'I'll be back,' I muttered.

Epilogue

Two and a half weeks after he was shot by PC Pat Hodgson, David Ewin died from his wounds.

On 17 October 1995 Pat Hodgson became the first British policeman ever to be charged with murder while in the execution of his duty.

In the short time that Pat had served with my team, I'd found him to be a mature, confident and honourable man. His actions that day have served to bring home to the public at large the tremendous amount of pressure and stress placed on the shoulders of each and every officer to whom a firearm is issued.

On 14 October 1997, after three trials spanning almost as many years, an Old Bailey jury unanimously found Pat Hodgson not guilty. During the six-day trial the jury had had the luxury of independent witnesses, the benefit of hindsight, the finest legal minds, and two hours of deliberation. That jury then came to the self same decision that Pat Hodgson had made in a split second on the street: that the threat had to be stopped.

In an age where the Home Secretary is calling for the police to scrap their 'macho' image while others are calling for the police to be armed, I would pose a series of simple questions . . .

How should we go about arming the police?

The training implications alone are enormous. Would we

make it a prerequisite that an officer pass a firearms course before sending him to training school?

Or would we train him first, then let him undertake firearms training? And what of all those officers still serving, many of whom – by reason of eyesight, judgement, or some type of physical disability – would under the present regulations be precluded from being issued a firearm? And what of those officers (of whom there are many) who simply do not wish to carry one?

Today many officers are unable to obtain the required score to pass a qualification shoot. Should we then lower the standard?

At present, under ACPO guidelines, a basic AFO within the Metropolitan Police area need only reach a qualifying standard of seventy per cent to pass. That means that for every ten rounds fired he is allowed to miss three.

Three lost bullets – three innocent bystanders?

Before we even talk about lowering standards, we must pose the question, are they currently acceptable?

On the other hand . . . If you happen to be an unarmed bobby out on the street and staring down the business end of a set of nostrils, knowing that an ARV is ten minutes away is hardly comforting.

I for one am the greatest advocate that a police officer has the moral right to defend himself. But to conclude the only suggestion I can make is one of a need for more highly trained, highly skilled and highly motivated firearms units. Such as SO19.

Steve Collins, June 1998

Glossary

Across the pavement	Term used for confronting robbers in the commission of an offence
Actions on	Actions on contact (Contingency plans)
A and E	Accident and Emergency (Hospital)
AFO	Authorised Firearms Officer
Armalite	Colt M16A1 assault rifle
ARV	Armed response vehicle
Asp	Small, lightweight alloy retractable baton carried by SO19
Assaulter	Term used for SO19 SFO member kitted for hostage rescue or rapid entry
ASU	Air support unit
ATF	Alcohol Tobacco and Firearms: US law enforcement agency
Bandit	Bad guy (usually armed robber)
Bang box	Box carried by SO19 SFO teams containing stun-grenades, specialist ammunition and gas
Baseman	SO19 communications officer at Old Street base
Bergen	Large army backpack issued to SO19
Black rat	Traffic officer (slang)
Black and white	American police patrol vehicle

Blagger	Armed robber (slang)
Blocked	Term used when an SO19 officer's personal vehicle details are 'blocked out' on the Police National Computer, preventing unauthorised access
Blue on blue	Accidental contact by friendly forces
Blue box	Security van (slang)
BNE	Bureau of Narcotics Enforcement: US drugs enforcement agency
CAA	Civil Aviation Authority
Cabbage-hat	Derogatory term given to Royal Marines, referring to the colour of their berets
CAD	Computer-aided despatch
Carrying	Armed
Cartel	Colombian drugs gang
Casevac	Casualty evacuation
Chetnick	Russian Mafiya (slang)
Chinese parliament	Team meeting to iron out tactics prior to an operation
Clacker	Handheld initiation device for explosives/distraction devices
Clocked	Seen/Identified
Clusterfuck	Term describing situation where everything goes wrong
Coke	Cocaine
Comms	Communications
Contractor	Hit man
Covert op	Plain-clothes (covert) operation
Cougar	Encripted radio
CPO	Close-protection officer
Crack joint	Premises used for smoking/dealing in crack cocaine (usually fortified)
Cred	Credibility
CRW	Counter-revolutionary warfare
CSF	Caribbean Security Force (set up

	after US invasion of Grenada)
CS launcher	L1A1 66mm, gas-canister launcher
Cyalume	Tube containing chemicals which, when broken and mixed, gives off light
DA	Deliberate action
Dancers	Feet (slang)
DC	Detective Constable
DCI	Detective Chief Inspector
DEA	(American) Drug Enforcement Administration
DI	Detective Inspector
D11	Forerunner of SO19
Dig-out	Early-morning raid by SO19
Dinosaur	Derogatory name for SO19 instructor
Double German	Double-width ladder for house assaults
DPG	Diplomatic Protection Group
Driveby	(American) term used for drive-by shooting
DS	Detective Sergeant
Duty officer	Duty inspector
Emerge	Operation Emerge
End-ex	End exercise
Enforcer	Portable hand-held ram used by SO19
ER	Emergency reaction
Eyeball	Surveillance speak for visual contact
Eyes about	Surveillance conscious
FAP	Final assault position
FBI	(American) Federal Bureau of Investigation
Feel his collar	Arrest
FHA	Forward holding area
Firm	Metropolitan Police
Fisheye	Covert surveillance camera

Five	Heckler & Koch MP5
Flashbang	Stun grenade
Flash	A show of money before a deal
Flounder	Black cab gunship
Footie	Surveillance foot officer
Full clip	Full magazine
Full SP (Starting price)	All the relevant facts
FUP	Forming-up point
Game on	Operation looks set to go off
Ganja	Rastafarian slang for cannabis
Gimpy	GPMG 7.62 calibre general-purpose machine-gun
Glock 17	Austrian-made 9mm self-loading pistol, standard issue to SO19
Goretex	Brand-name wet-weather clothing issued to SO19
Grot	Sleeping bag
Ground assigned	Designated position on an operation
Gunship	Unmarked vehicle containing firearms officers
HA	Home address
HAC	Honourable Artillery Company
Handler	Officer in charge of an informant
Happy-bag	Robber's bag containing firearms etc.
Hatton gun/round	Sawn-off Remington 870 pump-action shotgun firing a wax-and-powdered-lead round, used for shooting off door hinges and vehicle tyres
Head shed	SAS term for boss
Hit	Calling on an attack
Hooley	Hooligan bar: a jemmy with a spike at one end
Horse	A covert vehicle from which SO19 would deploy (Trojan horse)
Huey	Bell UH1 helicopter

HVC	High-visibility cap (donned when operating in plain clothes)
IIMAC	A tried and trusted method of planning a formula: Information, Intention, Method, Administration, Communications
India	Suspect, or Paramedic ambulance
India 99	Force helicopter
IR	Infra-red, or Information room
IRA	Irish Republican Army (Provisional)
Jurassic Park	Derogatory name for Lippitts Hill
Jobsworth	Derogatory name for security guard
Jump-off	Vehicle or premises where a team can wait out of sight ready to attack
Kick-off	Operation or attack has started
Kit up	Don body armour etc. prior to an attack
Kurtz	Fully automatic Heckler & Koch 9mm short-barrel machine-gun
Linkman	Liaison between SO19 and agency they are working for, usually the inspector
LOE	Limit of exploitation
LUP	Lying-up point
Manor	Ground or territory
Merc	Mercenary
Mini ground-burst	Pyrotechnic distraction device
M16	Colt M16A1 assault rifle
Misfire	Weapon stoppage or jam
MO	Modus Operandi (Method of operating)
Model 10/19	Smith & Wesson .38 six-shot revolver
MOE	Method of entry
Mothball	Pyrotechnic distraction device
MP5	Heckler & Koch 9mm carbine, issued to SO19 SFO teams

Narc	(American) Narcotics officer
Net	Radio network
Ninety-three	Heckler & Koch 93.223 rifle with telescopic sights
Nostrils (Set of)	Sawn-off double-barrelled shotgun
OIC	Officer in charge
OP	Observation Post
Ops	Operations
Opsec	Operational security
Paraffin parrot	Helicopter
PCA	Police Complaints Authority
Perp	(American) Perpetrator
Plasticuffs	Nylon ties used for handcuffing prisoners
Player(s)	Suspect(s)
Plod	Uniformed police officer
Plonk	Female police officer
Plot	Scene of an operation (i.e. Robbery plot)
PNG	Passive night goggles
Popped his clogs	Died
Posse	Term used for Yardie gangs
Principal	Bodyguard term for the person you are protecting
PSU	Police support unit
PTT	Press-to-talk switch
PT17	Forerunner of SO19 (Personnel and Training)
Pulsar	Specialist search teams
QRV	Quick-release vest
Raid jacket	(American) Nylon jacket worn over plain clothes to identify the wearer as a police officer during a raid
Rangey	Range Rover
Rapid entry	Fast entry into premises to preserve evidence
Rasta	Rastafarian

Ratshit	Term used when everything has gone wrong
Regiment	Special Air Service
Remington 870	Pump-action shotgun, also available in sawn-off version
Remount	Joint SO19–SAS counter-terrorist exercise
Reorg	Reorganisation phase of an operation
Resi	Standard S6 respirator worn by SO19
Respec	Yardie slang/greeting
Ride along	(American) Ride-along programme whereby citizens are encouraged to go out on patrol with regular police officers
Rifleman	SO19 team sniper
Riot gun	Heckler & Koch L104A1
Rupert	SAS term for officer
RVP	Rendezvous point
SAS	22 Special Air Service Regiment
SBS	Royal Marines Special Boat Service
SD	Silenced version of the Heckler & Koch MP5
Seated	Correctly engaged (weapons magazine)
SERCS	South East Regional Crime Squad
Seventy-five set	SO19 radio
SFO	Specialist Firearms Officer
Shooter	Gun or gunman
Shot	Authorised Firearms Officer
Sig	Sig-Sauer 9mm self-loading pistol with 15-round magazine
Simunition	A blank round filled with a soaplike substance, ideal for man-on-man training
SIS	Special Intelligence Section of the

	Metropolitan Police
SIO	Senior Investigating Officer
Skipper	Sergeant
Slot / slotted	To shoot somebody / Shot
Smudged	Photographed
Snout	Informant
SOCO	Scene of Crime Officer
SOP	Standard Operating Procedure
SO1	Organised and international crime group
SO8	Flying squad
SO10	Witness-protection unit
SO11	Metropolitan Police surveillance unit
SO19	Force tactical firearms unit
SP	SAS special projects team
Special	Special Constable
Special events	Metropolitan Police unit responsible for calculating the support needed to police any incident
Spieler	Illegal drinking and gambling den
Spyderco	Sharp knife issued to SFO teams
SPG	Special Patrol Group
SSU	Special Service Unit (St Kitts)
Staff	Staff instructor
Steyer	7.62 mm sniper rifle
Stick	A stave or small file of men
Stoppage	Jammed weapon
Stunnie	Stun grenade
Suit	CID detective
Supergrass	Heavy-duty informant who has agreed to turn Queen's evidence and testify against former colleagues
SWAT	(American) Special Weapons and Tactical
Sweeney	Flying squad (Sweeney Todd)
Sweep the plot	Have a look before committing a

	crime
Target	Suspect
Team leader	SO19 SFO team sergeant
Tec	Detective
Third Eye	Surveillance speak for lookout
Tiger kidnap	Extortion attempt involving hostages
Trojan	Call-sign of SO19 units
UC	Undercover detective
U101	Pager message for SO19 urgent call-out
Watcher	Surveillance officer
Wedge	Bundle of cash
Woody	Uniformed officer (as in Wooden-top)
Worry	Collective noun for three or more senior officers (slang)
Wrap	End of operation
Yardie	Jamaican gangster
Yellow-arse	Derogatory term for SO19 team member who considers himself pseudo-SAS
Zulu	Hostile